# GOODBYE LUCILLE

Segun Afolabi was born in Kaduna, Nigeria and grew up in various countries including Canada, the Congo, East Germany and Japan. He is the author of a collection of short stories, *A Life Elsewhere*, and has published in literary journals including the *London Magazine*, *Wasafiri* and *Granta*. His short story 'Monday Morning' was awarded the 2005 Caine Prize for African Writing. He lives in London.

GW00686164

By the same author

*A Life Elsewhere*

# GOODBYE LUCILLE

## SEGUN AFOLABI

JONATHAN CAPE
LONDON

Published by Jonathan Cape 2007

2 4 6 8 10 9 7 5 3 1

First published in Great Britain in 2007 by
Jonathan Cape
Random House, 20 Vauxhall Bridge Road,
London SW1V 2SA

www.randomhouse.co.uk

Addresses for companies within The Random House Group Limited
can be found at:
www.randomhouse.co.uk

The Random House Group Limited Reg. No. 954009

A CIP catalogue record for this book
is available from the British Library

ISBN 9780224076036

The Random House Group Limited makes every effort to ensure that
the papers used in its books are made from trees that have been
legally sourced from well-managed and credibly certified forests.
Our paper procurement policy can be found at:
www.randomhouse.co.uk/paper.htm

Typeset in Sabon by Palimpsest Book Production Limited,
Grangemouth, Stirlingshire

Printed and bound in Great Britain by
Mackays of Chatham plc, Chatham, Kent

*For my parents, and for Martha and Y*

'It is curious how people can build such warmth among themselves so swiftly.'

Kazuo Ishiguro – *The Remains of the Day*

# 1

I LEFT LONDON to get away from myself. The job that materialized in Berlin was simply an excuse to run, and when I ran I did not look behind to the past, only ahead to where the future lay. I arrived in the middle of a winter that made Kentish Town seem a tropical paradise. There were blizzards and the snow fell nearly every week like overzealous Christmas decorations. Hearts gave out when the temperature dropped beyond fifteen below; old hearts, tired hearts that had witnessed war and privation, people threshed and divided like fields of wheat. Or the newlyweds smashed by a runaway lorry on black ice across the autobahn. People whispered that it had been shame and blessing both that they had perished together at the start of their new lives. Or the children who skated to the bottom of the Fauler See when the ice sighed and swallowed them whole. School kids sang about the creature of Tiergarten that winter, but by spring it was all forgotten. I didn't know the language then, and when I asked, it seemed to me macabre that they should sing about such dreadful things.

Three years later things hadn't improved all that much.

But were they ever meant to? Had I ever really wanted to tame the wild heart of ambition? The job I came for fizzled out soon enough – assistant curator at Mattias Trommler on Fasanenstrasse, a poor imitation of a gallery, with only a thimbleful of staff stretched hopelessly on opening nights, withered with ennui the rest of the year. But here I was, away from myself once more, relieved to breathe freely again.

Now it was hot – a broiling summer, the kind a European city can become unused to. People complained from morning to night about the stultifying heat, the closeness, the stickiness of things, just as they would caw about the lack of sun or the poor summer had we been subjected to that instead.

Then came the Henkelmann affair. Whoever killed him left behind a string of clues. It couldn't have been a hit man; Henkelmann was bludgeoned to death. Not the work of a professional. Tyre marks were discovered at the scene. Two sets: Henkelmann's and his assailant's. A sliver of bright yellow plastic was lodged deep within the deceased's left cheek. I don't know what that means, other than he might have been killed with a toy or a dustpan brush. Could he have been killed with a toy? I'm not a detective; I am a photographer. I don't normally think about these things. I remember the Thursday morning, though, the rendezvous with Marie. 'Bliss café . . . the corner of Dieffenbachstrasse and Schönleinstrasse,' she had said. 'Don't be late.' By the end of the day Herr Henkelmann was dead.

# 2

For the past couple of years I have worked as a freelance photographer. It's not all I expected; there's never much work and what there is can be far from satisfying. I always wanted to be a high-profile photographer, taking pictures of the stars. Having to turn down Prince, say, because I had been booked for a shoot with Ella. Or packing my bags for South America for a year, photographing everything – the extremes of wealth and poverty – then observing people debate whether my pictures were art or reportage.

As things have turned out, it wasn't to be that way. I've had to turn to other areas to make a living and have veered away from what I most wanted to do. I haven't had much work now for several months. Things are slow and I have never been good at networking, spreading myself out. I don't have the inclination for hard toil. Only the need to pay rent has kept me relatively busy. When Marie phoned the other day, I realized I had been in a jobless stupor.

*Off the Wall* is a magazine devoted to the fringe sections of the city. It doesn't have a high circulation, but its reputation is sound. I once managed to sell a photograph to the

*Morgenpost* that Marie happened to spot. She got my number from a friend at the paper and phoned to ask if I could do some work for her. If you look at a particular back issue of the magazine, the one with King Sunny Ade on the cover, you'll see some early photographs of Wynton Marsalis on pages twenty-three and twenty-five. Those are mine. He wasn't so well established at the time, but now he's one of the giants of jazz. Last I heard, he'd even turned down *Rolling Stone*, so it appears I was lucky to photograph him when I did.

Marie edits the magazine, but since it's not a large operation, she always has her hands in other pockets and she will more than often pen an article herself. The magazine belongs to her and her husband, Stefan, an architect, who is only nominally involved, so she can do more or less as she likes. When she phoned the other day she said she was planning to cover a conference in Kreuzberg. The speaker, Heinrich Henkelmann, would be combining an entrepreneurial exercise with a little hands-on politics. Meeting ordinary people. Getting to know the neighbourhood. 'A common political ploy – being seen to take an interest in the people of a deprived area,' Marie scoffed. 'But I *have* heard interesting things about him and I don't want to miss out on the start of anything important.' Marie knows I switch off at the mention of politics, and she guessed I'd be reluctant to take the job, but she added that as I lived in the area, there would be hardly any travelling involved. 'You might even find it interesting,' she said. She knew I needed the money.

'Well . . . if you give me some more details,' I hesitated, 'I'll think about it.'

She said she would arrange for a press pack to be sent out to me, then slipped in, 'See you on the day,' as if I had already accepted. I suppose I had.

Marie is what I would call a handsome woman: not young enough to be pretty, not alluring enough to be beautiful. She is striking, though. I can't remember which, but one of her parents is Egyptian. She has only ever mentioned them once in all the time I've known her. Whenever I visit her office, I'm always surprised at how I tower over her. And I am not so tall, only fat. I wouldn't call her petite – she would hate that – but the woman has not got height on her side and she's very slender. Yet whenever I think about her, she seems very much larger than she is in reality. She fits the halfway mark of someone who is very attractive in an unusual, intelligent kind of way. You might catch yourself staring at her if you saw her in the street. You might glance, perhaps drawn by the sound of her melodic voice, then look back because her face, the way her hips tug at her dress, simply call out for your attention. I can't explain.

When the conversation ended I made a note on a scrap of paper and went through to the kitchen. When I say 'through', I mean I walked to the other end of the lounge as I rent an open-plan apartment where everything appears to be in the same room. This isn't strictly true; I have a separate bedroom, which is more than can be said for most of the apartments in this building. I also have extra space in what used to be a second bedroom, which I long ago converted into a darkroom – about six feet by eight, barely suitable for a child. Frau Lieser claims the other tenants 'manage just fine, thank you very much', but what else is she going to say? That's half the function of a landlady after all, to mollify without actually improving anything.

I stuck the piece of paper on the refrigerator door, which is covered in similar messages: *Must phone Johann – Don't forget! Call Lucille on the 27th! Lieser – 1st – Rent!!* I had no idea who Johann was. I told myself to remember to check all the notes as soon as I had an opportunity to do so in case there was something vital I had forgotten. I could have checked them there and then, but it didn't seem to be the right time. I would make time, I reasoned, when I had more time. Marie is always encouraging me to become more organized. That way, she argues, I would be better able to manage my workload, and people would come to rely on me more. I'll usually agree and promise to do something about it: join the Filofax craze, build a card index, something along those lines. But the idea will fizzle out a minute after I've thought about it, which usually comes as some relief to me.

I phone Lucille every other day or so, always in the evening. We have an on-off relationship that seems to be going round in circles, which cannot be all bad seeing as a circle never ends. I have one of those telephones that can memorize numbers. All you do is press a digit and it dials. That's the Eighties for you; technology is everything. It's ideal for someone like me; in the past I would invariably have had to phone the operator because I'd forgotten the code to London. Then I would have had trouble remembering Lucille's number. I could have written it down once and for all, stuck the note on the refrigerator door with all the others, but that would have required someone with far better organizational skills.

I dialled by pressing the number seven digit and waited for the connection. I visualized the hallway in the Caledonian Road house where she lives. I could see Rachel curled up on the burgundy sofa in front of the television or ironing clothes for work the next day. Then Sumitra was stepping into the shower, shampooing her hair, soaping herself liberally. I felt guilty, so I imagined her running down the stairs – still naked – to answer the telephone. Someone picked up the receiver.

'Can I speak to Lucille?'

'I'll just get her.' Rachel. 'One sec.' I could hear the sound of the television in the background, someone speaking in a clipped, formal manner. It sounded odd to hear English spoken that way after so long. I glanced at my watch and realized it must be the nine o'clock news.

'Hello,' Lucille said. 'What happened to you?'

'Nothing much.' My mind started to back pedal. 'How are you . . . What d'you mean, "What happened?"'

'You didn't phone last weekend. It was your turn.'

'It was?' I couldn't understand how I had forgotten.

'Never mind,' she continued. '*I* was supposed to phone this time, but you've done it now. It'll be your turn next as well.' It seemed fair enough, the way she explained it.

We talked about work – she's an exhibition sales executive – and then became sidetracked about how she was losing control of her life because of her MA, which she is studying for part-time.

'Well, you've got to organize properly,' I said. 'Make sure you prioritize, set yourself realistic deadlines. There's no need not to have leisure time as well.' Management speak. I felt the hypocrisy of it all racing down the telephone line. Lucille is one of the most efficient people I have ever met so my words to her were glib and insubstantial.

'I guess you're right,' she said. 'I should really plan things more in advance.' She was using her thinking voice; half in the conversation, half in her head. 'I'm still working on the final draft of an essay. If all goes well, it should be ready two days before deadline, but that's cutting it a bit close.'

I've never handed in anything on time in my life, so I was nonplussed at her anxiety. Nevertheless I said, 'Well, yes. That *is* leaving it a bit late. You don't want them to start getting a poor impression of you now. These things matter.'

I was pleased I had steered the conversation away from what I was doing with my own life.

'It's been almost a month now,' she said. 'Isn't it about time one of us visited?'

'One month? Already? It can't be,' I said. 'Well . . . things are busy at the moment. I'm not sure whether I'll be here in the next few weeks.'

'Oh! You're going somewhere?'

'Yeah . . . might have to cover a couple of concerts – Los Angeles and Montreal.' I didn't elaborate because I'm not so good at lying.

'You could come here for a change,' she suggested. 'On your way back. Sumitra's away every weekend. Rachel's always at her boyfriend's.'

'We'll see,' I said, but with such a lack of enthusiasm that she didn't mention the subject again.

We parted undecided and I felt bad about that. I thought I should phone her back, but realized I really didn't want to further the discussion. The thought of doing so brought on a kind of heaviness in me.

When I first moved to Berlin, Lucille and I used to visit each other nearly every weekend. I would travel to London, sometimes by train if I had the time, by plane if I could afford it. Lucille always flew; she can't stand the tedium of long journeys. This continued for almost six months and although I should have been saving my earnings, I didn't feel uncomfortable about spending money that way. But I had never taken to London. My trips grew more infrequent until it came to the stage where it was only Lucille who seemed to be making any effort. She made the physical effort, that's true, but we would always share the financial burden.

In the afternoon I made a start on the invoices that had been occupying a corner of my desk over the past few weeks. I sat and cleared a space so there would be a clean surface to work on. It didn't take long as I am unusually tidy, which sometimes confounds people because they know I'm not an organized man. Nevertheless, I am not good at untidiness.

I realized I hadn't had a drink and although it wasn't yet lunchtime, breakfast seemed a distant memory. I scanned the contents of the refrigerator: half a carton of orange juice, several cans of lager, two apple doughnuts and four eggs. The orange juice may have been there weeks, perhaps a month. I ambled back to the desk with a lager and the dough-nuts. The invoices loomed up at me. I needed a paper napkin so as not to soil the forms and leapt up and sauntered back to the kitchen.

It seemed like the ideal time to check the notices on the refrigerator door. There were three notes to ring Lucille. One contained her work telephone number, but I had copied it down incorrectly – two of the digits had been swapped round. I left it as it was. I ate a whole doughnut before realizing it was stale, and washed down the unpleasant taste with several gulps of beer.

There were several messages to ring people – picture editors mostly. One, for Thomas at *Zip* magazine, I had emphasized with large exclamation marks. I hadn't contacted him in over three weeks after making a point of telling myself to phone four days after he had written to me. That way, I reasoned,

I wouldn't appear too eager for work and I would also give the impression of being reliable. I was so perturbed about this omission I made my way back to the invoices.

I sat down with a groan and started to lift and shake the papers, arranging them in some kind of order. Once done, I picked up the top form, studied it for a moment, then returned it to the pile. I shuffled the invoices and knocked them against the desk to make them neat again, then put them to one side, in the corner, and finished off the lager and the second doughnut. The forms were in exactly the same position they had started in.

When B phoned, I was agonizing over whether I could deal with the humiliation of ringing Thomas for work. I knew I would need a valid excuse for failing to contact him weeks ago, but as I'm loath to lie I was having a difficult time of it. B wanted to come round for a chat because he had thought of an angle for an article about foreign students and prostitution.

'Undercover Education?' he suggested as a headline. It didn't bear comment.

When B is serious about anything, he discusses it hurriedly over the phone. He usually comes round to talk when he wants to have a drink, though he is too polite to admit this. I went through the pretence of being interested in what he had to say regarding the prostitutes. I even got as far as mentioning contacts I could use for photographs. But after a while, I suggested it would be better if we discussed the matter over a drink. He immediately agreed.

The Café Rio isn't the least bit exotic. Save for a few faded posters of Corcovado's Christ and some bathing beauties on a beach, it could be any run-down bar in any city. It can be sombre during the day; the windows don't appear to have been cleaned in years, and the lighting isn't effective. In the evenings, however, the dreariness lends the bar a certain worn ambience. Several nights a month, Claus, the proprietor, hires a jazz band. He isn't very discerning – I suppose he can't pay them much – and although they are hardly ever outstanding, it's always refreshing to listen to new acts. Occasionally he will hire a rock band, but that happens rarely as it tends to ruin the atmosphere and drives the regulars away.

There was a group called Blue Grit that evening, and although I'm not partial to rock, I can tolerate it after a couple of beers. I tried unsuccessfully to order our drinks above the maze of other people's heads. I noticed B had failed to register the clamour as we walked in. He smiled inanely as he nodded to the music, which was odd considering he hates rock.

'We're not getting anywhere at this rate,' I said.

'No problem, man,' he replied, still nodding. 'Patience.'

I looked at him, turned and ploughed to the front of the bar. A woman in tight leather trousers muttered, 'That's right, queue jump, fat arse.'

I ignored her.

'It's not bad,' B shouted, 'this rock'n'roll.' His Cameroonian timbre made it sound like an academic subject.

'Since when have you liked this music?' I asked.

He shrugged as if he didn't understand the question, then pointed to two women who were pretending to bang their heads against a wall.

'How is Lucille?' he asked.

'Fine,' I shouted. 'She's fine.' I tried not to betray my

uncertainty about this. 'She's very busy at the moment. Says hello.'

We turned back to the band. The rock chicks were now playing ferocious air guitar. The lead singer turned occasionally and sang specifically for them. This only encouraged more head banging. I drained my bottle of beer while B went to replenish the drinks. I scanned the room, but the only attractive woman was the leather-wearing complainer by the bar.

'How's work?' I asked when B returned.

'Quite well,' he smiled. 'Quite well indeed.'

'Really?'

B works as a journalist on a small community newspaper and as a part-time household removals man. He never enthuses about work. Neither of us does. There is either too much or too little of it, or there's something about it that isn't quite right. There is too much stress involved, the lifting and carrying hurts his back, the pay is inadequate, or it simply doesn't stimulate him.

'Yes, I have a few projects on the go at the moment.' He didn't elaborate. 'Hey, have you thought any more about joining us with the moving? There are still vacancies, you know.' B is always trying to get me involved in the removals business, but I will have none of it.

I rocked back and forth on my heels for a moment. 'Okay B, what's the story?' I said. 'What's her name?'

He gave me a look of false incredulousness, but I could trace the ghost of a grin in his eyes.

'Whose name?'

'Come on, don't make me beg. I know you're up to something.'

A laugh boomed up and tumbled out of his deep brown

face. Frown marks and worry lines made him seem older than thirty-two.

'Well, my friend.' He looked down at his feet, then back at the band. 'I have, actually, been seeing someone – for several weeks now . . . Angelika is her name,' he announced. 'Things have been going very well, I must say. Very well indeed, man.'

'Weeks? You didn't say anything.'

'Well . . . you know, I wasn't too sure. These things, they are tricky sometimes. I didn't know how it would turn out.'

B is not one for secrecy. I must have let my disappointment show with my silence. He cradled his beer in both hands and we stared out at the stage.

'You know, I think this might be the one, my friend,' he added, regarding me closely. 'She could be the one.' And from the way he had said it, I knew it was probably true.

I could tell he was getting drunk and that pleased me. It doesn't take him long. He didn't need much convincing in order to proceed to the club.


By the time we reached the Atlantic, Tunde was already on the dance floor. He waved, but didn't bother tearing himself away to say hello. One wave and then he was flush up against a perfect stranger. That was nothing new. The atmosphere was frantic. B's glasses steamed up the instant we entered the room. People squirmed about on the floor like so many eels in a bathtub. A Latin American woman writhed in her own space. Every so often she hiked up her dress for an instant, followed by the whoops and cheers of other dancers. This only encouraged her. Looking at her face I could tell she was very happy, very crazy or very high. Probably all three. Merengue and salsa oozed from every pore in the room. Condensed sweat dripped from the ceilings. I went to fetch the drinks while B perched on the edge of the dance floor, not quite drunk enough to venture forth.

At the bar I noticed a woman with a mane of blonde and copper-coloured hair, wearing a ruffled white skirt and pastel blue blouse. I was about to look away when she smiled and turned to a woman standing beside her. I paid the barman and stole another glance at her. She had the most cheerful-looking face I had ever seen, even when she wasn't smiling. I couldn't imagine her ever being morose.

I drank one of the beers at the bar, pausing once for breath. It didn't seem fair that B was already half drunk while I was still sober. The woman in pastel blue was talking to her friend. They had their backs to me. Once in a while they would look over, then turn away and begin their chatter again.

When I returned to the dance floor, B had disappeared. I thought he might have gone in search of me. I was about to circumnavigate the club when I noticed the Latin American woman in the middle of the floor, her arms draped around Tunde's neck. She reached up and stroked his hair, then let her hands drop to his buttocks and reined him in. I looked away. I noticed B dancing in a corner by himself, away from the fireworks of centre stage. I felt awkward standing there with a drink in each hand so I went to work on both of them. I looked back at the bar, at the cheery-faced woman, who glanced and smiled and turned again to her friend.

'Where's my drink?' Tunde shouted when he managed to disentangle himself. Perspiration dribbled from his sideburns.

'*I* don't know,' I said. 'This is mine. Look – someone's taken your place.' On the dance floor, the Latin American woman's legs were wrapped round another man's hips.

Tunde shrugged and moved off to buy more drinks.

'Good idea!' I shouted, but I don't think he heard.

By the time he returned I was feeling peculiar. People kept zooming in and out of focus. I'd drunk too much, too quickly. I like to drift into a gradual inebriation. I could have sworn he had brought along the cheery-faced woman and her friend.

'Claudia was just admiring your moves,' he said. 'Here's your drink.' He looked at me appraisingly. Then, quite suddenly, he seemed to find something else fascinating and promptly sped away.

I looked at Claudia. She was still grinning. I mumbled something even I could barely make sense of, but she only smiled.

'What's your name?' she shouted, leaning towards me. I shouted back. I knew her name already so there was nothing else to say. There was a moment of silence, which may have been a few seconds, but could just as easily have lasted minutes. I had no way of knowing. She reached up and half-whispered, 'My friend Claudia quite likes you.'

I wasn't sure what she meant. Did she refer to herself in the third person? She turned to indicate her friend who was still standing there, swaying slightly to the music, pretending she had no idea we were talking about her. I took a good look, but I couldn't place her. She looked North African or Latin American or mixed. She too had long hair, black this time, decorated with what looked like bits of coloured string. The pair of them wouldn't have been out of place at the circus.

'So . . . you're both called Claudia, then?' I ventured.

They burst into laughter, and the North African looked away. It was shyness, I suppose, or loss of interest, or both. But it seemed rude to me.

She turned back. 'I am Claudia,' she said.

15

'Ah! I see.' I turned to the blonde. 'And you – what's your . . . ?'

'Let's dance,' she cut in, and dragged us to the centre of the floor. Annoyingly, Claudia shuffled along behind us.

The cheery-faced woman seemed to find something about me amusing. Her smiles developed into giggles and soon she couldn't help but laugh. Then her guffaws began to irritate. I was grateful I'd become partly deaf on account of the volume of the music. It was obvious Claudia wasn't going to disappear in a hurry and I felt rude for not having said a word to her all evening.

'D'you want another drink?' I shouted. My shirt was wet with perspiration. I needed to prop myself against the bar and rest.

'Not really thirsty!' Claudia screeched. She and her friend continued to dance.

I shrugged and went anyway.

I couldn't find B anywhere and this surprised me because he never leaves without letting me know. I tried another level of the club, a more tranquil area. I sat at a round drinks table opposite a couple in the midst of an embrace. The woman's leg was straddled over the man's thigh.

'Don't mind me,' I said, but they ignored me. I put the beers on the table. I vaguely remembered something about Claudia not wanting anything. Maybe her grinning friend would appreciate a drink. I sat in a sort of stupor staring at the couple opposite, not really seeing them. Time was a hound on a leash I had lost a grip of. At one stage, the woman's eyes peered out at me from behind the head of her lover. She must have whispered something to him, because the next minute he was shouting – sharp monosyllabic profanities, but I couldn't really take anything in. I smiled at them through half-closed eyes and when I focused again, they had disappeared. I held onto the edge of the table and pushed myself up. I was going to leave the second drink there, then decided to take it back to the dance floor. By the time I returned to the main level, the two women were back at the bar. The smiler ignored me.

'What happened to you?' Claudia grilled. I didn't think *she* had a right to be annoyed. She had narrow, scrutinizing eyes, which sat in an over-made-up face, framed by the technicoloured hair. She had probably stored up years of resentment as the smiler's less glamorous sidekick.

'Been looking for B everywhere,' I explained. 'Can't find him.'

'Is that mine?' The smiler pointed to the beer.

'No . . . I'll get you one if you want.'

'Nah, don't bother.' She gave a little wave of dismissal. 'Not really thirsty.'

'Neither am I,' Claudia put in, as if I had asked her. No one said anything for a while.

We looked out at the dance floor: two women were screaming at each other, but it didn't get physical, which seemed to disappoint onlookers. The amorous couple I had earlier incensed swayed gently in the middle of the room, despite the liveliness of the number. I thought B might have already left. I closed my eyes for a minute to escape the cigarette smoke.

'Why d'you call him "B", anyway?' Claudia shouted, destroying my momentary peace.

'Yeah, doesn't he have a real name?' the friend chipped in.

I said the answer to the second question was probably 'yes', but regarding the first, I couldn't remember.

Claudia studied me for a moment. She wasn't sure whether

or not I was pulling her leg. Her friend continued to smile. It was a wonder she didn't pull any facial muscles.

'You speak English?' Claudia asked at length, in English.

The friend's eyes widened. I thought there might be some success after all.

'Sometimes. Only when I have to,' I replied.

'Cool! Fantastic!' the friend's language skills exploded. She brushed her blonde mane over her head with one hand and let it cascade down again, and shook it. I could envisage being lashed by her locks in bed.

'The discotheque we are in . . . it is very hot, no?' Claudia said. 'You believe it is so?' The words emerged like a goods train chugging past a railway crossing – you didn't know when it would ever end. She fanned her long neck with her fingers, more for the friend's attention.

'Hot, hot!' the smiler screamed. I didn't know why she had to start shouting simply because she was speaking another language. She bunched her hair together, then pulled the mess of it over her left shoulder exposing only one side of her face. She pouted and rubbed her lips together as if for the moisture, then reached up to her neck and began to massage it. I sipped my beer. She seemed completely oblivious to what she was doing. I had almost forgotten about Claudia.

'What is *your* name?' I asked the smiler, a little loudly, fearing she might be hard of hearing.

'Hot, hot!' she screamed again. She looked at me expectantly and smiled.

I was getting nowhere. The English was hopeless – it dragged like a two-legged dog at the end of a chase. My eyes must have glazed over because Claudia and the blonde had moved back into the vernacular. I watched them chirruping away, but I could hardly hear above the music.

'Hey, ladies!' Tunde sauntered up and slid a hand round each one's waist as if he had known them for years. 'What are we doing here? Why not dancing?'

Claudia's friend's eyes lit up. 'Yeah, dancing,' she parroted. She started to sway in Tunde's snaky clinch.

He withdrew his grasp of Claudia in order to envelop the smiler. He was my friend and she had no idea what he was like, but she would find out soon enough. There was comfort in that. Claudia and I tried not to look from either side. We glanced at the dance floor, while watching events unfold from the corners of our eyes.

Tunde wrapped his arms across the smiler's stomach while she reached up round his neck so that her breasts jutted out. I couldn't help but stare.

'Where's B?' I asked, attempting to distract them.

Tunde shrugged. They were rocking gently against each other now. They didn't seem to consider moving away. What hope was there for me if the smiler could fall for another man in a microsecond?

The Latin American woman wrenched free from the dance floor and began to sway towards us in heels the height of a table knife. Tunde started to disengage from the smiler's torso, while she continued to pitch and moan. The Latin American woman was barely five metres from us now. Still, Tunde kissed the smiler from behind, slowly, on one side of her neck. He gave her hips a firm squeeze, then he was off, his arm round the Latin American woman. The smiler looked dumbstruck.

'I should be going,' I shouted, to gauge a reaction. I glanced at my watch. 'It's getting late.'

'No, don't,' Claudia said. 'Why . . . why don't you come to ours?' She poked me in the ribs, becoming familiar. Did she mean the both of them? At the same time? She was wilder than she looked. I glanced at her friend's legs, the way they stretched from beneath the miniskirt and didn't seem to stop.

I remembered Lucille. An image of her face loomed up. For an instant I thought I should at least feign resistance or perhaps invent an excuse and leave. Uncle Raymond always said he could tell whether someone was lying or not. He simply had to focus on their breathing. If the person inhaled irregularly and appeared to hesitate before exhaling, then sure enough that person was lying. Invariably, most people were liars in Uncle Raymond's eyes. All the same, I always worried whether people could discern by their own secret method whether or not I was telling the truth. It annoyed me to think I could never tell a plain lie. I have never made a good liar. I accepted Claudia's invitation without giving it another thought.


I think Claudia may have had something entirely different in mind when she invited me to her apartment. I recall being helped up at the bottom of the stairs in the Atlantic. I don't remember falling. Claudia and her friend held on to me on either side. I seemed to spend the entire evening asking Claudia's friend her name. She repeated it once or twice, but I forgot almost as soon as it was given.

The woman with the elusive name attempted to bundle me into a car. I tried to protest, but what I really wanted was to lie down. Someone complained, 'He's no lightweight, is he?' but it could have been either of them. I must have passed out because the next moment I was being shaken awake by Claudia. The friend was standing to one side of the car, holding on to the open door. Her smile was a mere memory. When I got out I could feel the warm breath of the evening waft over me, and the whole world seemed to tilt. Claudia caught me by the arm and things stabilized for a while. The downtown lights had vanished.

The friend dashed to open the front door while Claudia and I staggered towards her. By the time we managed to clamber upstairs and fall into the apartment, the two women were exhausted. Then the friend disappeared. I kept expecting her to return, naked.

'Where's what's-her-name?' I asked.

Claudia was wandering round the apartment for no discernible reason, wringing her hands. 'Here, drink this.' She handed me a glass beaker of black coffee. 'Sylvie's gone home, silly. Why do you ask?'

I shrugged. Sylvie had left without so much as a 'good night', which struck me as rude. The night was racing away from me now and I longed for sleep. I sipped the coffee and reached across the sofa and kissed Claudia for what seemed like hours. She wriggled free and began to comb her fingers through her hair, undoing the multi-coloured extensions piecemeal.

'What's your line of work?' she asked as she placed another extension on the coffee table beside her, then smoothed down her dress. She was intent on readjusting herself every other minute, which seemed pointless at this stage.

'I'm twenty-four,' I said.

'No, work – what do you do?'

I wasn't up to any kind of conversation. I gave her what I thought was a seductive look and leaned forward again. I couldn't work the zip at the back of her dress. I yanked it down, then up again, but it moved only a centimetre. After a minute or so she began to resist. There seemed to be two of her now.

'If we don't do it now, I'll fall asleep. I'm dog-tired.' I was trying to be gentle, but I couldn't blame her for looking hurt. 'Where's the bedroom?'

We tottered along a corridor, fumbling kisses along the way, and then she rushed into the bathroom. I lay spread-eagled on the bed and began to twirl the tassels on the bedspread. A large Chinese paper lantern loomed down at me giving out a soft, pink glow. The next moment I was being slapped across the face.

'Wake up! Wake up!' Claudia kept on in a loud whisper.

'Stop. Please, stop,' I mumbled, unable to move. I thought: How have things come to this, begging not to be hit?

Claudia continued to provoke me until I was forced to open my eyes.

'Oh, thank God,' she sighed. 'I thought you'd never wake up.' She sounded more relieved than annoyed. 'You're a real sleeper, aren't you?'

Daylight oozed in around the edges of the curtains. I wondered what had happened to the night. It seemed unfair to be unaware of whether or not one had experienced any kind of pleasure. Claudia sat on the edge of the bed in an oversized yellow T-shirt and a man's striped pyjama bottoms. She had scraped off her make-up and wrapped her hair in a loose bun, providing clear access to her features: high forehead and cheek-bones and a smattering of freckles. She was neither Latin American nor North African, I could see that now.

'Well, I'm awake now,' I smiled. I reached across and kissed her and slipped a hand beneath the yellow T-shirt. I took her nipples in my mouth, one after the other. She moaned quietly and lay back. I tugged at the drawstring of her pyjamas, then tried to yank the material beyond her hips.

'Here, I'll do it.' Claudia released the knot, then attempted to remove the pyjamas, but I pushed her hand aside and was already thrusting by the time they were around her thighs. It was almost too late. In a moment it was over, barely three minutes since she had slapped me awake. She looked stupefied. I felt a pang of remorse, on the one hand for having been so quick, and on the other, for being unfaithful to Lucille. But then it wasn't the first time.

'I should go,' I said. I wanted to be in my own bed, without the complication of the situation.

'What do you mean?' Claudia said. 'Don't go.'

I was about to mention Lucille, but I decided against it. It seemed too much of an effort. I got up and staggered towards the bathroom. I was still drunk from the night before; my head felt like a calabash with a lead weight knocking about inside it. When I returned, Claudia had pulled on a pink dressing gown. She sat with her knees drawn up against her chest, arms wrapped round them. She watched closely as I dressed. I was worried she might break into hysterics at any moment. It had happened to me before and I had never forgotten. I felt powerless to assuage the situation.

'I don't suppose . . .' she said after a long silence, but she didn't finish the sentence. I didn't respond. I wanted to be away from there.

In the morning light I could envisage myself in her eyes and I seemed distant. That is how I must have appeared to her; very cold and far away.


On the U-Bahn home, some youths were causing a disturbance at the far end of the carriage. They were shouting and laughing at nothing in particular. I could tell their night of revelry was only just petering out. They seemed intent on clinging to whatever vestiges of frivolity remained.

At Hallesches Tor there was a splashing sound and the handful of passengers in the carriage kept turning round. I thought it might be a station cleaner washing down the platform. I heard a retching noise and realized one of the ruffians was being sick. The doors closed abruptly and the youth returned to sit with his friends. He was smiling now. They were all grinning and laughing. They seemed terribly pleased with themselves. 'Dirty rotten drunks,' I muttered. I turned away and didn't give the situation another thought.

# 3

I CALLED MARIE at the magazine. I tend to phone at random. I'm sure she doesn't appreciate this, but I do it, regardless. There was no work, of course, but an exhibition was being scheduled for the Andreas Grob gallery. She said she would notify me as soon as it was confirmed.

'You're still on for the Henkelmann assignment?' she asked. 'Next week, remember?'

'Of course,' I said, without hesitating. 'Just checking to see if there's anything else.' I had forgotten, actually, and it disturbed me to have lost a memory so easily. I wrote out a reminder of the job and stuck it on the refrigerator door. There was a note in place already:

**Henkelmann – Thursday – Marie**

No date.

Afterwards I rang Thomas at *Zip* to apologize for not contacting him earlier. I'd been away, I said. I didn't elaborate. He grunted and there was a moment's silence in which I was sure he was trying to think of a way to end the conversation.

I told him something terrible had happened – there had been a death. In the family. 'I can't talk about it,' I mumbled.

'I'm sorry to hear that,' he said, without emotion. He seemed to be mulling over something. 'Why don't I have a look in my diary and we'll see what we can do. I'll get my secretary to make another appointment.'

Once arranged, I wrote out another reminder and stuck it beside the two Henkelmann notes.

I began to work again on the photographs I had been trying to exhibit for the past four months, based on the lives of asylum seekers in the city. Christian, who manages Galerie Messinger on Knesebeckstrasse, keeps promising to show my work as soon as he sees 'something inspiring'. If you didn't know him you might think he was being tactless and insensitive. That's just his way and I appreciate the candour. The last time I saw him he said the photographs were interesting, but not quirky enough for his market.

I yawned and a moment later my stomach growled. I checked the hall clock and realized I had been working nonstop for nearly three hours. It worried me because there is no ventilation in the darkroom. I'm afraid of succumbing to the fumes one day, waking sometime in the future, emaciated, perhaps not regaining consciousness at all.

Apart from the eggs and a few tins of corned beef and sardines, there was no food in the kitchen, so I had to go out for lunch. Frau Lieser surprised me on the staircase.

'Good morning,' she warbled, even though it was well into afternoon. She has long been under the impression she possesses a fine singing voice. Her greetings are invariably delivered in the tune currently bustling through her head.

'Afternoon,' I replied, trying to steer round her. She seemed unaware she was blocking the way. Like me, Frau Lieser is not thin. I started to panic because I was sure she was going to mention the rent. I couldn't remember whether I had settled for the month, although it was remotely possible I was even ahead with the payments.

'These stairs,' she complained with a theatrical sigh. 'They're murder on the old bones, you know. You young people, you're up and down like squirrels. When you reach my age it's a chore simply to get out of bed.'

'You're still young, Frau Lieser,' I said, because to me she didn't look in any way enfeebled. That wasn't what she wanted to hear.

'Just wait and see,' she said. 'When you get to be my age you'll remember my words. You'll say, "She was right after all, old Marianne. I wish I'd listened." Look at you, jetting about the world every day. It would be the death of me.' Her fingers danced lightly above her scarf, over the place where her hair was thinning.

Frau Lieser thinks I travel a great deal more than I actually do. Whenever we meet she will ask if I have just arrived from somewhere, if I am about to set off again. I'll usually reply, Yes, I have been to New York or Marseilles in the past few days, that I'm planning to travel to Dakar or Reykjavik to cover a story. Whenever I mention the name of a country or city she has never heard of, she squeals and closes her eyes. 'Oh, the heat, the warm shifting sands,' she sighs, regardless of whether or not the place is blessed with a warm climate. 'The dancing girls!'

'I was making my way upstairs,' she gestured towards the ceiling, referring to the punks, Caroline and Dieter. 'They've got problems again. With the toilet. Am I in any fit state to do anything about it?'

I spotted her bag of tools beside her feet. Everyone in the

building has noticed this bag, but so far, no one has ever seen it open. When I first moved in she carried it upstairs to answer my complaint about a leaking radiator. She examined the problem briefly, rapped twice against the metal, and said, 'Needs professional attention.' Which is what she always says.

'As I was coming up to your floor,' she continued, ignoring my efforts to squeeze past her, 'I suddenly remembered that bread you brought me once. From Scotland. It's given me the most awful craving now, that lovely Scottish bread.' She smoothed down her apron with her palms and smiled coyly.

I couldn't remember ever giving her anything apart from the rent. She might have been confusing me with someone else, but then I couldn't imagine any of the tenants being generous towards her. Apart from Clariss, perhaps.

'That time you went to Scotland. There was a festival, remember?'

'Oh, *that* time,' I recalled. The episode had been fictitious, a ruse to encourage leniency towards me during another period of unemployment. I was afraid the lie had come back to haunt me.

'It's called shortbread, Frau Lieser. You can buy it down the road, you know.' I certainly had.

'Nonsense!' she snapped. 'Anyway, it wouldn't be the same. Only the Scottish know how to bake it that way. Properly. Next time you are in London, please visit Scotland and get me some of that bread.' She reached into her apron and retrieved a few crumpled marks. 'Here,' she said. 'You mustn't forget now. I'm relying on you.'

I did not tell her I hadn't been to London in over six months, that I had no intention of travelling there in the near future. She would have been bewildered to learn I had never been to Scotland.

'Frau Lieser,' I inhaled. 'I have an urgent assignment. Some musicians are, at this moment, waiting to be photographed at the InterContinental. I have to hurry.'

'Oh, of course, of course!' she exclaimed, managing only to become more involved. She shifted a few millimetres. 'These musicians, they are . . . are they? Do I know them?'

'No, Frau Lieser, you do not,' I said, squeezing past her. I muttered my excuses and left her to wheeze up the stairs.

The lunch menu had come and gone by the time I arrived at the Rio. I asked whether there was anything I could order. The waitress scurried into the kitchen and returned moments later saying the cook could prepare a Spanish omelette and French fries. I smiled in approval and she tweaked her ear and disappeared into the kitchen as quickly as she had arrived.

I sipped my beer at first in order to make it last the meal, but my thirst got the better of me and I drained the glass before the food came. I bought another straight away.

Apart from the waitress and myself, there were few other people in the room. In a corner towards the rear of the café, a man, perhaps in his late twenties, sat with his palm against his forehead. He began to write in a small pocket book next to his plate. After a moment, he stopped writing and started to pick at his food. He was wearing blue flip-flops and cut-off jeans, and a black T-shirt with faded gilt lettering. He took up his pen again and wrote for perhaps another minute. He wavered slightly, attempted to write something else, then brought his head towards his hand again. When my food arrived he was still clutching his head.

The chef had tossed slivers of red peppers into the omelette, and a heap of paprika. I spent the next couple of minutes picking out all the peppers, placing them carefully to one side of the plate. I thought we made a pernickety pair, the intermittent writer and I.

In the middle of this, a woman strode up to me from the side entrance. I didn't look up at once, but I could tell she was tall. She gave off a strong scent; like wading through the perfume section of a department store.

'Hello, Clariss,' I said without glancing up. I had nearly rid myself of all the peppers.

'What's shaking, honey?' She sat down and rested her chin in the cradle of her hands and looked at me.

'Nothing much,' I said. 'You?' The omelette minus the peppers was close to perfect.

'Go on and eat, sugar,' she waved. She lit a cigarette. 'I'm just fine.' She looked at the man in the corner. When he finally began to write, she started to applaud. 'Bravo!' she called in her American drawl, 'Bravo!' her claps like pistol shot.

He turned to look at her. Embarrassed, he swivelled back to his work, but he didn't write a word. He just sat there. The room was silent.

'I think you've interrupted his flow,' Clariss whispered.

'Interesting theory. Have a French fry.'

'Very generous, but no – I'm reducing.'

Clariss was wearing an indigo velvet trouser suit, with a sea-green and yellow silk scarf draped round her neck. Her hair fell in thick black curls round her face and shoulders. Her face was almost as black as her hair. Every time she took a drag on her cigarette, her bracelets slid down to her bony elbow. After a while she balanced the cigarette carefully on the side of the ashtray and shook the bracelets back into place. Clariss was taller than anyone I had ever met without the aid of heels. Today she was wearing stilettos.

'You look stunning,' I said.

'Aim to please, sweetpea.' She pointed a very long finger at me. She seemed thrilled with herself, but she was trying not to let it show. 'What has a girl got to do to get some service these days?' She snapped her fingers at the waitress, making a surprisingly loud crack.

The waitress traipsed over with absolutely no sense of urgency. 'What'll you have?' she barked.

Clariss gabbled something unintelligible.

'What's that?' the waitress glanced at me for an explanation, her palms held out. She didn't like Clariss. 'What'd she say?'

I shrugged. Clariss tried again. The waitress collected my empty glass and left.

'What's so funny?' Clariss asked.

'You – what language were you speaking?'

She glared at me and tutted. The writer in the corner had disappeared.

'I have to go now,' I said. 'I'm halfway through work.'

'Work? And leave a girl on her own? In a strange bar? How ungallant.'

'You're not a stranger here; this is practically your home,' I said. 'All right, I'll stay for one more.'

'Fine. Do as you please,' she sighed. 'Gentlemen are so hard to come by these days.'


I felt sluggish after the lunchtime drinks, but decided to continue. I had been working on a set of photographs of my neighbour, Arî. He looked uncomfortable in every print I had developed. Arî Jaziri is a Kurdish *Asylbewerber*. Asylum seeker. He fled Turkey over a year ago and has been waiting for a decision on his immigration status ever since. Every day he has some new worry more pressing than the previous day's. It will invariably be linked to his current state of limbo; he is not strictly a resident of any country at the moment.

The first time I asked if I could photograph him, he flatly refused. Then one day while he was having another one of his crises, I sat him down at my kitchen table. He began by telling me how the police had harassed him on the U-Bahn yet again. He halted in mid-tirade.

'Who are they, this people?' He pointed to the photographs on the walls.

'They're part of the project I'm working on at the moment,' I said. 'Partly why I've asked you to sit for me.'

He stood and scrutinized them, shoulders scrunched up, eyes hooded by thick eyebrows. He stopped in front of a triptych of three sisters.

'They're from Eritrea,' I explained.

'Why you take this pictures?' he asked.

I touched the triptych and straightened it, but it only teetered again. 'It's my job. And I want to.' I couldn't explain.

He smoked in silence for several minutes, then turned to me and said when I realized why I took the photographs, I should be sure to let him know. He had forgotten about the incident on the U-Bahn.

A few weeks later, I took Arî to a jazz club along Bleibtreustrasse. I'd been sent to cover a set by a band from Miami who had been touring Europe for the past five months. We were late. The air was viscous with smoke. Arî confessed he had never been inside a jazz club before. We sat as near to the front as possible and shared a table with three students from the Free University. The waitress arrived with our orders. In a moment I rose to take my photographs.

'Why you take this pictures?' Arî asked again when I returned. 'In your kitchen? Why?'

The musicians launched into a version of Charlie Parker's *Ornithology*. I wondered whether they missed Florida at all during their marathon tour. My fingers thrummed against the underside of the table.

'I'm not sure, Arî,' I said. 'I think I want to find out why people leave places. Their impulses. What makes them get up and go . . . What that can do to a person. I'm still not clear about it . . . Do you see what I mean?'

He made a slight *moue,* but didn't respond. He took a long drag on his cigarette and stopped badgering me with questions after that. We listened to the band until it grew late and Arî began to fret about returning to Kreuzberg. As we left, without my prompting, he invited me to take his picture if I still wanted to.

Looking at his photographs now, his irritation and anxiety visible, I was tempted to ask him if I could start all over again. After a while I reasoned it was the way he had felt at the time. I suppose I was fortunate to have captured the essence of him, that faraway look in his eyes. He seemed to be staring out into a distance I had been unaware of. I hadn't given him a set of instructions – what to wear, whether to smile, where to look. I had simply told him to do whatever he wanted – sit or stand – in his temporary home.

I had asked him about his family and he talked of his brothers, his mother, Hezar his fiancée, who was only sixteen. I imagined his journey from south-east Turkey to Germany, those he had left behind. I thought then that if you left the place you loved, that you were familiar with, if you changed it for another place, how could it not affect you? How could there not be pain?


I developed the prints and hung them up to dry. I had no idea which ones to choose so I arranged them on the kitchen walls and the cupboard doors to attain a clearer insight over the following days.

The telephone rang, startling me out of the silence.

'Hey, honey!' a voice sang out. Clariss. She wanted to know if Frau Lieser was still in the vicinity.

'Haven't seen her,' I said.

'Marvellous!' she screamed. She must have remained in the Rio all afternoon. 'I need to dash in and fix myself up for tonight. For the party. Wanna come?'

I knew Clariss's dash would mean a couple of hours parading round her apartment deciding what to wear, applying and removing make-up, gossiping with friends on the telephone. She always seemed to be on the way to a party or returning from one, emerging from a cab with groceries bought at KaDeWe. I could never wring out of her exactly how she earned a living; she never went to work, but she always wore long sequined dresses, expensive-looking gowns, power suits. I never once saw her in jeans.

'Sorry, can't come,' I said. 'Working.' I looked round at the prints for support.

'Your loss, sweetpea.' She hung up before I could reply.

Clariss was always inviting the tenants to her parties or to one of her favourite clubs. Sometimes Caroline and Dieter went, but I never accepted. I had heard too much, too often – the stories and the rumours. What had happened at a particular party, who had choked on their own vomit, who had been caught *in flagrante* with whom. The fights. Always Clariss only just managed to survive to tell the tale, escaping murder by fleeing down the Ku'damm wearing only a pair of stilettos, or out of a fourth floor window into the arms of a burly fireman; I'd heard the news about the inferno at the TicTac club, and I guessed she'd heard it too, and allowed her imagination to meld with reality.

# 4

WHEN THE TELEPHONE rang I was in the bath. I let it ring until the machine took the message, then tried to recover my previous state of calm. It didn't work. I drew more hot water into the tub and watched bubbles rise around me until islands of foam floated to the floor. I was trying to decipher who might have called. I got so agitated I dragged myself out of the bath to listen to the message.

Marie's voice was not what I'd wanted to hear; I was hoping it might be Lucille. Marie isn't good with technology – odd considering she spends most of her day on the telephone. She said, 'Hallo, it's Marie here . . . Hallo . . . Hallo? Oh, it's the machine . . . About tomorrow – there's something I need to do before the Henkelmann assignment, so it might be best if we meet there instead of at the office . . . say, in the auditorium . . . No! No! Why not . . . Let's make it outside the venue or, no! In the Bliss café. Yes? – On the corner of Dieffenbachstrasse and Schönleinstrasse? That's it. We'll meet there. Got it? Bliss café. Corner of Dieffenbach and Schönlein. At eleven. Don't be late, okay? See you there then . . . Hallo? Um, it's Marie!'

I was a few minutes late the following day, but was relieved to discover Marie hadn't arrived. I wolfed down a fried *croque-monsieur* and trained my eyes on the passing traffic. A woman with long coal-black hair and bedroom eyes stopped at the window and looked in. I smiled, trying to encourage her in, but it seemed to have the opposite effect and she couldn't get away quickly enough. When Marie drove up a moment later, I felt superior because, for once, I had given the impression of being on time. She parked her metallic grey Mercedes right outside the café.

'Something to drink? Tea, coffee?' She leaned down to kiss me.

I glanced at my watch. 'Won't we be late?'

'No, no, there's still plenty of time. I thought we should arrive early just in case.'

'In case of what?' I asked, suspicious, thinking it had to do with my timekeeping.

'In case, in case – don't be so querulous. What'll you have?'

I looked up at the board. 'Coffee, I suppose.' I didn't want anything, but it was a way to pass the time.

At the counter, Marie reached up on tiptoe in biscuit-beige heels to squint at the blackboard. Her calf muscles bulged. I turned away. In a moment, I looked back again. I followed the curve of her legs, the inverted wine bottles, the slight ankles flowing out to the swell of thick calves. A tan suede skirt hugged her ample behind. She exuded strength and sensuality. By the time she tottered back to the table with the tray of coffees and cakes I could feel my blood pumping.

'I shouldn't, I know.' She made an impish face as she set down the cups. 'I've got you some sachertorte. The pastries look as if they've been sitting there for days.'

I shook my head. 'I'm not hungry,' I said, even though the sight of the sachertorte made my heart swell. She pushed the plate towards me regardless.

'So, this Henkelmann character – you really think he's worth covering?' I asked. 'I mean, people – your readers – aren't they going to find this sort of thing dull? Politics? Agendas?'

'I disagree. I think we can approach this from another angle, not just concentrate on the politics, but personal stuff – home life, taste in music, opinions.' A few customers glanced in our direction, drawn by Marie's singsong voice. She reached over with a fork and cut herself a piece of cake. 'It's not as if he's a complete unknown. I reckon he's got as much voter appeal as Bauer.'

'Well, I guess it's best to reach them in their infancy, before they're inaccessible,' I said.

'My sentiments exactly,' she nodded. There was another lunge for the sachertorte. She didn't appear to realize what she was doing. 'He's a big fan of Bessie Corday, you know.'

'Corday? She's coming over for a concert, isn't she?' I cut a hefty triangle of cake with the knife, nibbled it, cradled the rest in my hand.

'Not only that, we're hoping to feature her. It'll make an interesting tie-in – politician/jazz singer.' She flashed her palms for emphasis, then helped herself to the final piece of cake. I finished my own slice, then considered getting up for another plate.

Marie glanced at her watch. 'Come on then!' She was almost stamping her feet. 'Don't want to be late.'

'I thought you said there was plenty of time?' She was always like this. Unpredictable.

'Time is money,' she chirped. 'The early bird and all that.

Don't forget, I need to secure an interview if any of this is going to be worthwhile. I'll need to corner Henkelmann when I get a chance.'

It took six minutes to trot to the half-empty auditorium. Six minutes to work up a sweat in the morning heat. I could feel the coffee and cake and fried food sloshing inside me during this uncustomary exercise. We shuffled into a row of vacant seats in the middle of the hall. Marie rummaged in her bag for a tape recorder and notebook.

'This is too far back,' I wheezed. I pointed to the recorder. 'You won't pick up anything with that.' I tucked in my shirt and leaned down to catch my breath.

Marie hadn't so much as a hair out of place. 'You think?' She glanced about, her head a sparrow's anxious twitch.

'Look, there are seats near the front,' I said. 'Why don't we move?'

Marie bundled her contraptions back into her bag and we were off again. The host had walked onto the stage and people were quiet now.

'Who is he?' I whispered.

'No idea,' Marie shrugged. 'Haven't got a name. Community leader, I suppose.'

I looked round at the rest of the auditorium, which was by now three-quarters full. The atmosphere was dull as a school assembly. There were mainly Turkish men wearing C&A suits that had been dragged out and pressed for the day. A few journalists huddled at the front, joined by a handful of photographers, one of whom kept clicking away from the centre aisle as if he had nothing better to do. Several bemused-looking men who might have wandered in off the street stood guard at the back. Marie was, as far as I could see, the only woman.

The host introduced the main speaker and people began to rouse a little. Perhaps it seemed that way to me because of the throat-clearing and feeble applause. Also, a photographer in the side aisle knelt down and began to peer through his viewfinder. I took that as my cue and moved into the centre aisle to take a few pictures of both the figures on stage and members of the audience. It didn't seem at all spirited and after being on my feet for two minutes, I promptly sat down again.

'He's broader than he looks on TV,' Marie whispered. She stared at the gesticulating grey-haired man on stage. Henkelmann was talking about capital injection and the revival of small business and industry. A few of the suits in the audience began to nod in appreciation.

'Business leaders in areas such as this need to band together,' he said. 'We have to support one another so that the community as a whole can prosper.' He spread out his arms as if to embrace the entire auditorium. I liked his use of 'we'; he probably lived along the Havel in a three-storey villa passed down through several generations.

If the Social Democrats came to power, he pledged, incentives would be provided for deprived areas such as Kreuzberg to ensure reinvigoration. That was a word he bandied about with increasing frequency. 'Reinvigoration!' he boomed, 'is at the top of our agenda, my friends, and this can only be accomplished with the skills and leadership of people such as yourselves.' There was a roar from the audience. Marie was scribbling furiously. Henkelmann had changed gear suddenly. Sweat marks bloomed from his armpits across his lilac shirt. All our cameras were clicking now.

Outside, the walkabout had been organized to follow a route past chosen local shops and buildings. These were meant to be representative of the area, but everything had a sheen suggesting the whole affair had been stage-managed. Graffiti had been scrubbed away. The exterior of *Flossi's* launderette still smelled of new paint. I had walked these streets often enough myself; it wasn't far from where I lived. I couldn't blame anyone for putting up appearances. We all like to show our best side when it matters most.

A little market ran along part of the street. Ordinarily the stallholders were brash, aggressive even, about selling their wares. Today they seemed to huddle together, glancing suspiciously at the oncoming entourage.

'I need to nip in closer,' Marie said. 'It's no good being way out here if I can't ask any questions. I can hardly hear what's being said.'

I hovered around the periphery to obtain a better overview. I watched Marie scramble towards the nucleus. As the procession approached the market, the stallholders grew more tense. Henkelmann seemed to be steering towards a butcher's shop. I stumbled through the throng to get to the centre of things.

One of the butchers, the one who appeared to be in charge, was a stout, bloated man with a string apron stretched across his waist. The apron cut into his stomach which bulged in a way I thought was slightly obscene. He had no hair except for a slight monastic fringe. His clean, broad face stretched like a moist balloon from his thick eyebrows to the back of his head where his neck disappeared. He resembled a well-fed pig. As the group approached the shop he tried to ready himself. Part of his face attempted to crease into what I took to be a smile, but then collapsed as if under too much strain. It looked as if, had you tapped him on the shoulder, he might well have bolted like one of his carcasses, had they still been alive. Occasionally he wiped a cloth across his brow and bald head, but the moisture rose to the surface again almost immediately. The heat was inescapable. The denuded chickens and wounds of beef and pork were making my head spin. The sight of so much raw meat in this weather seemed perverse. The smell was of quiet carnage.

As soon as Henkelmann entered the shop, the butcher shot out his hand so rapidly it seemed several minutes passed before they actually made physical contact. I waited, peering through the viewfinder, for Henkelmann to reach the man and shake his eager hand.

'Very pleased to meet you,' Henkelmann announced. The butcher only nodded his head. I didn't care; I photographed them, regardless. Then the politician started to talk to the journalists surrounding him and I could see Marie reaching in with her tape recorder. There was a lot of gesturing: Henkelmann indicated the butcher, pointed to various parts of the shop, the other workers, then nodded to the man by way of farewell, shook the overzealous hand again. The butcher nodded vigorously in return and I noticed his smile was more sustained this time. The group did an about-turn and left the shop to continue along the street. In all that time, the butcher hadn't uttered a single word.

I stayed behind to take more photographs of the butcher and his colleagues. For a while they pretended to ignore me. Then the butcher whirled about as if he had only just noticed.

'What d'you think you're doing there, eh?' he said, with a hint of aggression or cocky humour. I couldn't tell. He was putting on a show for his team.

'I'm just taking pictures of you and your fine shop,' I said. I waved at the other men, the hunks of meat.

'Taking pictures of our shop?' he bellowed. 'Unbelievable! They come in here. They like what they see. They talk, they take pictures, but do they give us a single pfennig for it? This is a pauper's game, my friend.' He turned to his colleagues who all broke out into raucous laughter. It didn't seem malicious. I could tell he was elated that the politician had chosen to enter his shop. He was guffawing so much he began to wheeze; single tears squeezed out of the piggy eyes. I laughed along with the men, and continued to take my photographs.

Henkelmann came to a halt near the centre of the market where a small crowd had gathered to hear what he had to say. A group of Turkish women scuttled over to see what the commotion was about. They clutched shopping bags and tried to squeeze in as close as possible. Occasionally they glanced at one another and pouted as if they couldn't discern who or what was at the centre of attention, what it was all about.

'This district's already had several cash handouts. What d'you say to those who think you're only jumping on the bandwagon of a lost cause?' one of the journalists shouted. Antje Kiesinger.

Henkelmann smiled. 'What handouts? Show me! Point out all the wonderful improvements and then we'll talk.'

One of the Turkish women had two small children with her: a boy and an older girl. At one stage the boy, who couldn't see above the heads of the adults, squeezed to the front of the crowd. A moment later he was whisked up into the air, brought to rest against Henkelmann's shoulder. He didn't seem at all anxious, rather he looked vaguely bored by the whole affair as he squinted against the sun. But Henkelmann was grinning now and our cameras went into overdrive. Even the child's mother seemed pleased. His sister beamed. I knew it would be the photograph to grace the pages of the newspapers the next day. It was too obvious and it annoyed me.

In the centre of my viewfinder, a cyclist wearing a mustard-coloured jacket was staring at me from the other side of the crowd. When he realized he was in my frame, he immediately shielded his face with his helmet and turned one way and then another. Abruptly, he weaved his bicycle through the crowd, mounted and cycled quickly down the street. It was an overreaction, but I dismissed it. People are always shying away from the camera.

The Turkish boy soon grew restless with the attention. Henkelmann set him back down on the ground and he ran to his mother. I thought of Uncle Raymond, when I was little. Whenever he lifted me up, I would always want to return to ground level. I never wanted him to carry me. I don't know why. I used to feel guilty because I realized it was peculiar for a child not to want to be held, to be carried.

Some of the other photographers had already drifted away. It was clear the most important photographs of the day had already been taken, so I pushed forward to Marie who was still trying to obtain her quotes.

'Aren't you continuing with the rest of the tour?' she asked. 'It'll be interesting to hear what else he has to say.'

'I'll take some pictures of the neighbourhood,' I said half-heartedly. 'At least it'll be more representative of the area.'

Marie shrugged as if she didn't care one way or the other.

'I'll bring in the photographs first thing Monday,' I said.

'Just don't be late with them this . . . Look, they're away again.' And she was off.

I crossed the street, walking in the opposite direction. I looked back at the crowd and from a distance it seemed small, insignificant. Only a few streets away and life was already different. The buildings were dirtier and daubed with graffiti: *Turks Out! Down with the Wall! The SDP is shit!* Henkelmann was unlikely to see any of this.

I had almost decided against taking more photographs when I spotted a café on the other side of the road. I wanted to sit and drink something cold. Get out of the sun. Perhaps it would encourage me to continue. The heat had sapped my energy. As I approached the café, however, I realized I had made an error, but I was already over the threshold and momentum seemed to carry me through. The place was drab and ill lit, the floor covered in torn orange and brown linoleum. Three pinball machines stood at one end of the room, only one of which seemed to be functioning, although no one was using it. On the left, behind the counter, lounged a rotund woman of indeterminate age with a helmet of oily black hair. She looked as if she had always been there, had never moved from that position – like a waxwork dummy. There was no discernible expression on her face, simply a mask of ennui. I had an urge to prod her, to confirm she was still alive. I took a few shots with the wide angle to capture her at one end of the room, the pinball machines at the other. No one seemed to react to my presence.

The only other occupants were two men and a girl of about six or seven. One of the men looked Turkish or Middle Eastern. He sat in an overstuffed chair with one leg slung over the side, as if he were in his own sitting room. He wasn't drinking or occupied in any way I could discern. He sat watching me as if I had walked into his line of vision and he was simply waiting for me to move. Had I stepped to one side, I thought, he would merely have continued to stare straight ahead. He looked almost as bored as the woman.

The only sign of life came from the girl who began to run at the other end of the café. She kept making noises, presumably in imitation of some object – a bird, a crying baby. I couldn't tell. The screeching grated. She spun around the chairs throughout the café, then ran up and tapped each of the pinball machines in turn. Then she sidled up to the counter, where the woman ignored her completely, all the time making the strange noises. I wondered whether they were related in any way, whether her bird's plea was a reaction against a mute mother. At one point she ran up to me, stopped and tilted her head back, making great moon eyes, until I thought she might fall over. I was sure she was going to say something, the way most curious children do, but then she snapped her head upright again and sped towards the back of the room, to the pinball machines.

The other man was from somewhere in East Africa. I could read it in his features, the shape of his face, his narrow nose. I thought he might be Ethiopian, Somali maybe. He too was looking at me – then after a moment, I thought I glimpsed the hint of a nod, but he didn't smile. I nodded in return, in any case, then turned and left. Walking away, it troubled me to realize no one had spoken in all the time I had been there.

In the evening I felt disconnected. I called Lucille, although I couldn't remember whether it was my turn to phone.

'Fine time to call.' She sounded distracted. 'Dirty Den's at it again. I don't know why Angie puts up with him.'

'What's that? Is everything all right?' I had no idea what she was talking about.

'Fine,' she said, which could have meant anything.

I was anxious about bringing up the subject of travelling to Berlin again, but she didn't ask any questions and appeared uninterested in attempting any kind of conversation.

'You heard from Pat and Louis lately?' I couldn't stand her parents, but I asked in order to have something to say.

'They're fine,' she sighed.

I felt the distance stretch between us like a taut wire about to snap. 'What's wrong?' I asked.

'What do you mean, "what's wrong"?'

'You sound . . . tired,' I said. 'I haven't called at a bad time, have I?'

'No, no, now is good. I'm not tired at all.'

'Oh.' I was so used to Lucille talking all the time, I found it impossible to deal with this taciturn creature at the other end of the line. 'Suppose you're busy at the moment – with work and everything?'

'Why do you say that?'

'Well, I was wondering . . . perhaps it's the wrong time for either of us to visit?'

'I thought you said you were travelling soon?'

'I . . . I don't think so,' I said. 'What I mean is, I'm not sure. Even if I am, it doesn't mean we can't see each other.'

'Were you thinking of coming over?'

'Well, I don't know about that. I didn't say . . .'

'Or I could come to you,' she suggested.

'Well . . .'

'It's been ages, you know. It's unnatural to spend so much time apart. I have to get out of this city.' She had discarded her earlier reserve. 'Let's decide on a date now,' she said. 'Tell me when's good for you and I'll arrange my holiday around that. Sound fair?' She went to fetch her diary. I sat down, then lay on my back against the cool floorboards, and waited.

'How about this weekend?' she asked when she returned.

'I'm busy all week.'

'Next weekend then. I can take from Thursday off and part of the next week too.'

'Well . . .'

'I won't be able to book time off for three weeks after that. It's either around this weekend or the next. You decide.'

'Next then,' I said, although it didn't feel like my decision. I hung up, stupefied.

I drew a bath, despite the warm weather. I had been on my feet all day and the city grime felt like a second skin. I drew it the way I like it – steaming hot so I could barely stand the temperature – and lowered myself in by degrees. Aunt Ama used to warn that a too-hot bath was harmful. She claimed it wouldn't get you any cleaner, and that you might be scalded, or, worse, you would never be able to have children. Half the time I hardly listened to her.

After my bath I put on Wes Montgomery's *A Day in the Life* and fussed about in the kitchen before settling on two tins of sardines and half a loaf of bread. I sank into a cushion on the sitting-room floor and devoured the sandwiches, drained a bottle of beer. I thought it a shame not to savour the taste properly, but I was hungry. I had a fleeting memory of Uncle Raymond asking me not to bolt my food, but then I wasn't sure whether it was an actual memory or a fantasy I had conjured up out of guilt. I drifted back into the kitchen and opened another beer, trying to concentrate on the warm, rich sounds of the music. But the heat and the alcohol had made me drowsy. It seemed only moments later when the telephone screamed, jolting me out of unconsciousness.

'Hallo, hallo . . . Vincent? Have you . . . have you heard?'
A voice garbled.

'What? What? Who's that?' I groaned in my half-sleep.
'Marie? What is it?' Morning sunshine streamed in through
the windows of the apartment. I wondered how I had been
able to sleep so comfortably on the sitting-room floor.

'Henk . . . Henkelmann's dead,' she panted. 'Henkelmann.'

'What d'you mean?'

'He was killed. Yesterday. Last night, I think.' She sounded
as if she had been running up stairs. 'It's not on the news
yet, but rumours are circulating. I got a call from a friend
at a news agency.'

Thoughts spilled into my head. If I had stayed yesterday,
I might have taken a better, more valuable photograph. More
pictures for the archive.

'It was long after I had gone. I was one of the last people
there,' she continued. 'I didn't even get a chance to interview him properly. I don't understand it. Why would anyone
want to kill him?'

'Listen, I'll work on the pictures now and get them to you
as soon as I can.' There was no rush for them as the magazine is published monthly, but I felt I ought to do something
immediately.

I worked all day on the photographs, snacking on boiled
eggs and sardines, drinking cold beer. I threw open all the
windows and then the front door. Clariss's clip-clop clam-
oured up and down the stairs, the Zimmermans opposite left
early for work, Frau Lieser hollered from her window on
the ground floor, a dog barked intermittently from her apartment. I couldn't seem to keep out the heat. Early next morning
the newspapers were full of it.

# MYSTERY OF
# SLAIN POLITICIAN

*Berliner Morgenpost* 6 July 1985

A body believed to be that of Social Democratic Party politician Heinrich Henkelmann was discovered early yesterday morning beside an overgrown path in the outlying village of Lübars, *writes Peter Müller*. At 6.35 a.m. on Friday, police received a telephone call from a young farmer out exercising the family dog at the location where, according to police reports, the body of the politician lay drenched in blood. As details begin to emerge about the killing, the full extent of the horrific act is only now coming to light.

According to Detective Chief Inspector Udo Schlottke, 'It [the body] is almost certainly that of Heinrich Henkelmann. Documentation discovered on the deceased and in a nearby abandoned vehicle points to this, although official confirmation is still pending following conclusive ID.'

Difficulties surrounding a swift identification relate to the particularly gruesome nature of the crime. The attack was of such a frenzied nature, according to Dr Alexander Riesner, head of Accident and Emergency at Humboldt Hospital where the body was examined, that 'much of the cranium had collapsed, the zygomatic bone was crushed on one side. The frontal bone, the temporal and sphenoid bones, the maxilla, the list goes on – even a section of the parietal – all had been openly fractured. Repeatedly', Dr Riesner explained to a group of waiting reporters. 'Several of the victim's fingers had been broken, smashed in various directions in an apparently futile attempt to ward off the blows. Whatever kind of instrument was used – and one can only speculate here – it would have taken a considerable degree of strength or length of time, probably both, to inflict such extensive damage. The attack may, in all probability, have continued long after the victim had expired. No human being would have been able to withstand such savagery for more than a few minutes.'

The victim was left unrecognisable. 'It was,' continued Dr Riesner, 'as if the assailant or assailants had been trying to remove all trace of the subject's identity – namely, his face.'

Henkelmann, a successful entrepreneur in his own right, was known to maintain interests in many private fields. Rumours suggest that the killing may be connected to a business endeavour gone awry. Perhaps there were links to a mafia-type organization? A more plausible motive, however, lies with his political career, a career that was beginning to scale new heights. He was popular with younger Berliners and minorities, those eager for more effective change,

and some suggest that the killing may have had a connection with one of several neo-Nazi organizations. Some even go so far as to hint at foul play among one of the opposition parties, although this has been merely speculative. Inspector Schlottke, heading the search for the attacker/s, has dismissed speculation saying, 'No motive for this attack will ever be discovered until the murderer or murderers have been apprehended.'

What is certain, however, is that the central office of the SPD now lies in a state of shock and incomprehension at the murder of the ebullient politician who had been strongly tipped to succeed at the next elections. Berliners also remain quietly stunned, and residents of the peaceful hamlet of Lübars are trying to come to terms with the fact that their once idyllic village community is now the site of one of Berlin's most horrific recent crimes.

Mayor Joachim Olbrich has described Thursday's attack as 'an act of madness' and has appealed for calm and vigilance in the apprehension of the murderer/s.

Police investigators have stated that no weapons have yet been discovered at the site, although teams of officers and local volunteers are painstakingly sifting through surrounding fields and countryside. Heinrich Henkelmann leaves behind a wife and two teenaged sons.

Murder of a politician, pages 2–3
Leader comment, page 15
Obituary, page 16

# 5

A Rî RAPPED ON the door and then lingered on the landing as if he had forgotten why he had knocked. I asked him in and returned to work. From the darkroom, I could hear him pacing about the apartment.

'You'll have a drink?' I asked when I emerged for a beer.

He shook his head and smiled, but his eyes were bloodshot and he seemed shrunken in his grey suit.

'You've heard about Henkelmann?'

'Yes.' He waved away the question as if it were age-old news. 'It's what everybody talks about – Henkelmann, Henkelmann,' he said. 'I tell Ezmîr you take his picture.' Ezmîr was a fellow Kurd who had been stabbed in the eye with a soldier's knife.

'What did he say?'

'Ezmîr no likes politician,' he said.

'What do *you* think?'

'I do not think too much about it. Is a bad thing, this thing that happen. They decide law. They say for you to come or go. They have power over my life, so sometimes I listen to what they say. But I don't care even one pfennig for them.' He sat down heavily and was quiet again.

I took a swig from the can.

'I have bad feeling,' he said eventually. 'I think they will not let me stay.'

'What makes you think that?'

'Just bad feeling, is all,' he said. 'Sometimes . . . Sometimes I think someone follows me.'

I was used to hearing about Arî's trials. He confided in me at least once a month, told me someone was either stalking or harassing him. I wasn't overly concerned this time. 'Why do you think you're being followed?'

'Last week, I go to Pfaueninsel. It is hot. We are feeling very good, you know? I am with my friends – Karwan, Mehmet, Ezmîr.' He counted them on his fingers. 'I am feeling very happy. When we are coming back, at first I do not notice – but on train, I see a man sitting. I see him before, I am sure. He is looking at us. When I look at him, he look away, so I know he is watching. I thinking he will get off at next stop, but no.' Arî shook his head.

'We change train and he follows. Karwan ask me why I am like this, being so nervous. I tell him someone from police is following.'

'Then what happened?'

'Well . . . soon he get off train,' he said.

'You know, Arî, no one is keeping you under surveillance. The police don't do things like that. Even if they had the resources, they wouldn't. What are you to them, anyway?'

He shrugged; he was never convinced when I tried to assuage him. He could always find a loophole, a no man's land where there was no justice.

At the end of the day I had to confess I didn't know all that much about Arî, about his life before, where he had been, what he had been involved in. I didn't really know

56

whether people were followed, whether immigration officials ever tried to catch people out in order to deport them. It wasn't something that concerned me. I knew Arî suffered, though, each day as he waited for the result of his asylum application. I could only try to ease his paranoia, which, to me, seemed limitless.

'I'll keep my eyes and ears open,' I said. Empty words designed only to fill space.

'Karwan say to me, if they take us to Turkey again, we will go – maybe to Holland.' He was already planning the next move when he seemed to have a perfectly strong case to stay here.

The phone rang and he looked at me as if here was news he had been dreading all along.

'Hallo!' A voice, artificially breezy, a mediocre saleswoman. I couldn't place it. There was a short silence. 'Hallo, this is Claudia.'

Claudia, I thought. Who *is* she? I glanced at Arî, who looked as if he thought I was going to hand him over to the authorities.

'Claudia . . .' I rolled out the name as far as possible, making it flat and thin like pastry.

'You don't remember me?' Gone was any artifice and in its place something more hesitant.

'Yes, of course I do!' I laughed. 'Claudia, how could I forget?'

'You don't remember? At the Atlantic.' She mentioned B and Tunde, and a woman's name I didn't know. The Atlantic, of course. The vivacious smiler; her less glamorous friend.

'Claudia!' I didn't recall giving her my number, but then much of that night was lost to me. What did she want? Was she angry? Was she pregnant?

'You didn't call,' she said, 'for such a long time. I thought I would phone. To see how you are.'

'Oh . . . I've been very busy, you know . . . work.' I didn't even have her number.

'Yes, of course. Work.' She sounded relieved and frightened at the same time.

'In fact, I was working when you phoned.'

'Oh, I'm sorry. Should I call later?'

'No, no, it's all right.'

Arî watched me, but now with more an expression of bemusement than concern.

'I was just phoning to see how you are,' she said again.

What did she want me to say, this woman whose name and face I had forgotten?

'Yeah, doing good. Busy.' I dragged out the nonsense words.

'Well, perhaps when you're free some time, we could meet up for a drink or something?' It was an effort for her. The dogged persistence impressed me.

'Yeah, sounds good to me,' I said. 'Listen, I'll phone you.' The relief of knowing there was no way I could reach her went some way to easing the guilt.


'This one isn't bad. It's a bit grainy, though,' Marie murmured as she pored over the transparencies. I had decided to show them all to her, not only the ones I thought were suitable. A considerable section of the magazine was to be devoted to Henkelmann, and Marie needed additional material.

'They're saying it was neo-Nazis. One of the splinter groups. Probably unsanctioned,' she said as she appraised two near-identical images of the politician.

'That's hardly surprising,' I said. 'He was popular with people they hated. That's reason enough.'

'It's a mad world, isn't it, when you kill someone simply because you don't like them, or what they stand for.' She sighed and gripped one of the transparencies and stared at it until I was sure she had forgotten I was there.

'Are you all right?' I asked.

'I'm sorry,' she said, surfacing. 'I've hardly slept. These are good, you know. I may use one on the cover. What d'you say?'

'Of course, yes,' I replied. 'Whichever you choose is fine by me.' Only two of my photographs had ever featured on covers.

She glanced at the images again. 'You know, I asked him that day, what he thought his chances were at the next election.'

'What did he say?'

'Oh, some rehearsed line about waiting and seeing. How it all depended on the electorate and one could never be too confident about the outcome. He didn't answer the question, but then I didn't really expect him to. I could tell he thought he had a good chance, though. I think that was the last thing I remember him saying.'

I looked out of her office window into the sunshine, at the passers-by below on Zähringerstrasse.

'You've been to see Thomas, I trust?'

'Um . . . not yet,' I wavered. I tried not to recall the forgotten appointment, the humiliating phone call.

'Really, you shouldn't miss opportunities like that,' she said. 'Some of these are good. Very good indeed.' She looked up at me once more with a glazed expression, not really seeing me.

\* \* \*

Frau Lieser was standing half in, half out of the front door. That was the first thing. I hadn't quite crossed the street when she called out shrilly, 'Quickly, quickly!' as I ambled towards the building. 'You must come quickly!' She beckoned me with her fat fingers, but I didn't alter my pace. I hate to run. It seemed pointless for her to have gone to so much trouble.

'What's the matter?' I asked when I reached her.

She shooed me in and waved me upstairs. 'Not a moment to lose!' she puffed, lumbering behind me.

When I reached my door, she was still on the landing below. 'Up, still up!' she called.

I continued my ascent.

The door to Arî's apartment stood wide open. I stopped outside and waited for Frau Lieser to chug up the stairs.

'Better to go in!' she wheezed when she finally arrived.

There was an acrid smell; for a moment I feared Arî had self-immolated, or worse, had been torched by racists. I had a vision of his charred skeleton, crisp as ten-minute toast, spread out on his sitting-room floor. Then he emerged from the kitchen with Clariss in tow, looking the same as always. How did my mind jump so wildly to these awful conclusions? There was the sound of other voices. Caroline and Dieter were sitting at the kitchen table. She was newly bald and dazed-looking while he had acquired a blue mohican. Dieter raised a hand in greeting. 'There's been a terrible fire,' he explained, his tone flat as a ship's horn. He waved limply at the wall, to a small charred area by the cooker, no bigger than a dinner plate. 'You've just missed the fire brigade. The public services, they've saved us all,' he continued in the monotone.

Caroline tittered.

Frau Lieser threw her a hateful look. 'What's to laugh about when we all could have been burned to cinders?' she snapped.

Caroline giggled even more.

'It's all my fault,' Clariss said. 'I called the fire department. Big mistake.'

'You're right there,' Dieter yawned. 'We could be having a peaceful afternoon now.'

The fact that it *was* afternoon, in the middle of the week, seemed to have escaped his attention. Apart from the few tenants who had regular jobs, no one in the building seemed prepared to work. The punks slept and took drugs all day, Clariss spent the daylight hours trying on outfits or entertaining friends, Arî wasn't allowed to work, the man occupying the apartment opposite Clariss's rarely emerged; I wouldn't have been able to identify him in a police line-up. The only inhabitants who led 'productive' lives were Frau Lieser, Helena, the woman who lived opposite her, and the Zimmermans, who worked enough for the entire building combined. They were never at home. Even on a Saturday morning I would catch one of them sprinting out of the building clutching a briefcase. I didn't know their occupations, but they couldn't have been very successful, judging from their accommodation.

'I'm only glad someone quick-thinking was here.' Frau Lieser sprang to Clariss's defence. 'Who knows? I could have had a pile of rubble on my hands. Even deaths.'

I looked at the spot of damage on the wall and the cooker, and then at Arî who had kept out of it all. He seemed fascinated by the discussion, as if he were merely an observer rather than the cause of the trouble in the first place.

'Well, I guess it's all over now,' I said. 'We can go back to our apartments.'

'I thought we'd be here for ever,' Caroline moaned without getting up from the chair. 'I'm dying for a nap.'

# 6

THE FIRST TIME we went swimming together, I took Lucille to my local pool in Kentish Town. It was crowded with families that swam in packs and screaming school children. People moved about in short, maniacal hops, unable to swim for more than a few metres. All one could do was splash and paddle, then rest momentarily. We remained for an hour, darting about idiotically. After ten minutes, I was tired of getting nowhere.

'Come on, it's fun!' Lucille cried. She waved her hands, flicking water delicately as if she were having the time of her life. Despite growing up surrounded by the Indian Ocean, she didn't know how to swim. I asked if she wanted to learn; I could teach her, I suggested. Lucille pushed her hands in front of her as if about to launch into an elegant stroke. At the vital moment her face rumpled and her arms waved the water aside.

'That's better,' I said, encouragingly.

'Really?' She looked dubious. 'Do you really think so?' Then, when she had summoned up enough courage, she began the manoeuvre all over again.

'Your legs,' I called. 'Try to move your legs, like this.' And I showed her. I held her afloat with my arms curled underneath her stomach. I felt her kick and sway and I imagined us together, naked in the pool, without the interfering crowd. Her body was lithe and strong, but lacked coordination in the water. She wasted energy thrashing to no avail. We made a proper pair – her tall and slender, me taller still, but spread out like a great soufflé.

People clung to the edge of the pool – kicking their legs, laughing, sinking, spluttering – still managing to almost drown. We found a space by the side and stayed there.

'Why don't you show me a dive?' Lucille said. She had seen others diving at the deep end.

'Too many people,' I squinted, wiping the water from my eyes. 'It's not safe.' I was loath to heave myself out of the pool, beached then waddling on the side. I didn't want people snickering at my body, the way they had when I was a child. Not in front of Lucille. 'Some other time,' I promised. I would have dived for her, over and over again, had it been only the two of us.

A man using small, elegant breaststrokes swam past. His head dipped beneath the surface without the slightest splash, then rose slowly, a few thin strands of silky hair clinging to his scalp. His pale, thin arms sliced through the water before him, though his skin hung in folds as he swam. On land he might have been a frail, arthritic creature, but the water seemed to make him supple, loosening his joints, invigorating the muscles. He smiled as he swam, navigating his way patiently through the crowd.

'Look! Over there!' Lucille pointed. There was a flurry of activity at the deep end, a commotion caused by a group of boys racing in some of the lanes. The frantic whirr of arms and legs churned the water to a white froth. When the first boy touched the wall at the shallow end, other swimmers applauded. He tried to appear nonchalant, wiping his face, taking deep exaggerated breaths. When the last boy struggled to the end, people clapped again, but more enthusiastically this time, and he looked about himself, pleased and slightly bashful.

A lifeguard approached the group, crouched down, and spoke quietly to them. He was probably handing out a warning. He didn't seem annoyed, though, and he smiled and sauntered back to his chair.

'Look at that,' I sneered. 'Give them a scrap of power and it goes straight to the head.'

'Oh, but he's fit, though,' Lucille replied, more to the woman beside her, dismissing my comment. They both cackled and kicked out their legs and sighed and giggled again.

I didn't have a reply to that and fell silent until Lucille nudged me and laughed. After that I forgot about it.

One of the boys from the racing group moved to an isolated corner by the ladder at the shallow end. He seemed to have lost something and kept peering into the water through the slits of his eyes. He stooped and focused suddenly and I thought he had found whatever he was looking for, because he made a lurching movement with his head. But then something poured out of him and I realized he had been sick. He was quick and secretive about it, and when he finished, he looked about himself. Thinking no one had noticed, he splashed the water in order to disperse the mess.

'Did you see that?' I said to Lucille.

'See what?'

I told her we had to leave, so we inched our way towards

the ladder at the deep end. I looked back at the boy who had vomited; he had joined his friends again. People were swimming in the area where he had been sick and I told myself I would never swim in a public pool again.

B was pacing in the entrance hall when we arrived. He glanced at his watch.

'We're not late, are we?' I asked.

'No, no, no!' he protested. 'Not at all, at all, man. What's a few minutes, eh? Come in, come in.'

We were definitely late.

'Lucille, it's been too long. Why does he hide you away all the time?'

'I'm beginning to wonder that myself,' she smiled.

'Oh, Angelika!' he called to a woman striding towards us. 'Angelika dear, my friends are here at last.'

Angelika also checked the time, but she flicked out her arm and adjusted the watchstrap, then squinted at the face for several seconds.

'What wonderful weather we are having,' B began to gabble. He was ordinarily placid, but now he seemed on edge.

I ignored him.

We went through the formality of introductions.

Tunde was already seated when we arrived at the table. Next to him was the type of woman who could cause heads to turn, cars to crash – the only kind Tunde ever dated. This one had deep olive skin, black hair that licked her waist, penetrating green eyes, breasts the size of cantaloupes.

'This is Isabel,' he announced. I had seen her before, but

couldn't remember where. On a billboard or on television, perhaps the cover of a magazine.

'Why don't you sit next to Angelika?' B nudged me. 'You can get to know one another.' It was a round table so it hardly made any difference, but in his nervousness he didn't appear to notice. He plumped down beside Lucille, already exhausted, and removed his glasses, wiped them with a napkin, then put them on again. 'Angelika recommended the restaurant. She says it's the best Chinese food outside China.' He laughed a little hysterically, then turned to his belle and winked.

I got a good look at Angelika as she turned to grin at B. I had imagined someone else, not the sturdy matron sitting next to me. She wasn't fat, but she must have had a constant struggle keeping off the pounds. It was the way she was built – big bones. I could relate to that. B's previous girlfriends had verged on the glamorous, though they were never in Tunde's league. She looked thirty going on fifty. She appeared to be flouting all the rules.

'It's not so expensive here,' she said to Lucille. 'The best food at the best prices, yes?' She seemed pleased with herself. 'We speak English, okay?' she continued, as though we hadn't been speaking in English all along. 'It's better, so we all understand, only . . .' She glanced pitifully at Isabel, then looked hurriedly away. 'See, even the locals come here!' She pointed to an adjacent table. We all turned. A young Chinese family was sharing out dishes. They halted momentarily when they noticed the sudden attention. I hoped they hadn't understood.

Lucille asked for wine while B and I ordered beers.

'Only half a glass of your finest white wine for me please,' Angelika warned the waiter. 'And a glass of cold spring water, yes? I am a woman, after all, and I must keep my figure,' she giggled. She tucked a loose lock of auburn hair coquettishly behind her right ear. She seemed like a woman who might once have been beautiful for the briefest moment, and known it, and never quite come to terms with the loss.

'Let us have champagne,' Tunde beckoned the waiter. 'Make it two bottles.' He proceeded to order the most expensive item on the wine list, then turned to Isabel and continued to coo. He was a true sybarite; his parents had provided amply for him in his pursuit of pleasure. His taste was so keen it needed no fine-tuning, whereas my discernment was blunt as the back of a bus. My own parents were gone. They had been smashed in a car crash long ago and there was no accounting for that.

'What do you recommend?' I summoned up the courage to speak to Isabel.

She looked at my held-out menu and smiled sweetly and shrugged. Perhaps that was another asset to being beautiful; you could leave your manners at home and still be desired.

Angelika was locked in conversation with B and Lucille, while Isabel and Tunde hooted over nothing in particular. The drinks arrived and they kept the champagne for themselves.

'We should take a trip to Wannsee,' B announced. 'All of us. Maybe this weekend. What do you say?'

'Good idea,' I replied, glancing at Lucille.

'Yes, I'd love to come,' she said. She looked at me and it was understood; we would find an excuse not to go. The thought of spending more time with Angelika dismayed me.

'Someone's made a wrong choice here,' Angelika pointed out in a kind of singsong, jabbing a chopstick in the direction of a slab of meat, drowned in a pool of oil. 'Don't touch that one, dear,' she warned B. 'It will make you fat, yes? Not so good for the heart.'

I realized the odious-looking dish was mine, as everyone else had already claimed their meals.

'There's an art to ordering good food, yes?' Angelika continued, waving her chopsticks at B. 'It's like painting, dear. One false stroke and you have ruined a masterpiece. Some people have a gift for it, and some . . . are not so fortunate.'

Angelika and I must have started off on the wrong foot. Halfway through the meal, it dawned on me she did not like me one bit. I harboured similar feelings about her. It was unfortunate we shared the same friend. She was in the middle of explaining to Lucille the high drama of being a secondary school teacher when she spotted the waiter.

'China tea for the ladies!' she shrieked at the passing man. She half raised her hand and waved to him as if she were imitating her unbelievably eager pupils.

'Beer for me,' B said. 'And another for my friend.'

The waiter started to clear away a few of our empty dishes.

'Don't you think tea would be better, dear?' Angelika said sweetly. 'Three beers – it's a bit much, no?'

'Yes. Yes, you're right, dear,' B agreed without pause.

Angelika smiled.

'So, tea for five?' the waiter clarified.

'No. Tea for four. Beer for one!' I had begun to shout.

There was a silence. B glanced at Angelika. Angelika looked at Lucille as if she felt pity for her. Lucille gazed down at the table. Isabel and Tunde had left the conversation long ago. I stared at the offending piece of meat. No one had dared touch it and I could see it being carried away at the end of the meal, a look of triumph smeared across Angelika's face. I picked up my chopsticks and tried to winch the meat onto my plate. It was heavy, far too bulky for chopsticks. I kept lifting it a few inches above the table before it fell back into the dish with a splash. I tried again. Everyone stared in silence. Even Isabel.

'Stop that!' Lucille gasped.

I must have been drunk because I didn't think anything of it. I picked up the meat with my fingers and proceeded to devour it. It was cold now; it had been ignored for too long. It was tough and gristly and I could feel the oil coating my mouth and throat, but I was determined to finish it.

'Do you have any plans for the summer?' I heard Lucille ask Angelika, but she couldn't be distracted from the spectacle of me.

'We're not sure,' B said. He passed more food round the table, first to Angelika and then to Lucille and Isabel. 'It depends on money. It's so hot this year, we might stay here.'

'Oh no, we will go away, even for one weekend,' Angelika stated.

'Yes, of course, dear,' B said. 'Maybe to Spain.'

'Spain!' Angelika shrieked. 'Maybe you go on your own!'

'No, not Spain. Somewhere else,' B panicked. 'We're still deciding.'

It was difficult to know what B actually thought now. As far as I was concerned he had wandered into a maze with no exit.

'What is it that you do, exactly?' Angelika turned to me.

'Me? I take pictures.' I did a hand mime.

She scowled.

'A photographer.'

'Oh!' she said, then went quiet.

I took a long swig of beer and felt the elixir spread to my

limbs and spill into my head. All the irritations of the evening were beginning to dissolve. B dropped some noodles onto the table. Isabel sipped her champagne. From time to time Tunde reached under the table and stroked her thigh. I could not help but notice the way her cleavage floated above her half-eaten sweet and sour pork. She sipped champagne and bobbed her head about in a mock dance. I realized where I had seen her before – the Latin American woman at the club. The clothes and the hair were different now, but she was the same person who had electrified the dance floor.

'You were at the Atlantic the other night, weren't you?' I exclaimed.

She smiled and made a slight purring noise as if she were searching for the appropriate words. She turned to Tunde, her shoulders hunched.

'Izzi doesn't speak English, do you baby?' Tunde was also on his way to being very drunk. No one else had been allowed to touch their champagne.

I tried again in German, but she shook her head helplessly. 'Little, little,' she apologized. 'Brasilien.' She let out a giggle.

I wondered how they had been communicating as there was no way she could comprehend Yoruba. Tunde knew no other languages, apart from German and English.

'Everything is all right?' the waiter asked.

'Very good,' Angelika replied. 'Very good. Seven and a half out of ten.' She turned and began to relate an article she had read in the previous day's newspaper. 'It was all about this actor – I forget his name – and a hammer that had become stuck. He had to be taken to the hospital. To have it removed,' she said mysteriously.

'What do you mean, "removed"?' Lucille asked. '"Stuck"?'

'It needed to be removed,' Angelika repeated. 'Removed!' She fluttered her hands by way of explanation.

'Oh, up his rear end?' I said. 'What kind of newspaper was this?'

She turned away from me. 'There was a picture of the doctor holding a hammer in the air. Very big,' she continued, illustrating the size of it with the span of her hands. 'He was wearing gloves, of course. The doctor.' There was a humorous headline suggesting the patient had got carried away with his DIY. 'But you'll know all about that,' Angelika said. 'That must be your kind of scoop.'

'Scoop?' I said. I wondered about Angelika's reading habits. She had it that I was a member of the paparazzi, that I was constantly popping up in other people's homes when they were engaged in unspeakable acts. I'd had enough of Angelika and her allusions to painting, her obvious disapproval of me.

She was still pontificating about photographers and the ways in which they ruin people's lives. 'You don't see ladies running around, being intrusive like that,' she said, appealing to Lucille.

'Cartier-Bresson would be so proud,' I smiled wearily at Tunde, 'that it's come to this.'

'Huh?' he said.

'Huh?' Angelika echoed.

I said, 'The lens is a window to the soul.'

Angelika peered at me and shook a stray thought from her head. 'But he's a drunkard,' she whispered, quite loudly to B, puckering her face as if fending off a bad smell.

'Don't listen to him,' Lucille said. 'He's just had too much.'

'No, I haven't,' I protested. 'I haven't had as much as those two.' I pointed to Tunde and Isabel.

Isabel glanced at Tunde for an explanation, but he only blew her a kiss.

'I don't know how you can mix with these people,' Angelika cried, getting to her feet.

'Darling, where are you going?' B stood up. 'He doesn't mean anything. Sit down, please.'

'Nonsense!' she said. 'Lucille, the pleasure was too brief. I must depart.' And she was off, with B in tow.

'Man, what a bitch,' Tunde chuckled. 'What a mad mess that man's in.'

Isabel swayed in her chair with her eyes closed, her long black hair swishing from side to side. She was probably on a dance floor somewhere, her legs wrapped round the hips of another man. Not Tunde's. She seemed wild even by his standards. I watched her breasts swing away and then draw back towards me.

## 7

'BERLINERS TOGETHER,' Henkelmann's poster campaign had declared, his face a composed stare of compassion. One of his appeals had been his concern for integration, for including new arrivals: Turks, Greeks, Africans, Kurds, East Europeans. Social issues. Frau Bowker was not impressed.

'Why does he want to go and spoil everything?' she rasped, squinting at the politician on Frau Lieser's television screen.

'He's dead,' I replied.

Frau Bowker glanced at me. Schnapps studied her, then turned to me and growled.

I waited for Frau Lieser to return with the tea, wishing the ordeal were over. She always entertained when it came time to receive the rent. It put her at ease, she claimed; she was awkward with money and wanted to conduct affairs properly. Rather than simply have her tenants push an envelope under her door, she insisted on receiving us individually, prolonging the agony for her and for everyone else.

Henkelmann brayed from the television set in a retrospective documentary. He was claiming that the children of today would be responsible for tomorrow's Berlin, extolling the virtues of a well-funded education system.

'Leave the children alone!' Frau Bowker barked. 'What is he doing, meddling with the little ones?' She gathered her bony body together like a sack of old sticks, clutching at the buttons of her cardigan. She hated summer and always dressed for the depths of winter. 'Why is he involving the children?' she muttered furiously. 'Silly little man!' And then she said something I didn't understand. She craned her head towards me; I realized she had asked a question.

'Beg your pardon?' I said. Frau Bowker came from a tiny village outside Cologne; sometimes I had difficulty with her accent.

'What's that, young man?' she growled.

'What?'

'Eh?'

We got confused as to what the confusion was all about. I could feel my anxiety mounting. I could have asked her to repeat herself, knowing she had probably forgotten her question, or simply made some comment concerning Henkelmann. She would have been none the wiser. Instead, I sought to placate her and stoke her anger in the same breath.

'Sorry Frau Bowker, I didn't quite catch what you said. Are your sinuses giving you trouble again?' I knew her sinuses weren't blocked, although she constantly complained about them. She seemed perfectly mucus-free today.

She gazed at me wild-eyed. I feared she might become bellicose. Schnapps rose from her haunches and assumed the attack position.

'Sit!' Frau Bowker screamed, still focusing on the television screen. Schnapps did not need a reminder.

Frau Lieser bumbled in from the kitchen carrying a tray.

'Tea anyone?' she sang.

'Please!' Frau Bowker snapped with exaggerated relief. 'This man,' she exclaimed, flicking her fingers at the television set, 'is irritating me!'

My heart jumped.

'I need to turn it off,' she scowled, still pointing accusingly at the television. She writhed in her chair like a creature possessed, as if that would have the desired effect. 'Is there no labour-saving instrument?' she complained after she had grown tired of her performance.

'Elsa,' Frau Lieser chuckled. 'You are impossible. You know there's no remote control.' And then she wobbled quite nimbly among the bric-a-brac of her front room – around the overstuffed chairs, the laden tables, the dainty porcelain of her life – to switch off the television set. She bustled back and poured the tea while Frau Bowker scrutinized her with a look of horror and absolute hatred. It was the way Frau Bowker was put together – she couldn't help it – so I thought nothing of it. I couldn't imagine how the pair of them had ended up best friends.

'Tea's too hot!' Frau Bowker announced.

'Just the way you like it,' her friend put in without missing a beat.

Frau Bowker swung her head towards Frau Lieser. She glared hotly at her for a moment. 'True!' she said. Then she went quiet. Her craggy old face fractured and she started to make an odd choking noise, a kind of hiccupping. In a moment I realized she was laughing.

Frau Lieser's bosom bounced up and down and she touched the side of her head where her scarf dipped behind her ear. I watched the pair of them cackling, one hand clutching my tea cup, the other gripping the envelope in my pocket.

Schnapps glanced nervously at her mistress, then back to Frau Lieser. She let out a yelp, which put an end to the laughter. She was a young dog, Schnapps, who preferred to act old, like her mistress and her mistress's friend. She couldn't abide children or revelry of any kind. She would have been a menace were her appearance not so ridiculous – a little snow puff and the explosion of white hair around the bewitching black marbles of her eyes. I once asked Frau Bowker what type of dog Schnapps was and she barked, 'Bichon! Bichon Frisé!' as if I were a halfwit, then turned away and sniffed.

'Don't like your tea, young man?' Frau Bowker swung round. 'Don't stare at Schnapps! It will make her cross!'

'It's a bit hot,' I replied, knowing the tea was all that lay between this awfulness and my departure.

'Just the way I like it,' Frau Bowker repeated and her face split up again, a scattered jigsaw puzzle. She sighed into her cup, apparently content now, and leaned back against a soiled antimacassar. 'I remember once,' she continued, to no one in particular, 'in Düsseldorf, with my daughter. We had tea in an old Viennese café. Very civilized. Those were splendid days.' She hummed a random tune.

Frau Lieser leaned forward for the next instalment. I blew harshly on the surface of my tea, spilling a little into the saucer, not really caring.

'Yes,' Frau Bowker continued. 'Such refined clientele. And the interior . . . without comparison. You can't imagine, Marianne. The tea was not so good, though. Not hot and scented like this, the way you make it, my dear.'

Frau Lieser perched on the edge of her chair, eager for another compliment.

'This was before she married,' Frau Bowker went on,

absently patting her flat bosom. 'Or it could have been after . . .' She seemed to lose her thread. She paused, thought about it for a while, then appeared ready to launch into something else. Instead she raised her cup to her meagre lips, and said nothing. It was obvious she had forgotten what she was talking about.

'Oh?' Frau Lieser uttered, surprised. But that was all. She got up and left to fuss in the kitchen again.

I looked at Frau Bowker and forced a smile. She shot a glance at me, turned away and muttered, 'Humph!' before falling silent again. We sipped our tea.

Frau Bowker's silences were terrifying; they were wells, deep and unfathomable. You never knew how to fill them.

'You've lived in Düsseldorf?' I ventured.

'Düsseldorf?' she cried. 'Düsseldorf? Whoever heard of such a thing? Who said I lived in Düsseldorf?' she half-screamed looking round for Frau Lieser. 'It's not true, it's not true.' Schnapps stood and skittered towards me. 'Sit!' Frau Bowker shrieked. The dog winced and scampered back beside her mistress.

'Your daughter,' I tried again. 'Does she live there?'

'My daughter?' she asked, as if she didn't have one. 'Monika?'

'Yes,' I said. 'That's the one.'

'Monika? In Argentina?' she said. Her face was a picture of incredulousness.

'No . . . no, Düsseldorf,' I tried.

She got confused, exasperated to an extent that I thought I had misunderstood everything she had said.

'What are you talking about, young man? Monika . . . Monika lives in Argentina.'

I sipped my tea again and thought I should leave it at

that. I tried gingerly to remove the envelope from my pocket. It was grubby from where I had been clutching it. When I thought Frau Bowker wasn't looking, I slipped it onto the table. Schnapps yelped.

'What's that?' Frau Bowker said, alert again.

'What's what?' Frau Lieser sang, bustling into the front room.

'There!' she panted urgently. 'The young man! There! He's put something on your table.' She pointed, eyeing me suspiciously. 'Just there! Look! Good girl! Schnapps caught him. Look!' she squealed.

'Oh?' Frau Lieser said, glancing at the envelope. She went crimson, as if a switch had been flicked and she had instantly changed colour.

'I have to go now,' I mumbled, getting up, fleeing the dainty sitting room.


I examined the negatives on the counter top until I found the ones I would print for Lucille. She wanted to know what Henkelmann had looked like, and I thought I would show her exactly how he had appeared before he died. I printed out the images from the rally. It was like reliving the day all over again through the sequence of photographs: the Turkish women, the butcher and his petrified grimace, Marie pushing her way through the crowd, the little Turkish boy in Henkelmann's arms, the comatose café. They were all there, frozen in time, but in a way that told a kind of fluid story: rooms and street scenes, the expressions on people's faces. It wasn't really static; there was a life to it. Marie in her white linen blouse and the too-tight skirt. Her reach on tiptoe to read the café menu, the way her calf muscles bulged.

It was hot, a little noxious in that narrow room, so I came

out for a while, leaving the door ajar for ventilation. The day was already warm and the aroma of brewed coffee hung in the air. Lucille must have brought it from London as I didn't keep any in the apartment. She would have woken earlier, made a pot and returned to bed while I was working. I poured myself a cup of the now tepid coffee and ate bread without butter or conserve, standing up, looking out of the kitchen at the buildings at the back. Two girls were leaping up and down on a bed near a wide-open window. Both were wearing pigtails. I could see one of them misjudging a jump and crashing to street level in my mind's eye. I could hear the sirens, the mother's hysterics. I sipped my coffee and turned away.

Lucille was knotted up in a cotton sheet. I lay on the bed beside her, watching her sleeping face react to my presence. Her nose twitched and she turned her head away, but she slowly returned to her original position. The breathing settled again. I traced my fingers along her bare arm, from the elbow to the hollow of her neck, then up across her chin to her lips. She moved her head again and when she stopped, I brushed the back of my hand against her cheek.

'What are you doing?' she whispered.

'I'm looking at you,' I whispered back. I didn't know when she had woken.

She sighed, from sleep, and seemed to drift into unconsciousness again.

'You're beautiful like this,' I said.

She inhaled deeply and sighed again, and I thought I would lie there and stare at her until I fell asleep.

'What do you mean, "like this"?' She opened one eye. She seemed far from sleep now. 'The rest of the time I'm an old bag, am I?'

I smiled and kissed her. '*My* old bag,' I whispered and

found an entrance among the nest of sheets and her T-shirt, to the heat of her stomach and breasts. I eased off her shirt and she moaned as I kneaded her nipples in my mouth. I reached up to kiss her, then worked my tongue against her stomach, her belly button, easing my way downwards.

'No, not that,' she said, feebly. 'Just come inside me. I need you inside me.' In a moment we were moving together, unhurried, trying to prolong the intensity.

When it was over, I lay back, exhausted by the morning heat and the exertion of pacing myself. There were tears running down her face, disappearing into the pillow. She had been crying and I hadn't noticed.

'What's wrong?' I said, reaching out to her. 'Luce, what's wrong?'

'It's nothing,' she said. 'Really, it's nothing. Just hold me.'

And I held her as the sunlight expanded from a corner of the room, occupying more and more space until the warmth made us drowsy and we drifted into a new sleep.


I was eight and I was at home, sitting at the dining table, waiting for the food to arrive. Aunt Ama sat opposite me, my brother Matty beside me, my cousins around the table. We were all waiting for something to begin. This was home and yet it was not home. I tried not to fidget in my chair, but I couldn't help it. I was aware of everyone as they sat still as pieces on a chessboard. I felt the disapproving eyes. I was hungry and uncomfortable and there was nothing to do but wait. At one point Aunt Ama laughed, but no one had spoken. I couldn't understand what had prompted her. It seemed a long time before anything happened. I wanted to turn to whisper to Matty, but I could not. I was afraid of the disapproving looks.

Then Uncle Raymond was at the head of the table. He stood as he handed out plates of food. He looked at me once and I knew it was my turn to be fed. The plate was passed slowly, to my cousin Roli and then to Matty. Somehow it bypassed me because my aunt was holding it next, then Kayode and Bunmi and Uncle Raymond again. I watched as the scene was played out repeatedly. Each time I determined to seize the plate, it mysteriously escaped from me. Uncle Raymond sat down and nodded, so I knew we could commence. I looked down and there were my mother and father, their heads staring up at me, without expression. I couldn't understand why they were on my plate. I glanced at Matty for an explanation, but he was eating, oblivious. I looked back at the heads on the plate and screamed, but no sound emerged. Then a white light washed over everything.

Sunlight had inched across to the head of the bed. I looked across at Lucille, who was still sleeping, her face puffy from rest and crying. Her breaths were short, but regular. She seemed to stop for a long while, before she inhaled deeply and the cycle began again. I got up and drew the curtains, allowing a gap for the breeze. The window with the jumping girls was shut now, the bedroom empty. I returned to the darkroom to work on the prints. While they were still drying I took them into the kitchen. I could smell frankfurters and eggs, recently fried, and a fresh pot of coffee. Lucille was sitting at the table in her underwear. She looked up at me and smiled but didn't say anything. I lay the photographs in sequence on the table in front of her so she could observe for herself the narrative of Henkelmann's last day.

# 8

WE CAUGHT THE S-Bahn from Zoo on Saturday. It was almost eleven and already the faint cool of the morning had lifted. Lucille held our swimming things, which she had packed neatly into a holdall. I carried two plastic bags filled with fruit, sandwiches, chicken drumsticks and bottles of beer and lemonade. There was pandemonium at the station with people racing to find seats. My heart sank. Everybody, it seemed, had had the same idea and now we were all heading in one direction. When the train finally jolted into motion around a dozen passengers were forced to stand in our compartment. All the windows had been pushed open as far as possible, but people fanned themselves with magazines and paperbacks, some even using their hands. As the train pulled away from the station, a warm current swirled through the carriage and there was a collective sigh. I thought it was all exaggerated, this re-action to uncommon heat, but I savoured it nonetheless.

'It's good we arrive early,' Angelika announced. 'You see, we all get seats.'

'Yes, you were right about that,' I agreed.

B beamed at her. Now we were here I was determined to

get on with Angelika. B had persuaded us to come, almost pleaded. It was too hot to quarrel, in any case.

'What happened to Isabel?' Lucille asked. Tunde had invited a woman I had never seen before.

'She's fine,' he replied. 'She couldn't make it. Famke agreed to come instead.'

Famke smiled, her cheekbones vying for attention with her watery blue eyes and her lips, which were full and moist. I couldn't decide who was more stunning – Famke or Isabel.

'We're at the Free University,' Famke said in perfect English. 'I'm studying the Classics at the moment,' she continued, 'but Tunde's introduced me to Ngũgĩ and Achebe – such a revelation. It makes my education so much more – how do you say it – rounded? Complete?'

I didn't know what she was talking about, so I kept quiet, but Lucille and B picked up the thread and soon they were discussing authors they enjoyed. I had read a few science fiction novels when I was a teenager, but the length of books easily defeated me. I wondered how Tunde was able to recommend books to Famke, he who had never completed anything in his life.

'There's Baldwin – both the fiction and the essays,' Lucille was saying. 'Toni Morrison's a must.'

'Baldwin?' Famke asked.

'James Baldwin,' Angelika put in. 'American. Better is Narayan or Coetzee.' They were skipping continents with alacrity now.

A man sitting opposite held up his newspaper like a form of defence. All I could see were his pale chicken legs, swallowed up by a pair of enormous red shorts. He flicked each page as if he were annoyed. At one point I caught a glimpse of a headline – *Hunt for Henkelmann's Killer Goes Cold,* before he folded the paper and slapped it on his knees.

I was uncomfortable in my jeans; I could feel the moisture begin to gather between my thighs, inside the crook of my knees. I looked across at Lucille's legs as she chatted with Famke. They were a perfect smooth almond brown, without blemish, except for the mark – like a small sable moon – where she had scraped her shin against a nail that jutted out from a rowing boat when she was a child.

We hadn't yet pulled into Nikolassee when people started stretching and getting up. There was an air of suppressed hysteria, as if there was only one remaining square metre of sand on the beach and we were all going to have to fight for it.

Two sullen children gripped the door handles as we approached the platform. They looked between seven and nine. I thought they might be brother and sister. A woman I took to be their mother kept warning them to stand away from the exit, but they hung on relentlessly with a look of panic on their faces.

'Leave it!' the mother shouted at one stage. She appeared embarrassed by her children, who seemed intent on ignoring her. If I were her, I thought, I would have given them each a good wallop, put them straight back on a train to the city. But all she did was turn away, pretending not to care. She stared out of the window, pinch-mouthed, defeated. When the train finally came to a stop, the two children dashed outside. They appeared to be following their own itinerary without giving their mother a second thought.

'Come back here!' she shouted after them. 'Gunther! Mina! Come back, right now! You hear me!' She was already going hoarse.

We all trooped to the same bus stand; I knew we were going to the same location. Sure enough, the beach at Wannsee was more crowded than the Ku'damm on Christmas Eve. The sight of all that frying, near-naked flesh made me wince.

'There's hardly any room left,' Lucille said.

'Always there is somewhere,' Angelika replied, scanning the area like a border patrol guard at Checkpoint Charlie. 'Look!' she pointed. 'We go towards the front!' And she was off before anyone had time to think.

When we reached her clear spot, very near the centre of the beach, Angelika stopped and looked about. 'Perfect,' she said. She kicked off her sandals and sank to her knees. 'Just perfect,' she repeated. 'Benoît, come and help me.'

B ran to assist with the blanket, while the rest of us, city slickers, stood about like lost souls.

I reached into one of the bags to retrieve a folded blanket, and soon we were all, with the exception of Tunde, spreading out towels and mats. Tunde was gawping at a pair of size-able bare breasts emerging from the lake.

'Aren't you hot in those jeans?' Lucille asked.

'I'm fine, really.' I lay back on the blanket. I had no intention of removing my clothes. It was enough being fat without having to broadcast it.

She squinted at me and tutted. Then she shuffled beside me. I smiled to indicate I wasn't annoyed and closed my eyes. I could sense her hovering.

'What is it?' I asked.

'Come on then,' she said. 'Let's go for a swim.'

'A swim?'

'Brilliant idea!' Famke announced. She grinned at Tunde. 'We'll all go swimming.'

'Here, these are yours.' Lucille threw my trunks at me.

'Luce!' I said, sitting up. I looked round at the rest of the beach. People were thin and pink and laughing. 'I'm not going swimming! I'm not in the mood. You go on. I'll watch.'

Before I could think, she stood and unzipped her print dress. I thought I might pass out. Then I realized she was wearing a bikini underneath. Nature girl, I thought. It was the upbringing in the Seychelles that did it; all the aquamarine and clear skies of her youth.

'I've never heard anything so ridiculous,' she said. 'We haven't come all this way just to sit on the sand.'

I closed my eyes.

Uncle Raymond always said I was fat. From the start he never minced his words, never called me chubby or big or plump. He would simply announce that I was fat, as if it were a sin, then laugh out loud like a lunatic.

When I opened my eyes only B and Angelika had remained on the sand. Angelika had commandeered a covered love seat – number 259 – one of hundreds that littered the beach. She had put on a floppy pink sun hat and cloaked herself in something resembling sackcloth. A paperback lay open on her lap, but her eyes were closed.

B cowered under the parasol, reading a newspaper. 'You will cook out there,' he said to me and laughed.

'I know,' I sighed. 'I should go for a swim. How about you?'

'Yes, good idea!' Angelika's disembodied voice spoke for him from beneath the sun hat.

'Why not,' he shrugged.

I wrapped a towel round my waist and pulled on my barely worn Hawaiian trunks. When we were ready, B and I walked slowly down to the shore.

'Look – the blacks!' a girl screeched, little more than a

toddler. What seemed like a sea of faces whipped round to stare, but B and I carried on, regardless.

When we reached the water's edge, I ran through the shallows and plunged straight in. The water was cool, but bearably so. Lucille stood knee deep, grimacing in her mauve bikini. I couldn't understand why she had been so eager to swim in the first place. She was wearing a bright yellow bathing cap bordered with tiny violets – which she had purchased the day before – so as not to ruin her permed curls.

'Where's Tunde and Famke?' I called.

Lucille looked up, shading her eyes with one hand and pointing with the other. 'Somewhere out there. I can't see them.'

'What are you waiting for?' I asked. People were leaping about, playing ball games, trying to manoeuvre plastic floats between bathers. Many simply stood on the shore, like Lucille, trying to decide whether or not to brave the initial cold.

B sidled up to Lucille in what appeared to be his underwear and grinned sheepishly. I didn't comment.

'Come on, you two!' I kicked my legs in their direction. I was eager to swim out towards the centre of the lake.

'Don't splash!' Lucille screamed, 'or I won't come in.'

'Don't splash!' I mimicked. 'I won't come in.'

She glared at me.

I kicked my legs again, and then a group of children beside us decided to kick up a storm, and soon Lucille and B were drenched.

'You fucker!' she screamed at me and proceeded to march out of the lake.

B retaliated, splashing the children in return. There was a cacophony of screams and churning water I hadn't bargained for, a war zone on a pleasant day.

I pushed further out where it was easier to swim, the temperature dipping as the water deepened. I swam towards the sailing boats and the odd canoe we had seen from the shore. I dived beneath the surface until I could touch the floor of the lake, then bounced back towards the sky light.

'There you are!' A woman's voice.

I swivelled round. Famke, and Tunde beside her.

'It's too crowded over there.' Tunde nodded towards the shore.

'I wish we had brought the Lilo,' Famke said. 'My legs are exhausted out here.' She dived beneath the surface, her legs and feet hardly producing ripples. Tunde grinned at me and dived after her. I waited for them to reappear.

After thirty seconds or so, when they still hadn't surfaced, I began to have visions of how the day would end. I could see Famke and Tunde laid out on the beach, surrounded by hundreds of onlookers. An ambulance would drive up to the shore and the two corpses would be lugged into the vehicle. Lucille and Angelika would be inconsolable.

'Ooowee! Ooowee!' a woman's voice shrilled and when I looked, in the distance, there were Famke and Tunde waving cheerily. I waved back and we swam towards each other.

'I didn't know you could swim,' I said to Tunde.

'Oh, well. I'm not too good,' he puffed. 'I'm still learning.'

He seemed beyond the learning stage to me. 'Let's race back to the beach then,' I suggested. I was growing weary of treading water. I couldn't recall the last time I had exercised.

I gave the signal and Tunde shot off like a starting gun, with Famke close behind. I thought I would give them a slight advantage and then surprise them near the shore, but halfway to the beach, they had increased their lead by almost five metres. I stood and watched as they raced each other, Tunde in front, Famke gaining on him. Perfect front crawls, the pair of them. Olympians. Their strokes hardly disturbed the water. Some learner, I thought, and drifted to the shore on my back.

We fell onto the blankets and I could feel the heat of the sun evaporating the moisture on my skin. Lucille was still annoyed; she sat next to Angelika, talking inaudibly. We shared out the chicken Lucille had fried the night before, and I was pressed to accept one of Angelika's Gouda cheese and lettuce sandwiches. Famke and Tunde had bought spare ribs and spring rolls from a Chinese restaurant, and had filled a large plastic container with fruit salad. They had also brought two bottles of champagne for all of us.

After lunch I lay down to rest beside Lucille while she flicked through a magazine. I closed my eyes and let the sun toast my eyelids until everything began to dissolve. I could hear the yelps of children as they splashed in the water. Occasionally an aeroplane would roar from above. Lucille would comment on something she was reading and I'd mutter a reply and our words seemed to emerge rather drunkenly.

'Do you love me?' she said at one stage, but I pretended to be asleep. She nudged me. 'Do you love me, Vincent?' she asked again.

'Eh?' I turned to look at her.

'Do you . . .'

'I heard you the first time, for goodness' sake. Of course I do. What a time to ask.'

We didn't speak for a while and I must have fallen asleep because when next I opened my eyes everyone apart from Angelika had disappeared. I felt momentarily dazzled and disoriented by the sun. The temperature seemed to have climbed by at least five degrees. I opened a beer, but it had lost its chill. I drank it anyway. Angelika was sitting in the same position in the wicker love seat, absorbed in the paperback. Her eyes swept across the pages, barely lifting to take in the revelry around her. I felt for her then, a large woman in a sackcloth dress, lost in fantasy.

'Where have the others gone?' I asked.

She looked up, as if she had heard a voice but could not discern where it had come from.

'They are out there, in the water, I think,' she replied. 'I cannot see them, but they went straight this way.' She pointed with the spine of her open book, which fluttered like an ostrich, unable to take flight. She turned to look at me and I realized she hardly ever smiled.

'Aren't you going to swim?' I asked. 'It's not as cold as you think. I can look after our things.'

'Well . . . no. I don't think so. It is nice to sit here. Just to relax and read.' She held up the paperback.

I nodded but didn't say anything. I didn't feel like swimming myself. Angelika returned to her adventures while I examined Lucille's magazine.

I turned and lay on my stomach to assess what was happening behind me. There were so many near-naked women it was impossible to focus on anyone for long. A cloud hid the sun for a spell and I almost shivered with the change in temperature. It felt like foolishness, lying out there without clothes, all of us. But then the sun emerged again and it grew warm.

Two women were walking towards the water. They both hid behind oversized sunglasses. As they moved closer, I became intrigued. The blonde was perfect: not too tall, ample breasts and soft curves, which she accentuated with a rolling gait. The other one was shorter, dark, her hair tied back in a bunch. She didn't seem as self-conscious as her friend and as she strolled towards the shore she kept her focus on the lake ahead. She wore a sober navy one-piece swimming costume, while the blonde showed off her figure in a white floral bikini. As she approached I could make out the butternut smudge of her nipples.

I looked down at the magazine to avoid leering at them.

'Hello again!'

I glanced up. The woman in the navy swimsuit was gazing down at me.

'Er . . . hello,' I replied. I'd been preparing to turn to watch them enter the water.

'You don't remember us?' The blonde smiled down. There was a hint of something in the voice. Mischief. Menace.

'I'm exhausted!' Lucille panted behind me. I turned. Famke, Tunde and B were behind her. 'We waited for you,' Lucille said. 'Have you been asleep all this time?'

'Um . . . no. I didn't fancy it.'

She looked across at the two women, as if she had only just noticed them, although she had probably seen them some time ago. 'Oh, hello,' she looked at them and back to me, waiting for introductions.

'Hallo, B,' the blonde said in English, taking her queue from Lucille.

Angelika had torn herself away from the book and was watching from beneath the rim of her sun hat.

'Hello.' B looked from me to them, frowning.

'You do not remember me, is it so?' The blonde removed her sunglasses. It was odd to see them in the daylight, removed from the effects of excess alcohol and strobe lights.

'Um . . . that's right. The Atlantic,' I said. I noticed the blonde was doing all the talking. I didn't like her tone or her fixed smiled.

94

'Yes, Atlantic. You remember.' She smiled at Tunde and then Famke, but the eyes spoke pure hatred. 'Hey, big man.' She placed her fists on her hips and wiggled, glaring at Tunde. She had no finesse, the manners dragging behind her like a string of tin cans.

I thought of sprinting into the water to be away from this awfulness. I couldn't tell whether Claudia was staring at me from behind her sunglasses. She kept quiet, allowing her diabolical friend to do all the talking.

'Hallo, I am Sylvie.' She introduced herself to Lucille. 'Here is Claudia.' The women were all forced smiles. All I could think of was our ten-second coitus, Claudia's disbelieving expression as I left that morning.

'Well, it's good to meet you again.' I tried to summon a smile, but it wouldn't come.

Sylvie turned to look at me as if she had never seen anyone so ridiculous.

'We should go now,' Claudia urged at last, in German, tugging at her friend's arm.

'Oh . . . well. To meet you has been wonderful.' Sylvie continued stubbornly in English.

'Bye,' Lucille replied.

No one said anything.

They walked leisurely towards the lake shore. Sylvie; I would never forget her name now.

'Wow, what a head case,' Famke yawned.

Tunde burst out laughing, but the rest of us stayed silent. He was still sniggering when Angelika abruptly took off. By the time B had struggled into his clothes, she had sped past the sunbathers and had almost reached the entrance to the beach.

'Who the hell were they?' Lucille said.

I shrugged. 'Just some people we met a while ago. It's nothing.'

'What do you mean "nothing"? The woman was livid. What the hell did you do to her?'

'Nothing,' I said. 'Nothing at all. What's the matter with you?'

'"Oh, hi, I am Sylvie. To meet you has been wonderful,"' she mimicked, her voice high and piercing. We were racing back to our familiar pattern, Lucille and I. All the old tensions had rushed to the surface in no time. 'Nothing!' she scoffed, and began to stuff our rubbish into plastic bags.


We were all sluggish on the journey back to town. People dragged about like drowsy bluebottles. All the heat and food and energy expended seemed to have sapped the collective spirit. It was like watching a film in slow motion, the edges blurred, the silence surreal. I felt the sun weaken as the day began to wane. No one shouted at their children or fanned themselves frenetically. Only a few reedy voices could be heard above the chatter of the train. A woman sitting next to me sneezed five times in rapid succession. She unfolded a paper napkin and blew her nose. Shards of material flew in all directions like tiny snowflakes swirling in the late afternoon sun. Famke rested her head against Tunde while they spoke in a barely audible murmur. Her hand rested on his thigh and he stroked her hair tenderly. I wondered what would become of Isabel, whether Famke would last the summer. Angelika stared out of the window while Lucille pretended to doze.

'We should come here again one day,' B said to me. I smiled. He looked across at Angelika, but she refused to acknowledge him.

# 9

I T WAS LATE by the time I returned from the Rio. I couldn't
remember saying goodbye to Clariss or B, whether they
had left me or I had left them.

I was having difficulty with the front door. I stood on the
pavement flicking through my bunch of keys. It seemed a
simple enough task, but I couldn't locate the appropriate
one. I belched and the evening came back to me in a warm,
beery cloud.

I caught a glimpse of movement from the corner of Frau
Lieser's ground floor window. I turned to look and a head
shot back inside. When I managed to let myself in, I tripped
on the threshold and fell into the hall. I felt no pain, but I
cried out in surprise. Then the barking began. The door to
Frau Lieser's apartment drew open a crack. I looked up at
a slit of face peering down at me, a thin, craggy, ghostly
white face.

'Who's there?' the face uttered in a strangulated whisper.
'Who's there?'

The door opened wider and another voice started. 'What's
happening out there? What's all that racket?'

The second voice belonged to Frau Lieser even though I could not see her face. She was obscured behind the figure of the first. I sat up to confront Frau Bowker.

'What are you doing down there, young man?' she growled when she realized who it was. She didn't seem as frightened as before. 'Why's the young man sitting on the floor?' she demanded to no one in particular. Schnapps slipped out of the apartment and confronted me with little yaps.

Frau Lieser squeezed past her friend and ventured into the hall in her nightdress.

'Heavens!' she said. 'You gave us both a fright.'

'Your floors . . . I'm sorry, Frau Lieser . . . your floors . . . very slippery . . . you polish them so well.' I could hear my words attempting to follow a straight line, trying to navigate themselves, failing miserably. Schnapps would not be quiet.

'But you didn't polish today, did you?' Frau Bowker demanded.

'Dear me, I can't remember.' Frau Lieser reddened.

'There's been no polishing today, young man,' Frau Bowker snarled. A deep gurgle leapt out from the back of her throat, which only encouraged Schnapps.

'We were in the middle of our sing-song,' Frau Lieser explained, trying to pacify her friend. 'We heard a noise. Maybe someone has broken in, we thought.'

'No . . . just me,' I said. 'Always forget about your polish . . .' I paused and looked up at the two elderly women. 'Won't happen again . . . Promise!'

'No, not a problem, really,' Frau Lieser said. 'You're quite right. Yes, perhaps I won't be so thorough next time. After all, I can't afford to have young people breaking their bones . . . Vincent?'

I must have passed out and come to again, because there she was, still barking at me as if I were the devil himself. It didn't surprise me; I always assumed Schnapps was a stupid dog.

'Aren't you getting up? . . . Why's the young man sitting on the floor?' Frau Bowker asked, as if she had only then noticed me. 'What with the police and the fire brigade and people trooping up and down the stairs all day long – what's the world coming to?' She let out a shrill cry. 'It's too distressing. We want to live in peace.' She swirled about. 'We see them, young man, coming and going, from the window. Don't think we don't know. Police driving by every hour, men wearing women's clothes, people with blue hair, and the stupid one – you can hardly understand what he's saying. And drunkards!'

'What's the problem?' I said. 'You're . . .' I tried to continue, but the words wouldn't arrive. I belched again and a fountain of vomit threatened to leap past my throat. I didn't see what any of it had to do with Frau Bowker. She glared viciously at me as if she were about to burst.

'*Ausländer!*' she spat. She stamped her doll's foot against the parquet floor, but it only emerged as a nervous tic.

'Time to go back to our sing-song, Elsa,' Frau Lieser said, tussling a little with her friend. Frau Bowker wasn't at all pleased at this intervention, but the mass of her friend's body was no match for her own slight frame. Schnapps was still yelping and skipping to and fro, happy now with the bedlam. She often hobbled and implored to be carried, but when she grew excited, the imaginary years fell away and the legs became pistons, her bark as fierce as a Rottweiler's.

'Foreigners!' Frau Bowker screeched once more from behind the closing door. Schnapps let out another yelp and

I could hear her scamper into the sitting room, then scramble back, pawing at the door.

I turned over onto my hands and knees and dragged myself into a standing position. As I climbed the stairs I could hear the beginning of one of Frau Lieser's songs. She didn't know many tunes and I guessed *Für Elise* as soon as the first bars were played. The old women made up their own lyrics. I could not tell whether Frau Bowker had started to sing, but her thin, reedy voice was seldom audible above the sound of the piano. I listened for a moment on the landing outside my apartment and then went in.


'What happened to you?' Lucille asked. 'Where've you been all this time?'

'Out,' I grunted.

'Out? What d'you mean out? You disappear for half the day and all you can say is out.' She stood up and sat down again, but her mouth kept moving.

'What are you talking about?' I groaned. On the radio Sarah Vaughan was singing *It Shouldn't Happen to a Dream*. I couldn't focus on Lucille's words. Out, out, out she seemed to be shouting and then she started bickering in a way I thought would soon bring on a headache. I only wanted to listen to the song. I closed my eyes and tried to think of something to take me away.

The music reminded me of Uncle Raymond, the slow drunken way he moved his gangling body when he danced with Aunt Ama or one of his children. I remembered the funeral, how he had approached me in the garden that late afternoon. He drew me aside during a quiet moment, after the burials, after most of the food had been consumed and people had started to drift back to their homes. Others milled about morosely with nothing particularly useful to do or say. Uncle Raymond had been drinking steadily all afternoon and now his eyes were bloodshot and moist.

'Well, it's just you and Matthew now,' he said, matter of fact, trying but failing to look me in the eye. He kept shifting his weight from one foot to the other. I remember aching for him to stop, to stand still. 'You will need to look after each other now. From now on. You will need to get along, okay?' He would already have had a similar talk with Matty.

It felt strange to hear him say those words because I felt *I* still needed looking after. I felt I, and Matty for that matter, did not know enough about the world to be responsible for anyone else. But I looked down at my Sunday shoes, which I had polished to a metallic gleam the night before, and obediently replied, 'Yes, Uncle Raymond.' And he smiled and said, 'Good boy,' because, after all, that was what he had wanted to hear.

'You're not even listening to me, are you?' Lucille said. 'I could be talking to myself for all I know.'

'Probably,' I said.

She glared at me. 'You're drunk!'

'Listen Luce, I'm really tired . . . I just want to go to sleep.'

'You never listen, do you? Everything simply passes you by. Water off a duck's back.'

'A duck's back?' I said, swimming back to things. 'What are you saying?'

She sat across from me, arms folded.

'Let's just go to bed, Luce,' I pleaded. 'Let's talk in the morning.'

She stood up, twisting her hair in one hand. 'What the hell am I doing here?' She walked out of the room and in a moment the apartment door slammed shut.

In the ensuing calm I became aware of noises from the floor above – moans and stifled screams, the sounds of bodies thumping across the room. It sounded as if there were multiple murders being carried out, but it was only sexual frenzy. I could only guess what Dieter, Caroline and their friends were doing. It would be at least half an hour before they either wore themselves out or killed each other. For once I wasn't annoyed. They seemed to have the right idea. I stood up and paced around the apartment.

It seemed odd we had been together for this long and yet Lucille did not know me. I knew her well enough, I thought, but it seemed unfair somehow for me to be so strange to her after all this time.

When she returned thirty minutes later, she went straight to the bedroom and locked the door. I walked slowly through the apartment turning off all the lights. As I bolted the front door and put the chain in the latch, I could make out, very faintly, the tinkle of the piano filtering up through the floors.


A cool breeze slipped through the window and slid gently over me. The net curtains billowed. The sounds from the street were slick and seamless. I opened my eyes and panicked for a moment. For an instant I thought I was somewhere else: another city, a forgotten country. Then the table legs loomed and I heard the disgruntled shudder of the refrigerator. Sleeping on the kitchen floor was never a sign that things were going well.

I sat up and looked out of the window, expecting rain.

Instead the sun beat down defiantly. It made me feel tired and heavy.

A sixth sense made me turn round. 'How long have you been there?' I rubbed the sleep from my eyes.

'Not long,' Lucille replied. 'I'm going to have a bath.' She got up and left the room.

I stayed hunched on the floor in my warm spot and drifted to sleep again and when I woke, Lucille was still in the bathroom. I sat up and hugged my knees. My temples throbbed after the alcohol of the night before. When Lucille had finished bathing she returned to the kitchen wearing a raspberry-coloured halter-neck dress.

'Coffee?' I asked.

She didn't answer, but I poured her a cup anyway. We sat in silence for several minutes. My shoulders ached.

'Why are you limping?' she asked.

'Probably from the floor . . . from sleeping on the floor.'

'Ah – I thought it might be from when you fell over. Your landlady said you fell over in the hall last night.'

'Did she?' I couldn't remember. Dust motes danced in the beams of light that fell across the kitchen. I had a hazy recollection of a face peering down at me from a doorway. A crazed dog.

'She said you were blind drunk.'

'I fell. So what?' I sighed. 'You've never fallen before?'

'That's not the point.'

'What *is* the point?'

'What do you mean "what's the point"! What is wrong with you!'

It was a shouting match already and it did not surprise me.

'You're drinking too much . . . I need *more* than this,

Vincent! You've got hardly any money, and this . . . this *awful* building.' She waved a hand at the apartment. 'It's not . . . it's not enough.'

'Money, is it now? Is that what this is all about?'

'Don't try to evade the issue. You know what I'm talking about.'

'I know exactly what you're saying. It's all you really care about when it comes down to it. Money, status – all of that. Well, fine. Fuck it. You know, there are plenty of women out there who don't give a shit about money. Just don't dress this up into something it's not.'

'Listen,' she laughed a little maniacally. 'It's got nothing to do with money, once and for all, so don't try and convince yourself that it has. And don't ever talk to me about other women again or I'll slap you into next week.'

All I could think of was Uncle Raymond and how that used to be his phrase. 'I'll slap you into next week,' he would warn, 'and you won't be smiling any more, believe me.' It brought to the surface how much I had hated him, how I still hated him after all this time. It occurred to me that whenever I was angry I began to think of Uncle Raymond and whenever I thought of Uncle Raymond, I was usually irate. I don't know why this should have been, but it unsettled me.

We argued and I walked out and when I returned Lucille had packed her things. I didn't try to stop her – it would have been futile in any case. When she left it was without commitment to the future on either side.

At the last minute I said, 'You know how it is. I didn't mean to get carried away. Sometimes I just . . . I can't help it. It won't happen again.' But I said it without conviction and she wasn't really listening anyway.

# 10

W HEN I ARRIVED at *Zip*, Thomas's secretary was in the middle of a telephone conversation that didn't appear to be work-related.

'Well, we must meet up soon,' she kept repeating. I could hear the excitement in her voice peak and dip, in a kind of rhythmic cycle.

'Let's meet up soon,' she said again. She glanced up at me, then started patting the air with her free hand, as if dribbling a basketball. She drew the receiver a fraction away from her ear so I could see she was making an effort to attend to me. Then she clasped it to her head again and narrowed her eyes in renewed concentration.

'One moment, Tina,' the secretary said, turning to me in annoyance. 'You've come to see Thomas, yes?' she asked hurriedly.

'Vincent. I phoned this morning.' I held up my portfolio. 'He said to come before noon.'

'Oh, that's right. Yes. Go right on in then,' she said. 'He's expecting you.'

I hesitated, unsure whether to take her at her word, but

when I glanced back she had resumed her conversation. I knocked on the door, but couldn't discern a reply, although I could make out a voice on the other side. I turned to appeal to the secretary who only looked up, made a waving motion to usher me in, but did not break her conversation.

As I creaked open the door I could hear Thomas speaking in raised tones. He too was in the middle of a telephone call. I looked from him to the secretary and it occurred to me they might be talking to each other. Thomas glanced up and waved me in. It felt awkward listening to his conversation. I sat down and looked about the office in an effort to appear preoccupied. There was a cactus on a corner of his desk, and begonias and ferns dotted along both windowsills. A potted palm occupied a corner of the room. It didn't look like the territory of a picture editor. The only decorations on the walls were a large poster of *The Seven Year Itch* and two framed book covers, which I assumed Thomas had illustrated – Alfred Dressler's *Collected Stories*, and *The Winter Waltz* by Cornelia Düring. The Düring was a photograph of a white-gowned woman dancing in the snow with an imaginary partner. I thought he had borrowed the idea from a painting, but the title escaped me.

'Why don't you reconsider?' Thomas was saying. 'The terms we offer are quite standard . . . Frankly Jürgen, I'm not one hundred per cent satisfied with the presentation . . . If I remember correctly, we agreed on something altogether different in the brief.' There was a long pause and Thomas twisted the tips of his moustache, one after the other, absent-mindedly. 'Why don't I give you some time to reconsider?' He was straining to keep his voice under control. He looked up at me. I smiled and turned towards the potted palm.

I was sitting on a black leather sofa three feet away from

a coffee table buried in back issues of *Zip*. I picked up a copy, but could not focus on it. I was concentrating hard on trying not to listen to Thomas, but it only had the opposite effect. His voice rose, but he didn't seem to be getting anywhere. Then in the middle of his tirade he said, 'Oh?' very quietly. I assumed the person on the other end of the line had hung up, but, in an effort to cover the indignity, Thomas continued to talk in a stilted, perfunctory manner. He ended with, 'Well, till next time Jürgen. Till next time. Goodbye. Bye.'

It felt odd sitting there, pretending I hadn't heard one side of the discussion, then witnessing his humiliation.

'Well then.' Thomas pulled his fingers through his long grey hair and growled, then shook his head free of the telephone conversation. Marie had said he was forty-five, but he looked older to me. 'Finally we meet. Sagemuller's told me all about you.'

I wondered who he was talking about, until I remembered Marie.

'Let's see what you've got there.'

I clutched my portfolio. I had half a mind to tell him I needed to leave and would only return when he was in a better frame of mind. I didn't think he was calm enough to be able to make impartial judgement. But I was there after all and after disappointing him already, I thought it doubtful I would get another chance.

'Well,' I said, trying to smile, giving him instead a kind of grimace. 'Why don't we start at the beginning.'


'Not there!' Clariss screeched, protecting the seat next to her. 'That one's taken. Pull up a chair.' She pointed to an adjacent table.

I peered round the room. 'Who's your guest? Someone I know?'

'Nosy. You'll see in a minute,' she said. 'Now hush and tell me what you've been up to, you and Lucy? Where is she anyway?'

I looked at her, then turned to the passing waitress. 'Ah, there you are,' I said.

She glared at me, hands-on-hips. I had never seen her before.

'Bratwurst and fries please. And a small salad. And a beer. And extra fries.' I glanced at Clariss.

'Nothing for me thanks,' she said. 'We've eaten already.'

The waitress sped away.

'Have to eat lunch by one or else it upsets my balance,' Clariss said. 'I get uncentred. Know what I mean, sweetie?'

I decided it wasn't worth the effort.

The waitress returned with the beer, then raced off again. A man emerged from the washroom, dressed in a navy blazer and check trousers. His hair was peppered grey and from the shade of his skin, he appeared to have spent his entire life under a sun lamp. He moved jauntily across the bar on the balls of his feet. By the time I realized he was heading in our direction, it was too late to interrogate Clariss.

'Frank, honey,' she beamed. 'We have a guest.' She unfurled one arm and wafted her fingers towards me. She made the same motions to Frank with her other hand. 'Frank, Vincent. Vincent, Frank.' The span of her outstretched arms made her seem like some great prehistoric bird.

'Ah, delighted, I must say,' Frank said, still standing. He looked about sixty, though he might easily have been seventy-five. Maybe older. It was difficult to tell with the tan and the impish, shifting smile.

I felt obliged to get up and shake the man's hand since he seemed intent on standing. His eyes were level with my collarbone; I wondered whether he walked on tiptoe to give the illusion of extra height.

In a swift, practised manner, he unbuttoned his blazer and sat down. It occurred to me he had buttoned up solely to make his way across the room.

'Any, ah, acquaintance of Miss Clariss is, ah, surely an acquaintance of mine,' he said.

'Ah . . . yes,' I said.

Clariss beamed.

'Bratwurst and fries,' the waitress announced with unnecessary volume. She flung several plates in front of me. 'Salad. Extra fries.'

'Thank you,' I said, unable to establish eye contact with her for more than a fraction of a second. She stood glowering as if waiting for me to taste the food.

'A bottle of wine, ah, miss, please. White wine, quite chilled, ah, yes? Something cool and refreshing for the warm afternoon, hmm? What ah, what weather we're experiencing.' He touched his brow with pygmy fingers as if he were about to expire.

The waitress glared at him. 'Very well,' she barked and reeled about.

'I remember guys like that in the army,' Clariss said. 'All they need is some *good* lovin'. All it takes. That's my advice. Am I right, Frank?'

'You are never wrong, my *cherie.*'

Clariss had been a colonel at one stage in her life. Her name had been Theodore then. But all that was past, save for the precipice of her Adam's apple.

'Frank here's in the movie business, Vinny,' Clariss said.

'Really?'

'Ah, well now. Come, come,' Frank said. 'Small projects here and there, you know. Very minor, ah, productions.'

'Movies, schmoovies! It's all the same thing,' Clariss purred. 'You said so yourself, honey, didn't ya.' She reached out and squeezed Frank's thigh. He gasped. I gulped my beer.

'Yes, ah, I suppose I did. But it's all interrelated, isn't it?' He chuckled nervously.

'Look, is that your handsome friend, Vinny?' Clariss asked. We turned and sure enough there was Tunde standing motionless in the doorway as if he had been caught in the glare of headlights. It seemed to take him some time to move in our direction. He was wary of Clariss; he had probably walked into the bar, spotted her, then tried to back out.

'Hey,' he said when he finally reached us. 'I'm late, I know. It's all *her* fault, okay?' He tilted his head towards a petite blonde trailing behind him. She giggled.

'We haven't seen you in such a long time,' Clariss said. 'Frankie, this here's Tundi.'

Frank rose to shake hands. He greeted the woman, whose name still eluded us.

'Tunde,' Tunde corrected, '"ay", "ay".'

'Well Tundi, honey, Frank was telling us about his movies. He makes movies, you know.' Clariss reached out to Tunde's friend. 'I'm sorry, candy. Didn't catch your name.'

The woman glanced anxiously at Tunde, then turned back to Clariss. I wondered whether she spoke English.

'Linda,' she said at last, making it sound like a question. She tugged the sockets of her sleeveless pink T-shirt and rubbed her palms along her slight arms as if she were unaware of the afternoon heat. Tunde reached out and placed a hand on her knee. She stopped fidgeting.

I turned to Frank. 'What films have you made, then?'

'Well,' he said, pouting. 'I am, well . . . ah, there is not such good distribution, and the market being what it is . . . Mostly they go to the United States.'

'Oh, honey!' Clariss yelped. 'Baby! Even better!' She looked at Linda and mouthed a silent 'Ho-lly-wooood.' She turned back to Frank. 'A house in Beverly Hills, haven't ya hon?'

'Yes, of course, and, ah, yes, not to forget St Tropez.'

'Boaster!' Clariss cried and rocked in her chair. She was like a child on its birthday; she didn't want the excitement to end.

The waitress marched back and set down three wine glasses and the bottle of white wine. She took Linda and Tunde's orders, then hurried away.

'She's new. She won't last the week. I won't let her,' Clariss said.

'Ah, the wine!' Frank clasped his hands together. 'The little joys of life. They're quite, ah, rare, you know. Hmm . . . One always appreciates the simple pleasures. Good food and drink. Pleasant company, yes?' He glanced round the table, then stole a long, yearning look at Clariss.

I winced.

'What are these films you make?' Tunde asked, salvaging the previous conversation.

'Yes,' Linda prompted. 'Tell us.' She seemed an odd choice for Tunde – pretty, but not devastating.

Frank pursed his lips and squinted. He tapped the edge of the table with his middle fingers. His eyes did not settle on anyone. 'Now, let me see. Let me see. One of my, ah, more memorable endeavours. Something, perhaps that has achieved some, ah, some degree of recognition. Hmm.'

Clariss studied him, rubbing her hands rapidly against one another as if rolling pastry dough.

'Ah, yes, of course! How forgetful. There have been so many, naturally, you understand. Bestsellers.' He turned to Tunde. 'Now, hmm . . . *Hot Nights in Havana*? It rings bells, yes?' He raised his eyebrows optimistically. 'Starring Kimberly Koenig?'

'Oh, yes honey! Yes!' Clariss shrilled before he had even finished his sentence. She began to clap wildly. 'You did that one, sweetpea? No! I don't believe it! Really?' It was obvious she had never heard of the film, but it seemed important for her to play along.

Linda tittered, her eyes darting anxiously from person to person, not really understanding, but laughing aimlessly. I wondered what had become of Famke and Isabel.

'*Hot Nights in Havana*?' I said. 'Are you making a film at the moment?'

'Well, as it happens, we are scouting for locations . . . right here in, ah, Berlin of all places.'

'Not just locations, honey,' Clariss said. 'Tell him.'

'Well, true my dear, as you well know,' Frank smiled. He looked at each of us in turn as if we were children. 'We have, ah, as is often the case, run into slight difficulties in the casting process. The principal actor, ah, actress in this particular scenario, is still unaccounted for, yes? It has been mentioned that in this case the role should perhaps not be given to someone of, ah, how should I say it – considerable renown. No! We, yes, my producers and I, feel that someone quite new and refreshing is needed. Someone who might inject some much required vitality and realism, yes, into things. Don't you think? Look at Otto, ah, Otto Ostermeyer. What he did for Wenders, yes? A complete unknown.'

I had never heard of Ostermeyer, or Wenders for that matter.

'You have some ideas?' Linda asked warily, 'about this actress?'

'Well, my dear. Let us just say that it is something we are working on at present.' He turned to Clariss. 'But we are, ah, very nearly there.' He gave her hand a prolonged squeeze.

'Oh?' I said. I looked at Clariss in disbelief. Clariss, a film star – I could see it now – her face, her near seven-foot frame splashed across every magazine cover in town.

She gazed at Frank, drinking him up, then peeled her eyes away from him to register our reactions.

'Very nearly there,' Clariss repeated in a kind of chant.

'Let me see,' Tunde said. 'You're shooting a film and you need a *woman* for the main part?'

'Ah, yes, quite right,' Frank replied. 'But not simply a woman, you understand – a heavenly creature. Someone to light up the screen.'

'No problem. I know some actresses,' Tunde said. '*Very* beautiful. You will not be disappointed.'

'Well, yes, we can always do with more faces on the set,' Frank said.

'Yes, but as Frank was saying, Tundi honey – you might not have understood,' Clariss said, 'is that he's more or less made up his mind about the lead. Isn't that so, sweetheart?'

'Of course, yes,' Frank added hastily. 'You see Mr Tindi, Miss Clariss has very kindly agreed to a screen test. She's perfect for the part.'

'It's Tunde – "ay".'

'I'm perfect for the part, don't you see?' Clariss echoed. 'But Tundi, your friends could be useful too. Frankie always needs extras, don't you, sugar?'

'Quite right. Absolutely. Another face or two always

adds a new, ah, should we say, a new dimension to the picture.'

Tunde chewed his food and frowned.

'That silk, sweetpea?' Clariss reached out and twisted the material of Tunde's ochre shirt between her fingers. 'Oh,' she pouted. 'My mistake.'

# 11

T HE ATMOSPHERE in the Atlantic was different on a
Saturday night. Gone was the salsa and the sense of
warm shores. In its place were old disco tunes and modern
dance tracks. Michael Jackson and DeBarge rubbed shoulders with the Bee Gees and Earth, Wind and Fire. The club
filled with a different clientele at the weekend – a younger,
more boisterous crowd that could only dance to hits played
at full volume.

Angelika looked on in horror as we approached the dance
floor. It already seemed full, but I knew in an hour there
would be many more flooding through the doors.

'I can't breathe,' she shouted at B.

'You'll get used to it in a minute,' I yelled. I didn't think
she would want to get used to anything here.

'Let's go up,' Tunde gestured. 'You will like it better there
– more quiet, less smoky.' He pulled Linda by the arm and
the rest of us followed.

Angelika sniffed and squinted as she allowed B to guide
her upstairs. 'You know it's a pity Lucille had to leave so
soon.' She swivelled round to me. 'Otherwise we would all

be couples now. It must feel very strange to live apart like this. I could not do it.'

'Well, you get used to it,' I said. 'Anyway, I might get lucky tonight.'

She started, then looked away. Tunde sniggered. B pretended he hadn't heard.

'I'll get the drinks,' I said. 'What's everyone having?' I would have to get drunk, I thought, if all we were going to do was mollycoddle Angelika.

On the way to the bar I had to steer past a group who seemed to think a staircase was the perfect place to congregate. They made a great show of moving to one side when I appeared, then re-formed like a wall of army ants, to block the stairs again.

The DJ played *A View to a Kill*, which cleared the dance floor, and I had to scramble to the bar because of the sudden crowd.

'I'll get these. What are you having?' I heard a man call in English.

He was speaking to two men who were further away from the bar. The accent was pure Yorkshire.

'I'll have a lager,' one shouted, but the other took an eternity to decide before saying, 'Make mine the same, then.'

I wondered whether they were army or tourist. I couldn't think why else they would be here.

The Supremes sang *Baby Love* and people began to drift back to the dance floor and I was able to surge forward.

'Push in, why don't you,' a familiar voice complained.

I wasn't sure whether to flee or simply ignore it. I could never forget Sylvie's acrid tones after that day at the beach.

'Hello,' I nodded. She had done something with her hair

– a perm or a frizz – so that it shot out of her head, then cascaded all around her.

'There's no getting away from you, is there?' she said.

I didn't even attempt to smile. A woman standing next to her stared at me. They must have been friends, but there was no introduction. There was no sign of Claudia, either. I caught the barman's eye and ordered.

'The least he could do is get us a drink,' the friend shouted. 'Honestly, after pushing in like that.'

'Never mind,' Sylvie said. 'There are gentlemen here, but they're not so easy to find.'

'Look, what would you . . .'

'Two Bloody Marys and a pina colada if you insist!' the friend screeched. She was an older version of Sylvie – her own bleached hair was similarly styled, but shorter, more plain. She looked nearer thirty, but she didn't have the self-assurance of the younger model.

'Drinking for two then, are you?' I said.

'We can't leave Claudia out, can we?' Sylvie said beneath the angry scream of hair. 'She'd be heartbroken to think you'd forgotten all about her.' She seemed capable of anything at that moment – a smile or a spit in the face.

The barman delivered the first round of drinks and I ordered again. I turned, but could not see Claudia.

'You come with anyone or you here on your own?' Sylvie's friend attempted to make conversation.

'On my lonesome,' I said. She had seen the drinks on the counter, so I wasn't impressed by the disingenuousness.

'Oh . . . I see,' she said, looking puzzled by the lie, but she had no retort.

'You in for a drinking marathon, then?' Sylvie said. 'You gonna to carry all those glasses yourself?'

'I'll manage.'

Their Bloody Marys arrived, followed by the cocktail. I felt like a fool standing there, wondering what to do with the other drinks.

'Here you go. One for you, and one for you, and, ah, one for Claudia.' I winked. 'She's drinking alcohol now?' From what I could remember, she had stuck to fruit juice that night.

'It's just a milk shake as far as she's concerned,' Sylvie said. She pointed. 'Isn't that your friend?'

I turned and there was Tunde.

'What's taking so long?' he asked, all the time squinting at Sylvie. I could see he was trying to work out who she was – he was waiting for introductions – the slow worm of recognition rising to the surface.

'Well, now your helper's arrived,' Sylvie said to me. 'Come on Gudren. We're overwhelmed with gentlemen here.'

And they were off, Gudren craning her neck for another peek at Tunde.

'That one again,' he said, as if he had completely forgotten about her personality. 'That's one foxy chick.'

I looked at him. He could spend the night with Sylvie even if she hated him and he wouldn't care.

Angelika had commandeered Linda by the time we returned.

'I see you have driven her away again,' B said.

'Who?'

'"Who?" he says. Lucille, of course.'

I swigged my lager. 'She had to go back a couple of days early. Work and stuff.'

'I see,' B said. 'Wasn't that the excuse last time?'

A gang of men ran past, shouting. One of them yelled,

'I'm taken tonight,' and the others guffawed as if he were being absurd.

I wanted to be taken too, occupied with another, instead of being a spare wheel on this motley vehicle of friends.

'These places, they attract rough types, yes?' Angelika said. 'Honestly, dear, we should have gone to the jazz club.'

'Next time, dear. But really, on a Friday night it's completely different. We're here on the wrong night. Isn't it?' he appealed to me.

'Well, I like it,' I said.

Angelika sniffed.

'I think it's quite fun, this place,' Linda piped up. 'The music really gets you moving.' She had been jiggling in her seat all evening.

Tunde didn't respond. He was usually first on the dance floor.

'Well, I'm going to dance,' I said. 'Anyone else?'

'Later,' Tunde said.

'Linda?'

'Okay.' She glanced at Tunde, but he only waved her away. 'He's being distant,' she said as we manoeuvred past the crowd on the stairs.

'He gets moody sometimes,' I lied. 'It never lasts. How long have you known each other?'

'Just over a week – that's why it's so strange; it was going great until yesterday. Suddenly he's Mr Ice. I don't understand.'

She was sweet, Linda. I hadn't taken much notice of her before perhaps because she was eclipsed by the glamour of Famke and Isabel. I guessed this was probably the last time we would see her. Tomorrow she would be yesterday's news. She would be hurt, but not heartbroken. Tunde was always careful never to get too involved.

'Let's dance and forget about it,' I said. 'I'm sure he'll come round.' We started to move to Shalamar's *Dead Giveaway*, and she began to laugh after a while, which made me feel good.

'It's funny,' she said. 'He says you're from the same place, the same country I mean. You sound so different.'

I shrugged. 'I lived most of my life in England. Tunde grew up in Lagos. We're not so different, though. We've both ended up in the same place, and basically . . . basically, we want the same things.'

'I suppose so. But no one wants exactly the same things. I know I don't.'

A man in baggy Levis and a yellow T-shirt attempted to impress onlookers with his dance routine. He seemed to spend most of the time spinning on the floor, flipping into the air, then repeating the exercise again. People cleared a space around him to watch, but, for me, the novelty began to fade almost instantly.

'What'll you have?' I made a motion with my cupped hand. Linda shouted back, but I couldn't hear. 'Some what?'

'Water!' she yelled. 'I'm going to stay here and dance.'

I brought the water to Linda and returned to the bar. I finished off another lager as I watched her move among the revellers, the human spinning top and the gang of youths who were dancing now, all the earlier menace drained away from them. I scanned the perimeter of the room, but Sylvie had disappeared.

I spotted the others at the bottom of the stairs and waved. Tunde walked towards me.

'She wants to leave,' he said, pointing his chin at Angelika. He didn't sound as peeved as I would have expected him to be.

'But it's early. It's not even midnight,' I said. 'What about you? You've hardly talked to Linda.'

He sighed and looked at her on the dance floor. B and Angelika joined us.

'At least one more dance before we go,' I said. 'Don't leave now. We've only just arrived.' But I was only thinking of myself. Of how young the night was and how I needed to share it with someone.

'Just one dance, dear,' B said. Angelika looked from his face to the floor and back again.

'I am not so fit,' she complained. 'I have not danced in years. If you want to go, it's okay. I'll wait.' She held her handbag against her stomach and B remained where he was.

Then Linda appeared and grabbed Angelika's hand. 'Just one,' she pleaded, inching back into the throng. In a moment both women were dancing. B and Tunde decided to join them. I watched for a while, then bought another drink. I figured it would be difficult for them to leave so soon now.

'I'd swear you're following us.' Sylvie's voice came from behind me.

I turned and there she was with her older friend and next to them stood Claudia. I wished I had listened to Angelika and left earlier. There was no escape now.

Claudia peered at her pointed red shoes, then at the dance floor, but she didn't say anything. All three were wearing short denim skirts and sleeveless T-shirts, like a set of triplets.

'Um . . . can I get you a drink or something?' I asked.

Gudren's eyes lit up. 'Well, if you're offering, another Bloody Mary.'

'Same again,' Sylvie said.

'Claudia . . . you want anything?'

She shook her head. I bought her a pina colada anyway.

'I see your friend's found himself another girl,' Sylvie sneered.

'Yes, it looks like it,' I said. 'This is yours.' I handed the cocktail to Claudia.

'Thanks,' she mumbled.

'Ooh, this is a good one!' Gudren shrilled, when *Tarzan Boy* began. 'This calls for a boogie. Anyone for a boogie?'

'Oh, all right then.' Sylvie put her drink down and joined Gudren. Claudia raced to her friends without a word.

I felt foolish all over again, standing there while everyone else enjoyed themselves. I finished my drink and started to move my body. I was beyond tipsy now.

'There you are,' Linda shouted. She waved and beckoned me. 'That was a long drink. I thought you'd left us.'

I shook my head. Angelika turned and smiled as she danced. I had been wrong about her; she moved fluidly, as if she had been dancing all her life. I gave her a wan smile in return and felt the music carry me away.

Tunde reached out for Linda and for a minute they danced in each other's arms. She threw back her head and laughed. When I first met Lucille, we often went to clubs in London. She had that same manoeuvre – head thrown back, eyes wide with excitement. She had been a different person then – we both had – flush with the discovery of one another. I wondered what she was doing now on a Saturday night in London.

'Come dance with me, Vincent.' Angelika was in front of me. The old antipathy no longer seemed to matter. Michael Jackson's *Working Day and Night* thundered out for the umpteenth time and we let ourselves go. She was a contradiction, Angelika; the frilly blouse buttoned up to the throat, the schoolteacher's long grey skirt, the sensible shoes. She didn't care what people thought.

'It's late.' Tunde slapped his watch.

B looked over at Angelika. 'What do you think?'

'Just a bit longer,' she pleaded.

Linda did not look as if she was willing to leave. Tunde stood still for a moment, then whispered in her ear. In a moment he was pushing through the bodies. I knew he would not return. Ten minutes later, I excused myself and went to the washrooms. Sure enough, he wasn't there. I walked to the upper floor where we had first sat. As I approached the staircase I saw his face. Sylvie was standing in front of him and he was nodding at her. I was about to interrupt when they leaned in towards each other and kissed. I veered abruptly to the side to avoid being noticed, and crashed into someone.

'You again.' Claudia rubbed her forehead.

'We must be stalking each other,' I said. 'I'm sorry. Does it hurt?'

'No. I'm all right,' she laughed.

'Let's move nearer the light.' I drew her away from the stairs.

She tried to peer over my shoulder. 'Who's that with Sylvie?' she asked.

'Who knows?' I said. 'I need to talk to you.'

'You do?' The anxiety in her eyes was unexpected. It gave me no time to think.

'Well . . . yes,' I said. 'Why don't we go over there.'

'No, tell me now,' she said.

'Oh, okay . . . well, then . . . what it involves is this.' I paused. 'Remember the other day on the beach, when you and Sylvie were, well, when Sylvie was having a go at us?'

'How could I forget.'

'Well, I thought that I'd been careless . . . I thought I should make things up to you.'

'You did?'

'Yes, well . . . yes.'

'Make things up how?'

'I don't know. I was thinking of dinner. We could go to an exhibition or a film. Something to eat?'

'Oh,' she said. 'That's not what I thought you were going to say.'

'It's not? What did you think?'

'I don't know. Not that anyway.' The tension had left her face as she contemplated the offer. I hoped she would turn me down.

'What are you two gossiping about?' Sylvie interrupted.

I looked round, but there was no sign of Tunde.

'We're going to an exhibition,' Claudia said. 'Who was that man?'

'An exhibition!' Sylvie exclaimed. 'That's not your thing, is it? What kind of exhibition?' She was aglow after the stolen kiss. Whatever was being discussed didn't matter to her.

'It's . . . it's at the Andreas Grob . . . gallery,' I said.

Sylvie looked nonplussed.

'An Italian exhibition,' I said, remembering what I had read in the press pack. 'Very avant-garde. You might like it.' It was work, but it was the first thing I could think of.

'Who, me? I don't think so,' Sylvie said. 'Life's too short for that kind of thing. I'm not a stare-at-a-painting kind of girl. I like movement. Dancing. Passion.'

'Where's Gudren?' Claudia asked.

Sylvie shook her head. 'Search me.' Then she drifted into the crowd.

'Why do you hang around with people like that?' I asked.

'Like what? Sylvie? . . . What's wrong with Sylvie? She's

no worse than your gigolo friend,' she said. 'Besides, she loves me. And I love her. We've been friends since school.'

'I shouldn't have said that. I'm sorry. I don't know what I was thinking. I've drunk too much.'

Claudia smiled and pinched her nose.

'I should go now. It's late.' I couldn't understand how I had got into this predicament in the first place. I had wasted precious moments protecting Tunde instead of staying on the dance floor. Now I had an unwanted date and no one to spend the night with. I was more than angry with myself.

'How do I get to the exhibition?' Claudia asked. 'You haven't got my number.' She rummaged through her bag for a pen and paper. 'Oh dear. I've nothing to write on.' She glanced at me.

I tried to smile, but I was tired and my face was set. I stared at the revellers on the dance floor.

She made another search in her bag, then looked at me again. 'You don't want to go, do you? To the exhibition? Why did you ask me if you weren't interested?' Her eyes were wide and wavering. I felt like a scoundrel all over again.

'No, I do. Really, I do,' I said. 'I'm drunk, that's all. Here, give me the pen.' I pulled a ten mark note from my pocket and wrote down her number as she recited it. 'Now we can both get in touch. Agreed?'

'Okay,' she said. 'Just don't forget.' She half smiled again. She was like a flower that bloomed or wilted depending on the gardener. I feared for her in the care of my clumsiness.

# 12

WE TOOK A taxi from Zwickauer Damm to Ezmîr's building. I stared out of the window at the bleak horizon, punctuated by intermittent green, wondering why the hostel was situated so far from anywhere.

'There!' Arî pointed, directing the driver.

We drew up to a large grey building that looked more like an office block or a warehouse than a home.

Ezmîr met us at the main door and ushered us through the entrance. The security guard attempted to glance up as we hurried by. He squinted slightly, but did not quite manage to break away from a well-thumbed paperback. We jogged up several flights of stairs and it occurred to me that what Ezmîr had planned might be, according to the rules of the hostel, quite illegal. I glanced at the patch over his right eye and wondered at the horror story that lay behind the cloth.

We walked through a set of double doors on the fourth floor, along a blue echoing hallway, past several individual doors. Ezmîr stopped outside a room, knocked and entered, then motioned for us to follow. Inside was a kind of makeshift dormitory with five or six interspersed bunk beds. Even though the windows had been flung wide open, the atmosphere inside was stifling.

On the lower half of some of the beds were several African men – in sitting positions, some lying down. They were all, without exception, smoking. I wondered why they weren't outside. Ezmîr slapped the hand of one of them, and gestured to Arî and myself.

'You're welcome,' the man on the end bed greeted in English.

I shook his outstretched hand. He leaned out to an ashtray on the floor, tapped his cigarette, and lay back. He stared up at me for a moment through spiralling smoke. Rivulets of sweat trickled down the sides of his face. I began to greet the other men. Arî waved to them and I wondered whether he was a regular here. Ezmîr glanced at his watch and spoke to Arî.

'After five, no more visit,' Arî translated. 'We must go. Five o'clock!'

I nodded.

'Where are you from?' I asked the man whose hand I had shaken. 'From which country?'

He exhaled slowly, watching the smoke plume out of his mouth until I thought he wouldn't answer. 'Ghana,' he said eventually, enunciating carefully as if he were afraid I might not hear. 'All of us,' he continued. 'And you, you want to take our photo, eh?'

'You don't need to move,' I said. 'Just relax. Ignore me.'

'What!' exclaimed another man, grinning widely. 'You're joking, surely?'

'Not joking,' I replied, setting myself up. The others laughed.

'And you, you're from where?' asked a man leaning against the windowsill.

'Nigeria,' I replied.

'Ah, you're our brother then.'

'But your people don't welcome us,' another man said, 'so we come here instead.'

There was a tension; I didn't know the history of it and I could not respond. I remembered Uncle Raymond's wife, Aunt Ama, who had been born in Ghana. 'My aunt, she's from Bimbilla. Ama,' I said.

'Okay, okay,' said the man whose hand I had shaken. 'I know it – my brother-in-law is from there.'

The cell filled with the sun-dappled haze of cigarette smoke. Ezmîr was explaining something to Arî in Kurdish. A minor disagreement ensued among the men to which I paid scant attention. Occasionally someone would look up, not completely at ease as I made my way about the room, but towards the end of the time there, I was ignored.

'So soon?' the joker asked when I announced I had finished.

'More?' I laughed. 'You want more?'

The joker frowned. 'But you're not in the photo. You need to be in the photo,' he said.

'No, I don't. I'm the photographer.'

He snapped his fingers impatiently for the camera.

The joker asked everyone to move to one side of the room so we would all be in a single frame. He took one photograph, then asked someone else to act as cameraman so he too could be included.

Afterwards Ezmîr led me to the end of the corridor, to a tiny room where his friend Sediq and his wife lived.

'Sediq,' Ezmîr announced. 'Afghanistan.'

We remained with them for only a short time while I photographed Sediq. He wouldn't allow his wife to sit for the camera and I did not try to persuade him.

We walked to different levels of the building, along endless corridors – into the refectory, Ezmîr's own dormitory, the recreation room behind the reception – meeting his ephemeral companions. As the deadline drew near, he started to become agitated.

'He cannot see one family. From Somali,' Arî explained.

'It's not important,' I said. 'Tell him I have enough material already. More than enough. Tell him not to worry.'

But Ezmîr wasn't satisfied and he left us for several minutes while he searched for his friends. He returned moments later with a giggling East African boy of no more than five or six.

'Come,' Ezmîr said in English, holding the boy's hand.

We made our way to the second floor, to the end of a hallway, into a secluded kitchen area. The boy ran ahead of us and hugged the covered legs of a thickset woman standing in front of a stove.

'Ahhh!' she sang out, raising a free hand to her mouth. 'Ezmîr!' With a deft movement, she drew her child away from the cooking area.

Ezmîr smiled broadly and made the introductions. I noticed, sitting on a chair beside the kitchen table, a slender man I took to be the child's father. Something about him seemed familiar.

The boy moved to the man, clutched him possessively, turned to peer at the strangers, then buried his face into his father's side once more. His father laughed and I realized where I had seen him before – in my photograph: the man in the run-down café with the sombre face. He had been in Kreuzberg on the day of Henkelmann's rally, the man I assumed was Ethiopian. I wondered what he had been doing there, alone, away from his family. His face betrayed no sign of recognition. He looked altered in some way, perhaps because he was here, within the warmth of his family. I was forced to recall the day all over again: the muted pinball machines, the enormous woman at the cash till, the Turkish boy on Henkelmann's shoulder, the butterball butcher, the murder ringing in my ears.

I took several photographs of the family as we had found them – the mother frenetic over the stove, the boy charging between his parents – then set up the tripod for their portrait. The woman was swathed in a traditional aquamarine gown, the material draped over her head, her shoulders, in the blue heat of the day. The boy fidgeted while his father attempted to calm him.

I peered through the lens then and I could see my mother and father, Matty, myself. I glanced up. There was the Somali family standing patiently, waiting for release. I could hear the Kurdish chatter of Ezmîr and Arî from the corridor.

'Okay!' I waved. 'Ready?'

The boy laughed, scratched the side of his head, held on to his father's hand.

I looked through the lens and this time it did not come as a surprise. I saw my mother's dimpled face, my father grinning at something Matty had said, my pink sandy tongue held out to the camera, like a gift. I saw their faces clearly, each feature, as if time had not dulled my memory. I released the shutter and everything seemed to decelerate.


In the car, Papa informed us that Grandma had been overjoyed to see us after such a long time. 'You have made her so very happy,' he said, turning to us in the back. Our mother added something in collusion and then they began to have their own private conversation. I felt smug, but uneasily so, as I felt Matty and I had done nothing to deserve praise. We had simply agreed to visit our grandmother in her village, hundreds of miles from Lagos.

The car sped through the humid atmosphere, the road mantled in the sepia tint of early evening. Matty held his arm out of the window, angling wind to his face. I tried to imitate him, but our mother noticed and told us to wind up our windows. I sighed and Matty glowered; I had ruined his fun yet again. In a moment the first drops of moisture grazed the windscreen, and before long rain was falling steadily in sheets across the landscape.

There was silence as we listened to the music of the shower, the gentle drumming. The conversation started up again in the front and I felt the pull of rain-induced sleep, tinged a little with boredom. I looked across at Matty and he seemed lost in thought as he stared out of the window.

'But who will look after her?' our father asked. 'Where will she live?'

Mama was quiet for a moment. She said, 'We can manage somehow. It would not be so difficult, you know. Besides, it is only a suggestion. There is always Raymond; it does not have to be us. I am only suggesting, that's all.'

'Yes,' Papa exhaled. 'I know.' And then they seemed to have the argument all over again, going over the same ground.

'Your brother . . . ' Papa said.

'Only for a short time . . .' Mama replied.

'Yes,' Papa said again. 'But it's not a question of time.'

I listened to their voices, picking out irritated snatches of rhythm, feeling my eyelids droop. Then they were quiet, and for a while I held sleep at bay. The car whistled through the night air, the tyres slick, greedy for the sodden road. Mama used to explain that rain was always a precursor to a fresh beginning. It washed away the accumulated filth. It was like a new day, a wiped slate.

The silence was broken by laughter. I thought either they had begun to talk again or I had slept and woken. Mama sighed the way she always did when she had laughed too much and it began to hurt; they were talking about a bumbling colleague in Papa's office and the previous gloom had now lifted. I must have fallen asleep.

When I woke again, when I was jolted awake, I could not understand why we had come to a standstill. Why there was glass on the seat beside me, rain stealing its way into the car. Papa made a long, strange, high-pitched noise – like singing – that did not seem to come from his mouth. Then he fell quiet. I kept thinking he would wake up, that he must have been very tired. Sleep was all he required and then we would move off again. Matty kept shaking our mother. He was crying and shaking her hysterically, but she never once stirred. I sat in the corner with the rain soaking me, watching the desperation in him, a little asleep, a little terrified, but I didn't say anything. I did nothing. Nothing came to me.

# 13

A BLUES BAND, fronted by a singer who seemed like a man leaning into a hurricane, played in a corner of the bar. There was nothing in front of him, no object behind, only the thin metallic pole of the microphone into which he poured the gravel of his voice.

'Of course it was suicide,' Claus said as he handed me the drinks across the bar. 'That's what they're saying now, and quite frankly, I'm giving it serious thought.'

'You shouldn't listen to rumours,' I said. 'And you shouldn't spread them either, especially when they're ridiculous. Have you forgotten that Henkelmann was beaten unrecognizable?'

'So far I've come up with twelve possible explanations for the death, so you can see I'm getting desperate for ideas.' Claus laughed and looked towards the stage. 'These fellows are something else, aren't they? A real find.'

The bass player began to sway, leaning forward into the crowd, thrumming the guitar furiously. The audience applauded after his solo. He leaned back again, his blue-black face soaked in sweat.

I carried the glasses to the table where Clariss, Arî and Frank sat. Frank kept slapping his hand against his thigh. I couldn't tell whether he was trying to get into the spirit of things or whether he genuinely enjoyed the music.

'I'm a year older,' Clariss's voice rose above the clamour, 'since you been gone. You make those drinks yourself, sweetpea?'

'Sounds like a song,' I said. 'I was chatting to Claus.' I put down the beer and the wine and Arî's ginger ale.

On stage the singer began to move, but he did so in halting, ungraceful movements. *Ease on down the river,* he sang, *damn, packed my bags, set myself free.* He lurched forward, came to a halt, then dragged one leg towards himself. His eyes were shut tight. Droplets of sweat clung to the end of his chin, but he didn't seem to mind. He turned his body to face a rotating fan to one side of the stage, but the crippled leg remained rooted to the spot, twisted, as if his foot had been nailed to the floor. *Gonna mosey on down that river, where ain't nobody gonna bother me.*

'Nigger – why don't you put your sorry self out!' Clariss shouted.

Frank looked at her, aghast.

'Pay Clari no mind.' She patted his thigh. 'I'm only teasing.'

He reached across and stroked the back of her hand and smiled. Arî tittered.

'Another drink anyone?' I asked.

'Already?' Clariss and Frank had barely touched their wine.

'Arî?' I waggled my empty glass.

He shook his head. Frank declined. I got up anyway.

At the bar Claus was serving a woman in a pink *I ♥ New York* T-shirt. Her breasts were so ample it seemed entirely possible the material might tear down the middle. Claus noticed me and waved as he served.

'Vincent – here's Ingrid,' he called. 'She doesn't believe me . . . about our blues singer. About the leg.' He turned to fetch a bottle of white wine from the refrigerator.

I had no way of knowing what he was talking about. I moved closer. 'What's not to believe?' I said.

'You know – the accident. The river.'

'Wait, wait, wait,' Ingrid interrupted. 'Let me hear it from *his* lips. You keep quiet there. No funny business. So, what happened then?'

'Well,' I said, glancing at Claus. 'Let's see if I can remember. It was so long ago – my memory's not great.'

Claus rolled his eyes and threw his hands up. 'The river – don't you remember anything? The accident. The branch . . .'

'Hey, hey, hey. What'd I tell you? No butting in mister. Let's hear the story from this guy. Go on.'

'Okay, okay. As you wish.' Claus held up his palms and smiled. 'But he'll probably get it all wrong. I've booked these guys before. I know the whole story.'

'Yes, the river . . . the river. In Florida I think it was, or somewhere South. But Claus always gets it wrong – about the branch. I'll tell you.'

She leaned forward and narrowed her eyes. She had biceps, Ingrid, and cyclist's thighs, which she had squeezed into tight faded blue jeans. She hooked her thumbs into the pockets and began strumming her fingers against her legs. I was both alarmed and amused by her aggression, her lack of humour. She seemed like a woman to wrestle and conquer on a waterbed, covered in oil.

'He was with a bunch of friends,' I said. 'They were playing

137

in the river – don't ask me which one because I don't know. They'd climbed up a tree and balanced on a branch stretching out over the water.' I used my hands to illustrate the jutting branch, the river below. 'Claus is partly right about the branch, by the way, but that wasn't the cause of it.'

'It wasn't?' Claus looked baffled.

'Oh?' Ingrid said. She was right there in the story.

I took a swig of the beer Claus had placed before me. I had no intention of paying.

'What happened was, he, they – it was a group of school friends – took it in turns to tiptoe out to the end of the branch and jump into the river. The papers all focused on how dangerous this was, but they'd done it a hundred times before. They were school kids. Boys. For them this was normal.

'After a while, the kid drifts off towards the opposite bank – he's a bit bored of the whole climbing/jumping-off routine. I can't remember how it happened, whether anyone saw it coming or not. Claus brought a photocopy of the article ages ago. He might still have it.'

Ingrid looked across at him, and he swung his head towards her. 'Yeah . . . of course, yeah. The article. Yeah.'

Ingrid frowned.

'Well, one minute the boy's just floating on his back in the water, the next he feels a tug on his leg, and under he goes. Then all hell breaks loose. The other kids are shouting and throwing whatever they can at him. Rocks, shoes. Turns out it's not *at* him, though. The ones on the bank are thrashing torn-off branches in the water. But not one of them dares go in. The ones in the water are scrambling out.'

'But – what was it?' Ingrid demanded. The heart shape kept heaving up and down her chest. She looked as if she might hurl me to the ground if I didn't finish the story.

'They confirmed that the bite marks were those of an alligator, but the boy himself never caught a glimpse of it. A couple of the boys in the tree swore they saw it, but it all happened so quickly.'

'Poor kids. They dragged him out, all of them terrified they might be next,' Claus added, as if he had been there. 'He was lucky, wasn't he, that he didn't bleed to death?'

Another barman called for Claus's assistance and he left us. Ingrid gazed over the crowd at the blues singer, her mouth open, a little undignified. 'Poor man. What a life. You know, I once broke my leg.' She patted her left thigh. 'I was skiing, in St Anton am Arlber. Seventeen I was at the time, but oh, do I remember the pain.'

I thought the two incidents were incomparable: breaking one's leg and nearly being chomped to death by an alligator. I was about to suggest this when I realized I was getting carried away with the story.

Ingrid sighed, but she did not continue. She sipped her wine and I thought how pleasant she looked – with her flushed cheeks, the cautious eyes – when she wasn't speaking or gesturing. At one stage she pinched the neckline of her T-shirt between forefinger and thumb, quite delicately. She pulled the material to and fro in an effort to cool down, exposing the slope of her breasts. There was no chance of the T-shirt splitting. I glanced at the outline of her nipples each time the cotton returned to the perspiring skin. She took another sip of wine and turned to meet my gaze over the rim of the glass and smiled. I smiled back.

'Never any peace,' Claus grumbled when he returned. 'They could manage for a single second without me, you'd think. The burden of responsibility is not an easy one.' He glanced down at Ingrid's cleavage. I noticed he was wearing a fresh shirt.

'So this is *your* place?' Ingrid's narrow gaze widened. 'I didn't know. Very nice. It's a bit different from your usual bar. I like what you've done with the plants and all these posters. Very artistic. Is that Spain?' She pointed.

'No, Brazil – Rio. Remember – Café Rio?' Claus said. He tapped his head and uncrossed his arms, pushed out his chest a little. 'I do my best with what I'm given.' He shrugged and Ingrid laughed as if he had made a joke. 'But staff,' he looked across the bar at his helpers and shook his head. 'It's hard to get decent workers in the first instance. You never know how long they'll stay, whether they'll rob you blind.' He fidgeted with the sleeve of his batik shirt and scratched his temple and crossed his arms again.

I didn't know why he was talking about his staff like that. He never usually had a negative word to say about them. Ingrid's presence, I thought. We both glanced at her chest again, her flushed, sweaty face.

'You know, I'm not sure I can go on if this weather keeps up.' Ingrid had lost interest in Claus's managerial responsibilities. 'It's not supposed to be this hot in Europe. We're just not used to it.'

'Come on,' I said. 'After the last winter it's great to have these Mediterranean temperatures, don't you think?'

'I'm with Ingrid on this one,' Claus said, playing the agreeing game. 'Summer's fine, but heatwaves are a pain; we're not used to them. No one has air conditioning. People start losing their heads. Look what happened to Henkelmann. Probably taken out by someone with sunstroke.'

'Don't remind me,' Ingrid said. 'Gosh – I'm as dry as a cotton ball.'

'Here, let me get you another.' He snatched her empty glass.

'Kind of you, Claus.' I handed him my glass. 'And I thought you said it was suicide?'

'See what I'm forced to put up with?' He nodded towards me. 'People constantly taking advantage of my generosity. What have you ever done for me, Vincent?'

'If it wasn't for me, this place would shut down in a minute.'

'You see? No shame.'

Ingrid laughed. I could see she was already half in his hands. Claus would struggle, but she wanted him to fight. My dream of spending the night with an athlete had been stripped away as fast as the hairs on Claus's scalp.

In no time, it seemed, I could barely stand. I had only eaten breakfast. And French fries for lunch. A tin of corned beef with bread after that. Bratwurst at the stand by the U-Bahn station at Bayerischer Platz, a chocolate bar for the journey home. It was coming back to me now. Two tins of creamed rice before leaving for the Rio. The alcohol, in any case, had gone straight to work. I trapped Ingrid into hearing about my trials with Lucille, while Claus served other customers.

'But you can hardly blame her when she's all the way in London,' Ingrid said. 'If it were me, I'd have, well, it wouldn't have happened in the first place – you end up living two separate lives. Before you know it, you're strangers. That can't be fun.'

I frowned. I had been trying to get Ingrid on my side. I blinked and it must have been some time before my eyes opened again, because Claus had ventured over to our side of the bar.

'Here we go, Vincent.' He raised my arm over his shoulder and hoisted me up. 'Hold on now. I don't want to drop you. What a crash that would make.' He chortled and Ingrid said, 'Stop that! – Let me get the other side.' Her girl guide's zeal was swift.

I didn't mind being carried out of the bar. I could have walked myself, but I liked the idea of being escorted.

'She was the tidiest person I ever met,' I said, continuing my saga about Lucille.

'Tidiness . . . now that's not a good sign,' Claus said, panting. 'My ex-wife . . . she was exactly the same . . . a perfectionist. Nearly drove me insane . . . Better to be a complete mess, I say.'

'You're right there,' Ingrid concurred. 'Never trust a tidy person. Always something going on under the surface.' Unlike Claus, she didn't sound as if she had just jogged up a mile-high staircase.

'Now listen, Lucille's not like that exactly,' I protested. I didn't entirely approve of the direction the conversation was taking.

'You know, I once went out with a guy who wouldn't leave the house unless all the laundry had been stuffed into the washing machine,' Ingrid continued. 'The thought of dirty clothes lying around was too much for him. Even at night, before we went to bed, the clothes we'd been wearing all day went straight into the mouth of the beast – otherwise he'd have lain there all night agonizing about the filth around him. You can guess what the rest of the house was like. That should have been a sign, but like a fool, I stayed with him for years and years.'

'I've got you exactly . . . Paula was just like that with the dust . . . And don't remind me about the rubbish bins. They had to be empty all the time . . . as if they were only there for show.' I could hear the anger in Claus's voice. 'No surprise she went insane.'

'Really! She was mad?'

They were talking around me as if I wasn't there, but it was an effort for me to construct a sentence anyway.

'Well, not really insane . . . but something had to give. All those years of doing things just so. It's not natural, is it?'

'I see,' Ingrid said. She paused, measuring what she should say next. 'But what happened . . . in the end?'

'Oh, well. You know. Someone discovers a taste for something and then "boom" – there you go. It's an addiction. In Paula's case it was adultery: my neighbour, Paula's friend's husband.' Claus paused. '*My* best friend, colleagues in her office. Who knows who else? It was a sickness really. It wasn't in her nature . . . but as I say, something snapped. Too many years of repression. Vincent, give me the keys. Give me the keys.'

'Oh, you poor man,' Ingrid said as Claus unlocked the door.

'Don't "poor man" me. I'm better off without her,' he said dismissively. 'You'll be all right from here, Vincent?' he shouted as if I was deaf as well as drunk.

'Yes . . . yes,' I said.

'No more drinking so much,' he chided. Ingrid stood to one side as Claus pressed the keys into my palm. He had never spoken about his wife before. He always seemed so jovial. Before he could withdraw I pulled him close and held him.

'That's enough now, Vincent. You get to bed, okay?'

Ingrid stood by the door with her arms crossed. I reached over, feeling her resistance until she gave in to my bear hug.

'Okay, okay,' Claus said. 'We'll be here all night at this rate.'

'Death to tidiness!' I bellowed as they headed back to the bar.

'Who's that? Who's making all that noise at this hour?' Frau Lieser opened her apartment door a fraction of an inch.

'Oh!' she cried, seeing me in the hall. She craned her head a little further. She had forgotten to wear her scarf and the bright hall light shone through the meagre hairs on her scalp. 'This is not good,' she said. 'Not good at all, Vincent. You must go upstairs at once. And please be quiet! You will disturb the other tenants.'

I waved. She sighed. She shut and bolted her door.

I was so tired it required a supreme effort to drag myself upstairs. I fell onto the bed. I wondered whether I could fall asleep without first tidying the apartment. I lay on the bed trying in vain to get up. I heard moans from above and then the ceiling began to rumble. The windows gibbered quietly. The noise grew louder. Dieter and Caroline were at it again.

I thought of Claus and Ingrid and their tidy exes, Angelika and B, the puzzle of Frank and Clariss. Arî's fiancée was still in Turkey and Frau Lieser's husband had died over a decade ago. Tunde was into his third or fourth relationship in as many weeks. I hardly saw Marie's husband, Stefan. Nothing was straightforward – there were moments of what passed for bliss, but, in life, chaos appeared to be the norm. Lucille and I were alone in different countries, although we hadn't really been together for several years.

The noise from upstairs drew to a gradual halt. There were a few post-coital cries. The windows stopped shaking, the ceiling shuddered, sighed and was silent. The night air was warm and still.

# 14

THE ANDREAS GROB gallery is a vast hangar of space whose façade is composed almost entirely of glass. I could see figures moving inside long before I reached the building. I had hoped to arrive before Jochen for once, but there he was flirting with a woman who was trying to ward off the attention of an excited child. As I approached I realized the woman was Claudia.

'You're late,' Jochen remarked without emotion.

'I know.' What could I say?

'He's always late,' he explained to Claudia as if they were old friends.

'Sorry.'

'No – I'm early. Really,' she said. 'I wasn't sure how to get here so I gave myself plenty of time. It's nice and cool in here anyway.'

'Cool? You could store meat in here, no problem,' Jochen said, chuckling to himself.

'As long as you're not bored. I'll take the pictures and then . . .'

'No, no,' Claudia said. 'You go ahead. Take your time. It looks interesting. Jochen was telling me all about it.'

I said, 'Well, why don't we get to work and I'll let you know when I'm done?'

'Okay, I'll see you later,' she said and wandered into the main exhibition area.

Jochen shook his head. 'Cheap date, eh?'

I didn't reply. I had never liked Jochen and that wasn't about to change.

'Now, you'll need to take pictures of him over there.' He pointed to a cluster of people in the centre of the hall. I couldn't make out the person he was referring to. 'And the bearded guy. Alessandro Strada and Ettore Mistretta – they're the artists.'

'Anyone else?'

'That bunch over there? They're teachers. I've talked to some of them. Dull as hell, but they might be useful in case no one else has anything to say.'

I hadn't reckoned on all the children, the cacophony of sound, the movement. Claudia was sitting at a giant grand piano with keys the size of paperbacks. Its legs were covered in dense padding. A boy sitting beside her bashed out random notes, but no one seemed to mind the clamour.

Claudia was wearing a pale blue summer dress, in a paisley print. She'd scraped her hair back into a chignon so her high-lights were almost invisible. As the boy hammered out the clanging notes, she pressed the pedals with her sandaled feet. It seemed, had she turned to face me, she would surely be the most beautiful woman in the world. But I knew it was only Claudia with whom I had once shared a drunken, pitiful night. Claudia, who claimed the horrific Sylvie as a good friend. I didn't know why she was here, sitting at the piano with a strange child, why I had invited her, why she had wanted to come.

Saucer-sized holes had been drilled into a section of wall. Visitors pressed their faces against the perimeter of each circle to observe or interact with the art: a feather duster tickle, a spray of water, a jelly mould that embraced the face, a Brothers Grimm narrative. Children wrestled with or lay upon outsized toy animals. A girl appeared to have fallen asleep on top of a six-foot crocodile; a string of saliva dangled out of her open mouth. Ropes unfurled from the ceiling, which the children tugged for effect, releasing bursts of confetti, a rainbow of lights, the shrill whistle of a steam train. Parents and teachers patiently accompanied the children around the exhibits.

I photographed a girl Jochen was trying to engage. She was far too excited to answer his questions and she skipped across the gallery, eager to join her friends. She collided into a vast, cushioned Mother Hubbard shoe and I frowned. She fell and struggled to recover her orientation. Only then did I realize, although I couldn't understand why it had taken so long, that all the children were blind or partially sighted. I noticed the hesitant movements now, the caution, the absence of resolute abandon.

A boy tiptoed beneath a hole in the wall, but could not reach it. I moved closer to the source; there was a sound of dripping water. He stretched up, making tiny fists, then unfurled them. He continued this repeatedly until I thought he would begin to wail. I placed my camera on the floor and lifted him so that his face was inside the circle.

'What's in there?' he asked, jerking his head sideways in order to listen.

Apart from the dripping water there was no activity. The space was completely dark. A sensor must have been triggered because the blackness turned to fluorescent yellow, then sapphire and then a shower of water swirled into a luminous pool. An instant oasis.

'What's in the water?' the boy asked. 'Fairies?'

'Well . . . no, not fairies. It's just water,' I said.

'But I can hear fairies,' he whispered.

I wondered where his parents were. He giggled as if someone else was speaking to him. The pool turned peacock green. And then I *could* hear something, a faint high-pitched mirth intermingled with the trickling water. There must have been a tape playing at very low volume. The boy made cooing noises as if he were able to see what lay ahead of him. I wondered what he did see, what his senses were telling him, what he imagined instead of the lush green glow, the encircling rings of water.

After dinner Claudia and I took the U-Bahn to Krumme Lanke and walked for fifteen minutes before stopping in front of a modern apartment block. A handful of tall pine trees decorated a parched manicured lawn. As we walked up several carpeted flights of stairs, I tried to recall the interior of the building, to no avail. I had been drunk that night. Apart from the memory of a disappointed Claudia, I could remember little else.

'This is unusual,' I said, relieved she hadn't witnessed the ruin I called home.

'It is, isn't it,' Claudia said. 'Spanish architect. I remember hearing that once. The balconies are huge – wide enough for tables and chairs. We could sit outside and have a drink, if you like.'

She turned the key in the lock and I wondered how soon we would begin. I dreaded the delay of coffee and small talk. I wanted to feel her soft skin, to be inside her again.

As we moved into the apartment I reached out to her shoulder, but she suddenly called out 'Mum!', perhaps from fear, so that I almost jumped.

'Claudi? Claudi, is that you?' A woman wearing a floor-length blue and white kimono emerged from the hallway. 'Oh, Claudi. This is the young man?' she asked, this time in English.

'Yes, this is Vincent. Vincent, my mother.'

In my confusion I reached out to shake her hand, but she offered me her cheek. I couldn't work out what was happening.

'Vanessa Schlegel,' she said, in perfect, accented English. 'Delighted to meet you.' The name sounded familiar, but I couldn't place it. She had drawn her strawberry blonde hair into a tight ponytail, which shot out at a seventy-five degree angle from the back of her head. She was several inches shorter than her daughter, and slim to the point of being gaunt. Her bare feet slapped against a gleaming wooden floor. Another memory came to me: leaving Claudia that first time I remembered the carpeting in her room, throughout the apartment. I had never been here before.

'Why don't you two sit down and I'll make some tea,' her mother said, reverting to German. Her voice was gravelly, which might have come from cigarettes or shouting or both. The kimono trailed behind her as she wandered into the kitchen. She didn't look older than forty-five.

'I thought we were going to your place?'

'Well, I think of this as my place, too. I spend a lot of time here,' Claudia said.

She led me outside to an oval wooden table and cloth-covered dining chairs. I caught my reflection in the glass of the sliding doors, oversized and burly. The walk up the stairs had generated an instant sweat and I wiped my face surreptitiously with the back of my hand. The pine trees on the lawn protected us from the gaze of passers-by on the other side of the road, but I could see the pavement we had used on our way from the station.

Claudia sat with her legs crossed at the ankle and closed her eyes against the breeze. She was silent for a moment, then said, 'I would have told you where we were going, but I thought you wouldn't come.'

'Well, I don't know. I might have come anyway.'

'No, you wouldn't have,' she said resolutely. 'I have to look after my mother sometimes, so I couldn't have gone anywhere else. Besides, she wanted to meet you.'

'She did?' We barely knew one another and after this would probably never see each other again.

The pine trees bristled in the breeze and I was grateful for the cool air. I went up to the metal railing where a row of potted plants lined the edge. The apartment was at the top, on the fourth floor, with an overview of the neighbourhood. There were mainly houses here instead of apartment blocks, and green spaces between buildings, a pleasant calm.

'Here we go, here's tea and coffee.' Claudia's mother came out onto the balcony. 'You like cheesecake, Vincent? This kind is delicious. Baked – American style.'

I sat down and drank coffee, while Claudia sipped tea. Her mother drank wine. I would have liked a glass myself, but it wasn't offered.

'It's very peaceful here. I like this place,' I said. 'You wouldn't know you were in the city.'

'I like it too, but it's hardly quiet,' she said. 'You can't hear the traffic?'

I closed my eyes and made out the faint ambition of

acceleration, the constant rally of cars in the distance. It didn't seem significant.

'You are from where, Vincent?' Frau Schlegel asked, and I told her. I had to explain about the Sahara and the Gulf of Guinea, the armpit of Africa.

'I have never been,' she said. 'I wanted to go in my twenties, on safari, but it was too expensive. Then Claudi arrived.' She smiled as if she had no regrets whatsoever.

'It must be interesting, Nigeria, so close to the equator. The climate. All that variety,' Claudia said.

'It's okay,' I shrugged. I wouldn't be drawn.

'My husband, he wanted to travel to Africa – he was American,' Frau Schlegel continued. 'He discovered that his ancestors were in all likelihood from Sierra Leone. He thought so. He always talked about going there one day. Who knows, maybe he went there eventually.'

Claudia looked down at the tiles. She seemed to be concentrating. After a silence, her mother pushed her chair out and stood.

'Time for bed. I'm sorry Vincent, but it's early to bed for me. We Schlegels, hey Claudi? It's annoying, I know.'

'I'll help you, Mum.' Claudia rose and reached for her mother, who did not seem to need any assistance.

We said good night and the two women returned indoors. I could see only the lights of the neighbourhood now. I hadn't noticed night's arrival, but it was still early. In town, people would only now be thinking of trickling into the clubs. The noise in the bars would be furious. I wondered whether B or Tunde were out – at the Atlantic or the Boogaloo. I thought I could join them later for a couple of hours if only I knew where they were.

After five minutes, when Claudia had still not appeared, I

went indoors in search of the toilet. I crept along an unlit corridor with only the illumination from the sitting room for guidance. There was a strip of light from a room at the end of the hall. The apartment seemed to stretch in different directions. I knocked and opened various doors until I came to a spacious bathroom whose brilliant whiteness was interrupted by a row of burgundy towels folded hotel-neat on a wooden bench. On one wall were four framed black-and-white photographs of women's shoes: stilettos, ankle boots, mules and sandals. I looked closely and realized the photographs had not been torn out of magazines, but were professional prints.

When I finished I closed the bathroom door behind me and stood for a moment in the dark corridor. I could make out the sound of muted singing, first hushed, then stronger – there was an unrecognizable tune – then falling again to barely a whisper. It seemed to come from the room at the end of the hall.

I returned to the balcony and sat for another ten minutes. When Claudia had still not come back, I went into the sitting room and located a light switch. A long black leather sofa hugged one side of the room, while a huge metallic wall unit covered up most of the wall on the other side. There were few books: several guides to South America, some illustrated hardbacks on shoes and fashion, and Hesse's *Siddhartha*. A large-screen television sat in the centre of the unit, and a hi-fi and speakers took up more space. I recognized a young Frau Schlegel in one photograph, a toddler, who must have been Claudia, and a tall, smiling black man in military uniform. I thought of Clariss and her years in the army, how she might have resembled the man smiling before me at one time. There were other photographs – of Claudia at various stages in her life, with her mother, with friends or simply alone – but only one featuring the soldier. I picked up the frame for a closer look. I noticed how beautiful Frau Schlegel had been – she was beautiful still, but she had had the advantage of youth then.

'There you are,' I said as Claudia appeared beside me. I hadn't heard her approach; it was too late to replace the picture frame.

'There are so many of you here,' I said.

'Mum likes to put things out on display,' she replied. She eased the frame gently out of my hands and returned it to its position in the wall unit.

'Is that your father?' I asked.

She nodded, but didn't say anything.

'Is something wrong?' She had been away for so long and now she seemed subdued.

'No, everything's fine. Mum's asleep now. She has trouble sleeping, that's all.'

I reached out to touch her face and moved closer to kiss her. I could see a vague resemblance to her mother in the shape of her almond eyes and the hue of exhaustion beneath them. She didn't resist and I wondered whether we would spend the night together after all.

'No, not here. I can't.' She shook herself free. She looked round as if someone might walk in at any moment.

'I thought you said she was asleep.'

'She is, but I just can't. Not here. Please.'

'Well, we can go to your place or mine,' I tried.

'I'm sorry, Vincent. I have to stay,' she continued doggedly. 'I told you before, remember?'

I nodded, although I didn't understand what was keeping her. I wanted to spend the night with the Claudia who was frivolous. Who danced and laughed and invited me to her bed even though we had been strangers.

'Well, perhaps I'll see you another time,' I said.

She smiled. 'I had a nice time today. I really enjoyed the exhibition and the meal. I'm glad you came here tonight.'

I nodded but I didn't see what there was to be so glad about.

# 15

T HE WOMAN WAS screeching. Her husband's inaudible responses were interrupted by a din of smashing crockery. It wouldn't have been so disturbing had the Zimmermans not been the quietest, most industrious tenants in the building.

'What *is* all that racket?' Frau Lieser demanded.

'I don't know. Sounds like they're rowing,' I said. 'Why are you phoning *me*?'

'I'm an old woman!' she exclaimed. 'I can't put myself in danger. Listen to them – who knows what's happening? They're just across from you. Please be a gentleman and ask them to stop.' She could have phoned them herself, but I didn't say anything.

I ignored her request in favour of a bath. I was thinking about the enigma of Claudia; how she could lead me on one moment, yet be completely cool the next.

When I emerged from the bathroom, perspiring and dehydrated, the commotion had become worse. Ingo Zimmerman had lost his reserve and was shouting now. I feared they would come to blows if they weren't interrupted. I pulled on a pair of shorts and a T-shirt and walked out to the landing.

She was a whore, the husband was a lobotomized pig-dog. I could hear them clearly now. I knocked heavily, and immediately the noise ceased. I knocked again, quietly this time, but no one came to the door. My telephone rang, so I ran back to my apartment.

'You spoke to them?' Frau Lieser asked.

'Yes,' I lied. 'I said you'd evict them if they didn't keep it down.'

'You told them *what*?' she blustered. 'Who told you to say that?'

'Frau Lieser, it's getting late. Some of us need to sleep.' I hung up.

I woke early the next day to buy beer, bread and milk at the supermarket on Manteuffelstrasse. I'd arranged to take photographs of Arî in his apartment – he often spent his days at the Kurdish centre or at the café overlooking the canal – and he wouldn't appreciate my being late.

It was cooler than the day before and I wondered whether this signalled the end of the heatwave. It still hadn't rained. I had hoped the high temperatures would continue for a few more weeks despite the complaints and the discomfort. In no time we would be shivering and dressing in layers again, recalling the summer as if it had been a dream.

When I returned Else Zimmerman was locking her apartment door, her back to me. She had on a black jacket and skirt combination, leather ankle boots like an East German waitress.

'Morning!' She turned and flashed a smile.

'Morning,' I smiled back, searching for bruises. Instead she looked like a woman who had just triumphed at the races. She tucked her briefcase underneath her arm and skipped downstairs as if she hadn't been shouting herself hoarse all night.

I shook my head and went in to make tea, tearing off a chunk of bread and dunking it without thinking. Then I remembered – that had been Uncle Raymond's routine, so I cut the loaf into thin slices and made buttered toast instead.

A moment later Arî knocked on the door, asking whether I had forgotten about our appointment.

'Of course not. How could I forget? Come and help me carry these things.'

He took the lamps while I managed the rest of the equipment and two cans of beer. On the landing he thrust his chin at the Zimmermans' door. 'You listen, in the night?'

I nodded, hoping Ingo Zimmerman couldn't hear on the other side. Arî shook his head.

Arî's apartment was austere. The surfaces gleamed. There were photographs of friends and relations throughout the room. A rolled-up woven mat was propped up against a wall, and a wooden flute lay on the bedside table. The air was stained thick with tobacco. I set up the lamps and unrolled my screen against a bare wall.

A photograph of Arî and a girl took centre stage on top of the black-and-white television set. On ZDF a woman was discussing the attributes of coffee grown in various parts of the world.

'Hecher?' I pointed.

'Hezar,' Arî corrected. 'Now she is seventeen.' He picked up the frame and handed it to me even though I had seen it several times before. I often thought she looked younger than her years – a child-woman in make-up and adult garb who knew little of the world, its joys, its disappointments.

Perhaps she had faced hardships and had witnessed things I could barely imagine. I didn't know.

Arî sat on the end of the bed with his legs outstretched, a cigarette dangling from his mouth, leaning back on one arm. I picked out a photograph of an old woman in a head-scarf through the viewfinder, above his head. I changed position so he had his back to the lens, with the bare room and the window and the opposite building in shot. We moved the lamps a hundred and eighty degrees to illuminate the other side of the apartment.

They were talking about excrement on television, how the government needed to clamp down before the pet problem became as hopeless as the situation in Paris. There were images of people dragging their Dobermans and schnauzers across the city, hunched poodles straining against the pavement, expelling faeces.

Arî laughed and said it was odd such high priority be given to pets. Then remembering something, he dropped his usual guard to tell me about an incident that had occurred where his family lived. One day, Turkish soldiers arrived and rounded up the men in the village they claimed were members of a resistance group responsible for terrorist activities. There were old men among them, Arî's father included, and there were young men, no more than boys. They had no idea about the claims, Arî said. They were made to lie face down on the soil while the soldiers trampled over their bodies. Arî stood to illustrate their actions. It looked as if he were crushing grapes.

'They think they play game,' he said, 'the way they play with us.'

The ZDF host was still talking about the subject of street hygiene. Her mouth was moving, but I couldn't make sense of what she was saying.

'They make them to eat shit, like this,' Arî said. He pointed to the television set. He gathered together the fingers of his right hand and made a scooping motion to illustrate, then blew a vapour trail of smoke across the room. 'To eat, like food.'

I didn't understand, and yet I did, but I couldn't comprehend it. He had said 'them', meaning 'us', for he had been present as well.

Heinrich Henkelmann – that was next on the agenda. There was the familiar photograph of the politician and then a reconstruction of the day he died. There was film footage of the rally in Kreuzberg – I spotted myself briefly, then Marie and Antje Kiesinger, and Oskar Vogel from the *Tagesschau*. They highlighted other locations where Henkelmann had been seen. Finally, the farm in Lübars was shown in great detail, the route his car had taken, the precise location of the attack. Guests had joined the presenter in the studio and a replica of a yellow wheel lock, discovered several yards from his body, was displayed on screen. This was presumed to be the instrument of murder.

Arî sat and I stood staring at the television set. He did not like to talk about his life, but now he had spoken. Was it a burden for him? A shameful thing? Being forced to eat excrement, the persecution? I didn't know all that much about Arî, his people, what he had or had not done, though I had heard about the PKK.

'You make picture of people.' He turned to me. 'Why?'

I inhaled. 'I don't know. It interests me, Arî. When you find something you like to do in life, you do it. What's the point otherwise?'

He nodded and thought for a while. 'Before you take picture, where are you, when you are a boy? In which place?'

He already knew where I was from, but I had never told him why I lived in Berlin.

'I don't have any stories like yours.' I continued to make adjustments to the camera and the lights. 'Where should we go now?' I asked. 'Outside? We could go to the Wall.'

'No more picture,' he said. 'Too many picture.' He stood up and took down a framed photograph and gathered a collection of others from around the apartment.

'Here is mother,' he said. He told me their names, their approximate ages, who worked on the farms, where they were in the world now: his grandparents, his brothers, the nieces and nephews, even a few of the neighbours in the village.

'My grandmother lived in a village too,' I told him. Arî nodded. It was like a trick he had played on me and now I couldn't help myself.

My grandmother had only once made the journey by bus to visit us in Lagos before she had grown too old. Before that I had never seen where she lived. The first time I remember visiting her we drove to a rambling village outside Kaduna. It was dry and desolate and did not feature on any map. We stepped into a low, crumbling building and walked through a large open compound where a young girl sat pounding yam. My mother spoke to her in Yoruba. The girl left her work and guided us to another section of the building. I inspected the area: the laundry hung up to dry, the open fire, the stack of charred pots, the mortar for pounding yam, its giant wooden pestle wet and gleaming. The sun burned onto the square of compound. I was dismayed we had come here: an outdoor kitchen, no air conditioning, no cars, no television. It seemed an incongruous place for my mother's mother to live.

Grandma spoke no English so Matty and I could not communicate directly with her. She took my face in her wrinkled, arthritic hands, her bony fingers, and attempted to read me as if I were Braille. She too was thin like Uncle Raymond, her eldest child, and I shrieked at her spider's touch.

'Fonny pickin,' she cackled. 'Heh, heh, heh.' She sounded like a hyena, slowed down by age, but equally mischievous.

She looked at me for long moments and simply smiled. Whenever I glanced at her she was watching me. Matty seemed oblivious. She called out our Yoruba names – no one else ever used them – whenever the feeling took hold of her, like a spirited evangelist.

'Demola!'

'Yes, ma?' I answered, startled.

She smiled again, the wrinkles on her face spreading like Plasticine, and stared at me a little longer. Now and then she tried out a few sentences to see if we could suddenly understand Yoruba.

'Fonny pickin,' she laughed when I couldn't reply, as if the thought of her rotund and anxious six-year-old grandson was a source of infinite mirth. I began to understand that she did not want anything of me apart from my presence.

In the evening Grandma and her housegirl – the one who had been pounding yam – made fish stew with onion rice, and roasted plantains.

'Eat all of it,' my mother advised, 'so she knows you like it.'

I gasped, the taste eluding me because of the pepper in the sauce.

'Fonny pickin,' Grandma giggled again when I began to cough.

'Stop that nonsense!' Papa warned.

'Make sure you finish it all,' Mama said.

I ate another spoonful, coughed again. Our grandmother laughed.

'My throat hurts,' I whimpered. I sipped water, but continued to cough. Then I began to dry retch.

Matty looked across at me dispassionately and frowned. Grandma stopped giggling. She spoke to my mother and called her housegirl. She took my hand and led me to the compound, my mother trailing behind. The sky was alive with stars. An open fire blazed in a corner.

The housegirl approached with a plastic container which she handed to my grandmother. In the other hand she held a glass of water. Grandma scooped a dollop of pounded yam with her fingers, smoothing it into a ball. She opened her mouth wide so I would mimic her. She pushed the yam into my mouth and even though it hurt to swallow, I followed her example. She took the glass from the girl and gave me a sip of water. Then she fashioned a second ball of yam and we continued the sequence another two times until she was satisfied.

'How does that feel?' my mother asked.

I hadn't realized the fish bone had become dislodged until my mother's question.

'I think it's gone now,' I said, coughing again for sympathy.

Grandma could do no wrong in my eyes after that, despite the mosquitoes that sang in my ears all night and the lack of air conditioning. She had saved me, after all. As we drove back to Lagos after the long weekend, it was as if we had known one another throughout our lives, rather than during our brief, intermittent visits. Even though we could not speak the same language, we had made ourselves understood. We had been strangers before, but now we were familiar. Family.

# 16

WHATEVER HAPPENS TO a person usually involves a degree of choice. It was Uncle Raymond's choice to be so unlike my mother and grandmother. He was a mystery – an abyss I could never fathom. One moment he would be guffawing infectiously, the next, without warning, his wrath would billow out. I was rarely able to gauge his moods and I often assumed he was cheerful when he was in a foul temper, or he was not to be disturbed when he was in good humour.

'Don't trouble your uncle now,' Aunt Ama would say, if she sensed a confrontation. I would stop immediately or leave the vicinity. With her things were very simple.

Uncle Raymond claimed I looked exactly like Papa and as far as I could gather, he had never approved of him. He always felt his sister had chosen unwisely, had married beneath her status. I don't know the history of it, where my uncle's anger came from, but Mama was cool and pleasant, so very different from her older brother, the adored Raymond of her youth.

I often felt I was the only one who experienced Uncle Raymond's anger. I don't know whether or not this was true. I don't know how others brushed against his life, but it perplexed people how rarely we got along. I seemed to be a constant source of irritation to him. It made Aunt Ama wary of situations, say a dinner party or a family outing. She was always struggling to keep us apart.

Uncle Raymond was always on the move, forever changing his place in the world. Whether this was due to a love of adventure or simply an inability to settle, I cannot say. He grew restless if he was in one place for too long, and he was always relieved to be moving elsewhere. It was like starting all over again for him. Living life from a clean slate. He worked for an oil company that sent him all round the globe. It was, for him, the ideal occupation. I don't remember being aware of my uncle until I was five or six years old, after he returned from Venezuela.

When Matty and I arrived in Uncle Raymond's world, it was unexpected. It had never been part of his plan to take us anywhere, for us to become a chapter in his life. But when our parents died he had no choice. He was the only relative familiar enough to look after us. We did not know our father's side of the family and my mother had only Raymond.

The news that he was being sent to Barbados seemed to lift something in me. We had lived with his family for almost a year and I hoped the strangeness of our altered lives would now bring some recompense. Matty and I had never travelled abroad.

My youngest cousin Kayode and I spent hours poring over the pages of my brother's atlas, charting the imaginary progress of the flight across the Atlantic. We made detours, stopping for fuel and additional passengers in various countries. We took the circuitous route to the Caribbean, flying over the Indian Ocean. As the time drew near to our departure, we must have diverted the plane to nearly every area on the globe, filling the aircraft with everyone from Icelanders to Argentinians, Indonesians to Senegalese. My altercations with Uncle Raymond subsided; my attention had been channelled in another direction.

I began to sort through my belongings, separating essential items from those I could afford to live without. I soon realized I would need more than one suitcase to transport half of what I owned. I reduced the essential pile infinitesimally only to stare longingly at what remained. I snatched back a favourite pair of shorts, a beloved T-shirt, familiar plimsolls I had cast aside the day before. Now and then I sat back and regarded the two heaps of clothes. I thought of Grandma. Would she fit into my suitcase? The prospect of leaving her behind induced pangs of guilt in me. Could I sacrifice everything I owned in order to smuggle her on board with us? I attempted to allay my feelings of guilt with the prospect of life in Barbados. Grandma invariably lost out.

No one minded about the chaos in my room, and this surprised me. Matty came and went and sometimes helped me come to a decision, but his heart wasn't in it. I asked him, was he not excited about the move? But he only shrugged and murmured and seemed preoccupied.

'What are you doing?' Aunt Ama asked one day. She gazed at me in the centre of my belongings, strewn across the bedroom floor.

'That's going to Barbados.' I indicated the larger pile.

'And that?' she pointed to the other.

I sighed and threw my hands up in the air. 'Grandma can keep it.'

She gave a brittle smile and left the room.

It was disappointing to have Aunt Ama walk out without comment. I had hoped for some encouragement, from her at least. Perhaps I had become so distracted, so drawn by the allure of the Caribbean, I had failed to notice developments around me. There was no charged atmosphere in the house. Old suitcases were eventually pulled out and items were placed in storage. Uncle Raymond, Roli and Kunle would travel ahead, while Aunt Ama and the rest of us would shut up house and follow two weeks later. Apart from me, no one else rushed around, frantic with expectation. Even Kayode now seemed relaxed about the move. No one else had learned the names of the major towns, the beaches, neighbouring islands. They were already used to upheaval, I reasoned, and I was not.

Perhaps I hadn't noticed how oddly people were behaving. They seemed kinder now, gentler. Even Uncle Raymond. Especially Uncle Raymond. I envisioned a time in the new country when we would be like a family, Aunt Ama and her husband the perfect surrogate parents. I knew I would try hard to please them both. I would strive to be quiet and well behaved.

But as we drove to the airport – Uncle Raymond, Matty and I – my method of blocking out the unthinkable had begun to crumble. I knew what was coming and I had only smothered it. Vague words and sentences had survived, although I had tried to strangle them: warm clothes, England, boarding school. I did not want to understand what it meant. I couldn't manage a second separation. Everything inside me had frozen somehow. Wherever Uncle Raymond was sending us would lie behind the pane of a window. I could see it, but it would never touch me. It would all pass by and I would see, not believing it, making it somehow unreal.

I carried Matty's atlas in my hand luggage. On the plane to London I touched my finger against Bridgetown, Barbados, guessing what the temperature would be at that precise moment.

# 17

I MISSED HER. LUCILLE. I didn't know what we were doing, not seeing one another, not even speaking. Things were vague between us and the business with Claudia was ill-defined. Claudia had struck me as a woman without scruples, a good-time girl; exactly what I needed. Now she seemed to be withholding from me – her body and parts of herself that were hidden.

I phoned Matty in London. He seemed surprised I should want to visit, but said he would expect me at the weekend.

I promised Marie I would deliver the prints of the Andreas Grob exhibition the next day. She laughed and said I was becoming conscientious at last, meeting deadlines before they were due. I explained about the trip to London.

'Pity,' she said. 'Kid Creole is in town next week. I was going to ask you to cover.'

I sighed. 'I don't know when I'm coming back. If I'm here, I'll do it. You'll probably have to pick someone else.'

B dropped by when I was working. He didn't mind that I was locked away. Each time I emerged from the darkroom, he was reading the newspaper or listening to the radio or standing at the window peering out at the activity on the street below. It was overcast and humid. I wondered if a storm was imminent. I couldn't remember the last time it had rained.

'It says here two men were arrested in Mannheim . . . In connection with Henkelmann's death,' B read from the paper.

'Mannheim? Why Mannheim? What's the connection?'

'It doesn't say . . . Taken into custody yesterday . . . They're being questioned . . . Mid-twenties . . . The other is past forty. That's all it says.'

I pulled two beers from the fridge and we drank as I worked. At one point I sat back to front on a dining chair and watched him as he spoke absentmindedly.

'Listen to this . . . Two children . . . Drowned . . . A lake outside Munich.' He scanned the article, but didn't look up to see if I was listening. 'Boys . . . Twins. Imagine, man.'

'How's Angelika?' I asked.

'Fine, fine,' he said breezily. 'Something's not right here. How can two children be drowned in one go? One perhaps, but two. It doesn't make sense.'

I sighed and got up to examine the prints. There was a photograph of the artists, Alessandro and Ettore, against the backdrop of the Old Mother Hubbard shoe. Ettore was smiling, but his eyes were half closed. I hoped the other prints would be an improvement. Claudia was sitting with the boy at the grand piano in her summer dress, their backs to the camera. The soles of the child's feet dangled far above the floor. I put it to one side. I knew Marie would like it.

I took a handful of prints to show B, but he didn't comment until he came to a photograph of Claudia and Jochen in conversation.

'When was this?' he asked. 'I thought you didn't like her?'

'She's okay,' I said. 'It's nothing.'

He nodded, but he was trying to puzzle something out.

'So, what's happening with Lucille?'

I took the prints back and flicked through them and paused at the image of the blind boy I had carried. 'I don't know. She's not speaking to me. I'm going to see her this weekend, if I can.'

'Ah, that's good. If you try, these things will sort themselves out.' He didn't seem as concerned as I thought he might be. 'Angelika wants me to live with her . . . Twenty-four hours a day.' He drew a circle in the air, then repeated it slowly.

I smiled and took a swig of beer. 'I thought she was living with you anyway?'

'She stays sometimes. I go to her place. Now she wants me to move in with her, or we should find a new place together.' He shook his head.

'But I thought you really liked Angelika? This is a good thing, right?'

'Yes, I do like her. But it's too much now, all this time with her. There's no space. I'm confused, man.' B lived in a three-bedroom apartment in Wedding, which he shared with two students from the Cameroon and a Togolese electrician. Someone always slept in the sitting room.

'Maybe you should stay at her place for a while, on a trial basis. Perhaps for a fortnight or a month.'

B scowled as if I had spat in his beer. 'I'm happy as we are *now*. Why does she have to go and change everything, man?'

'But she's crazy about you, and you love her, don't you? What's the problem? You have to try it sooner or later.'

I had lived with Lucille in London for nearly six months before I moved to Berlin. Perhaps we hadn't lived together long enough, because the relief of freedom was immediately gratifying. But I couldn't tell B that.

'Well, maybe you're right,' he said.

'Course I am. I haven't seen you with other women as you are with Angelika. You're really happy. And if it doesn't work out, well, at least you tried.'

'Why wouldn't it work out?' he snapped.

'Exactly,' I said and hoped he wouldn't pursue it any longer.


It was raining as the plane touched down at Heathrow, but by the time the Tube arrived at Finsbury Park the sun had emerged. It was almost as warm as it had been in Berlin, but the air was different – thick and gritty – despite the rain. I walked to the Victorian terrace near the end of Marriott Avenue and was met by Matty's wife.

'Ah, ah, you've changed-o!' Peju exclaimed, even though I hadn't. She had seen me only a few months earlier, after all. She, however, *had* changed. The roundness of her stomach was unmistakable now, and even though she wasn't due until October, she had slowed down considerably.

'Let me go and wake Asa,' she said. 'He wanted to see you as soon as you arrived. He's been asking every five minutes.'

'No, don't,' I pleaded. 'He'll wake up soon enough. Let him sleep.'

My nephew Asa was four years old and boisterous. He was the only child I had ever loved, but after five minutes I never knew what to do with him. The thought of having to entertain him always induced panic in me.

'You're right,' Peju said. 'He needs his rest, but not too much. I don't want him to sleep all day and then keep us awake at night.'

We went out to the garden – a tiny, ragged patch of land neither Matty nor Peju knew what to do with – and sat on the patio deck chairs. The grass was shin high and dishevelled, the area bordered by weeds and bushes. An apple and a hornbeam tree only further diminished the space.

Peju sighed as she stretched out on the chair and made exaggerated sounds of discomfort. She wore a navy and maroon wrapper, and an oversized watermelon-pink T-shirt which partly hid her stomach when she was standing, but only emphasized the pregnancy when she lay back. She'd braided her hair in long thin plaits that reached down to her shoulder blades. She brushed them away from her face from time to time, but they eventually fell back. I didn't think she was beautiful, but she was striking and hard to ignore.

'D'you know what it is yet?' I nodded at her stomach.

'No, not this time. We're going to wait until the birth,' she said. 'Boy or girl, it doesn't matter to me. We have Asa already.'

Matty had told me they both hoped for a girl after the rambunctious parcel of Asa, but they didn't dare voice their desire for fear of disappointment when the child was born.

We drank iced tea and – because they didn't keep alcohol in the house – pineapple juice and lemon squash. After a while I went indoors to use the telephone.

'I'm here,' I said as soon as Lucille answered.

'Why are you calling me at work?' she asked. She didn't seem surprised. 'Where are you, at Matt's?'

'Where else?'

'Okay, I'll call you back in five minutes.'

I had been to Lucille's office two or three times before and I remembered the vast ground-floor lobby and the bank of elevators, the smooth ride to the sixteenth floor, the give of the luxurious carpet that led to her office door. I didn't know where she would be making the call from, but guessed she would travel all the way down to use a phone in the lobby to avoid her colleagues overhearing.

'So, you've decided to visit,' she said coolly. 'Is there a special reason, or are you just passing through?'

'I thought we could meet, maybe, and talk,' I said.

'Talk about what?' There was a harshness to her tone that made me tread carefully.

'Just talk, Lucille, like sensible adults. I don't want to argue or discuss anything you don't want to talk about. I thought we could maybe meet, if only for five minutes. I don't want to pressurize you or anything. You don't have to talk to me at all if you don't want to. Seeing as I'm here at Matty's, I thought we could at least say something, or meet. What d'you say?'

'Why are you whispering?' she asked.

'Eh? Oh, it's Asa. He's asleep. I don't want to wake him.'

She laughed and sighed. I didn't speak for fear of saying the wrong thing.

'Okay, then. How about Sunday? I'll meet you in Hyde Park. At Speakers' Corner. Listen, I have to go, Vincent. I'm in the middle of something.'

I could hear Asa upstairs, calling for his mother, sounding sleepy and confused and already upset.

'Okay. What time, then?' I asked.

'At one. Wear comfortable shoes.' She hung up.

There was a thud on the landing. I looked up and there was my nephew frowning down at me.

'Hello, Asa,' I said, the receiver still in my hand.

He continued to stare as if I were an intruder.

'Asa, is that you?' I spoke into the receiver. 'Can I speak to Asa please?'

His frown moved to bewilderment and then he grinned.

He made a fist and used it as an imaginary mouthpiece and answered, 'Yes, I'm Asa.' He spoke quietly, uncertainly. 'Are you Asa too?'

'No, I'm Uncle,' I said. 'Don't you recognize me?'

He nodded and I replaced the receiver.

'Asa, Mummy's in the garden!' Peju called. 'Come downstairs and greet Uncle like a good boy.'

He refused to budge. He still held his fist to his ear.

'Come down and have some lemonade,' I said and moved outside.

'Hello, I'm Asa,' he called from the landing. The shyness was already leaving him. 'Can I speak to Uncle?'

'Asa, come outside and stop being naughty,' his mother said. She craned her neck to see if he had appeared.

'Is Asa there? It's Uncle. I want to speak with him.' It was far easier to collude than wait for the unexpected.

'Yes, Asa's here. Is that Uncle?' he asked brightly.

'Uncle wants to see Asa downstairs quickly before all the lemonade disappears.'

We could hear him bumping down the stairs on his bottom, and then he ran out to us looking wildly at the cartons of juice.

'What do you want – lemonade or pineapple?' Peju sat up.

'Lemonade, lemonade, lemonade!' he chanted. He hopped up and down as she poured the juice into a green plastic tumbler. Then he attempted to drain the contents in one gulp, spilling liquid onto his T-shirt.

'Wait now – ah, ah!' Peju pulled the tumbler away from him.

'No!' he screamed. He tried to grab the drink back, but she gave him such a severe look he didn't try again. Then the tears began.

'What's the crying for now, Asa?' Peju's voice was calm.

'You didn't even greet Uncle and now you're crying. What's he going to think?'

He looked at me with hatred, and sniffed, then stared at the tumbler in his mother's hand. He pointed to the lemonade and glanced at me again and giggled. Peju conceded defeat and handed him the drink.

Asa had been diagnosed as hyperactive. He was disruptive in the classroom, and a handful for Matty and Peju, who welcomed any outside assistance they could get. They even valued my presence, although I tried to spend as little time as possible with the boy.

He led me upstairs to the spare room and in great detail illustrated how all the lights worked, where to put my things, how to draw the curtains. A framed photograph of Matty and me, aged thirteen and seven, stood on top of the chest of drawers. On either side of that was a photograph of our parents and one of Aunt Ama and Uncle Raymond. I placed my clothes in the empty drawers and when I thought Asa wasn't looking, I stuffed the photograph of my aunt and uncle beneath my socks and underwear.

'Why are you hiding that?' Asa asked, alert as a Doberman.

'I . . . I don't want it broken, Asa,' I said. 'If I put it in the drawer, it won't fall and the glass won't break.' I smiled at him, but he didn't smile back. I thought of Frau Bowker and Schnapps, how similar they all seemed to be.

'Let's go downstairs and help Mummy,' I said.

'Mummy's in the kitchen,' he glowered.

'Yes, I know. Maybe we can give her a hand?'

He frowned and pursed his lips for a moment and then, when I feared he was going to throw a tantrum, he said brightly, 'Okay!'

Matty arrived shortly after six, and we stayed on the patio

for supper. Peju had boiled basmati rice and made a green salad and *efo* soup, along with fried plantain. Asa refused to touch anything other than the plantain.

'I'm going to count to ten,' Matty said. 'If you don't eat your food properly – and *dodo* doesn't count – you're not having dessert.'

'What are we having for dessert?' Asa asked. There was no dessert, but Matty didn't know that. It made no difference to Asa. He looked to his mother, who shrugged, then glanced at me. I winked.

'Uncle is hiding the picture of Granny and Grandy!' he burst out. 'He put it inside the drawer!' He beamed at his father as if this would excuse him from eating his food, but Matty began to count to ten regardless. On the count of eight Asa began to eat the rice, but the corners of his mouth were turned down and he took long gulps of juice in between.

'How's that place of yours?' Matty asked. 'Still the same one?'

'Still the same,' I replied. 'Suits me fine; the rent's low.'

'Lucille thinks you should move to a better place,' he said. 'Pay extra for a bit more comfort.'

'She told you that?' I said. 'When was this?'

'Hey, easy now. She didn't tell *me*.'

'She only mentioned it,' Peju said. 'You know we talk from time to time.'

'What else did she say?'

'Nothing. She just mentioned that you could do better, that's all,' Peju said.

'Why? Is there something else?' Matty asked, as he wiped his plate clean with a slice of *dodo*.

'No, of course not,' I said, but I guessed they knew more than they were saying.

'Does Uncle live in a nice house?' Asa asked.

'I live in a very interesting place, Asa,' I said. 'One day you'll come and visit me, won't you?'

He nodded vigorously, shovelling rice and soup into his mouth, forgetting his earlier aversion.

It was always like this, the reference to my existence, my choices. Matty was the one with the cars, the wife, the child, the baby on the way, a career others could only envy. He had worked at this thing called life and it had paid dividends. My own life seemed shameful and shabby compared to his.

It was barely 9.30 and they were already exhausted and I could stand it no longer. 'I'm going out for a drink,' I said.

'What, now?' Matty asked. 'It's going to ten.'

'It's not late. I won't be long.' I went upstairs to fetch my wallet. When I returned Matty had put on his shoes.

'I'll come for a round,' he said.

We walked, still in our shirtsleeves, to a pub three streets away. Streetlamps flickered on, but it was light outside. I pushed my way to the bar, and while I waited, turned to look for Matty as he stood outside with the other drinkers. He didn't like places where people gathered in crowds and drank and grew raucous and disgraced themselves. He stood on the pavement – a tall, slender man in a white linen shirt, beige chinos and polished brown brogues – and I thought no one would guess we were brothers; the pristine accountant and the hefty photographer. I didn't even think our faces looked similar.

'This your local?' I asked when I returned with the beer.

'I suppose so. First time I've been here, actually,' he chuckled. 'And probably the last.'

'So, what's with Asa calling Ray and Ama his grand-parents?' I asked.

'It's nothing,' he said. 'Most of his friends have grand-parents. There's no harm in it.'

'It might be nothing now, but it's going to confuse him later on, don't you think?'

He waved away the suggestion with a flick of his hand.

'No really, I don't like it when he calls them that,' I said. 'He'll never know his grandparents. *That's* the truth. You can't go putting ideas into his head. It's not right.'

'Like stuffing the photograph away because you can't stand Ray? Did you tell him the truth about that?'

'Come on, that's hardly the same thing.'

'Well, it's a question of the truth, fudging the truth for the child's benefit. Yes or no?'

'I suppose so, but . . .'

'Well, there you go,' he said. 'I don't even know what we're arguing for.'

'We're not arguing. I just don't think it's . . . Forget it,' I said. I hated arguing with Matty because, somehow, I was always wrong.

'They're getting older now, anyway,' Matty said. 'And Ray's not well. You never go and see them, and they're always asking about you.'

'How many times have they come to visit you here since Asa was born?' I asked.

'Two or three, I suppose.'

'Three. Three times in four years,' I said. 'And how many times have they visited me?'

'Come on, Vincent. You never write or phone or answer their letters. They didn't even have your address for years, and it wasn't for lack of trying. We go to see them every year, remember. How many times have you been?'

I shook my head. I had seen them occasionally over the past seventeen years, but what did we ever have to say to one another? What did I have to say to Uncle Raymond?

We dropped the subject – it always made me angry – and bought another round of drinks before the pub closed.

A glass smashed against the pavement and when we looked, two men were playing chest tag. In no time they were in full brawl. Some of their party attempted to separate them, but so half-heartedly it would have been better had they not bothered. The middle-aged publican and a titan from indoors came out and wrenched the brawlers apart. They were young, no older than twenty-one, and surprisingly slight when removed from the tussle. They had seemed formidable during the commotion.

The publican rang his bell, but many of the drinkers had already dispersed at the first sign of trouble. The atmosphere had soured. Only Matty and I and a handful of stragglers remained on the pavement under the streetlamp.

'What do you mean, Ray isn't well?' I asked.

'He's old now, Vincent. Older, in any case. The last time I saw him, he didn't look so good. Ama says he isn't eating properly. He's been in and out of hospital, but he's not so concerned.'

'It's just like him not to be concerned,' I said. 'If he showed a bit more concern, maybe I'd bother to write once in a while.'

'Come on Vincent,' Matty sighed. 'He's not well. How long are you going to go on hating him?'

'He never liked me, that man.' I shook my head. 'He never cared.' The anger had brought tears to my eyes; I couldn't help myself.

'Of course he cared,' Matty said. 'He did, Vincent. Of course he cared.' And I was seven years old again, at school, and Matty was having to comfort me as he always did when I was distressed and could not grasp the fact that our parents would never return.

# 18

PEJU AND MATTY had been invited to Sunday lunch at a colleague's house and thought Asa would prefer to spend the afternoon in the park. I said I didn't mind.

I soon regretted the decision on the Tube to Marble Arch when he refused to sit still. He stood on his seat, wiggling his hips for the benefit of other passengers. A woman glanced at his unsteady form and glared frostily ahead of her.

'Sit down, Asa,' I whispered, in the silence of the carriage. This only encouraged him.

At Oxford Circus he stepped down from his seat and moved towards the doors, looking at me uncertainly, as if he might bolt free of my gaze.

'It's here, Uncle!' he cried.

I gave him a hard stare. 'Come and sit down.'

At the last moment I realized we did indeed need to change lines. I rose quickly and Asa held out his hand for me to lead him to the platform.

'Asa, you have to listen to me when we're in public. You can't just go where you want to. What would happen if you got lost?'

'Can I have an ice-cream?' he asked, ignoring the question.

'Only if you're good. You'll be good, won't you?'

He nodded enthusiastically.

We arrived at Speakers' Corner at a quarter past one, but there was no sign of Lucille.

'Uncle, who are we waiting for?' Asa asked. 'Is it a lady or a big dog?' He giggled to himself, then snapped his head round as if someone had whistled. 'Is there ice-cream here? What kind of ice-cream do they have?'

I ignored him and glanced round for Lucille, but couldn't see her. The speakers were trying to out-shout one another. Their audiences shrank and swelled and I thought Lucille might be among them. A stretch of clouds appeared and the park grew dull and humid. The traffic on Park Lane purred.

'Hello, you two!' Lucille called.

We turned at the sound of her sunny voice.

'Sorry I'm late. Thought I'd make something to eat.' She held up a carrier bag.

'Ice-cream!' Asa screamed.

'No ice-cream, Asa, I'm afraid. Maybe they sell them over there.' She pointed towards a kiosk and Asa raced towards it.

'I'm sorry,' I said. 'They needed a hand with him. I didn't have a choice.'

'That's all right. It'll be nice to have him along.'

'You look well.' I kissed her and felt awkward when she didn't respond. I glanced round for Asa, but he was still by the kiosk.

'Something's different.' Lucille squinted at me.

'Really? That's what Peju said. What is it?'

She pursed her lips, shook her head. 'I'm not sure.'

'Nothing's different,' I said. 'Everything's still the same.'

'It's 20p!' Asa shouted, running towards us. 'It's 20p! The lady won't give me any ice-cream if you don't give 20p!' He was hopping from foot to foot. Tantrum speak. I gave him the coins and he sprinted back.

The sun reappeared as we strolled under the tidy avenue of plane trees before joining the crowds along the Serpentine. Asa had smeared his Softy across his mouth and T-shirt, then dropped the remainder of it on the grass. He didn't seem to miss it. He seized the end space on a bench, which drove the other occupants away. We ate a lunch of crisps and tuna fish sandwiches, and watched the pedal boaters zigzag across the water.

'I want to go on a boat!' Asa demanded.

'And what if you fell in the water?' I said.

He put a finger to his mouth and searched for an answer, but remained silent. He was afraid of water and I knew I could never coax him onto a boat even if I had wanted to.

'So,' I turned to Lucille, 'how are things with you?'

'I'm seeing someone,' she said. 'A lawyer. He's a lawyer.' There was no hesitation.

My stomach felt full and empty at the same time.

'That's nice,' I said, without thinking. 'I mean, that he's a lawyer. That's what you always wanted, isn't it?'

'What do you mean by that?'

'Well . . . Nothing. I'm sorry – I don't know what I'm saying.' I fell silent. I hadn't foreseen this situation.

'But if I'm on the boat, I won't fall in the water,' Asa reasoned.

'Shut up, Asa,' I said, but without force, so that he appeared confused by the signals. 'Lots of little boys have fallen in. Just look at the water. You'll see them all, lying at the bottom.'

His eyes grew wide.

'That's not true, Asa,' Lucille said. 'Don't listen to him. No one's fallen in. He's just joking, aren't you? Tell him you're joking.'

I looked at Asa, then squinted at the water. 'I can see one right now.'

'Where, where can you see him?' Asa squealed. He climbed onto the bench and put his arm round my neck and peered into the water. 'I can't see. Where is he?'

'Vincent's just joking,' Lucille said. 'Don't listen to him. Here Asa, have some juice.'

But he was intent on discovering a child's corpse in the lake. As we got up and walked further along, he pointed to ripples and the lap of the water against the bank as possible evidence of activity beneath the surface.

We held his hands as we crossed the road into Kensington Gardens and watched as he tried hopelessly to imitate a group of teenagers doing cartwheels on the grass.

'How long have you been seeing this guy then, this lawyer?' I asked.

She sighed, but didn't answer and I did not ask again.

'You were right; something is different,' I said.

'Yes,' she nodded, 'something's changed.'

'Is it serious?'

'I don't know, Vincent. Don't ask me that. Don't be angry. Even if I wasn't seeing him, we couldn't have carried on as before, could we? Could we now?'

But I wasn't angry, only confused and depleted.

We came to a statue and Asa asked, 'Who's that?' and Lucille replied, 'Peter Pan,' and we moved on. A knot of tourists took our place, their cameras clicking and flashing. It was a relief for once to be without my own equipment.

On the way to the washrooms I played a game of hide and seek with Asa between a maze of hedges. He ran and hid while I counted to ten, and then tried to find him. He giggled and breathed so asthmatically, it was impossible not to discover him. He found me eventually on two occasions, but I had lost interest by then. I could feel my face beginning to set into a grimace after Lucille's revelation.

'Please!' he insisted. 'Let me find you.'

I feared we would have to continue the game all afternoon if I was to be spared a crying jag.

'Just one more time, Asa. Then we have to go home.'

He began his feverish count. I squeezed through a gap in a hedge and knelt on the ground so I couldn't easily be seen. He ran up and down the path, calling for me. I didn't move. When he walked further away I called his name and he drew near, but I didn't speak. I thought about Lucille and her lawyer and wondered when it had begun; before her recent trip to Berlin, immediately afterwards? Was he a colleague; had it been going on for years? Asa crept in another direction muttering, 'Uncle, where are you? Uncle?' I coughed and he returned to the space in front of me. He stopped and whispered, 'Uncle?' a couple of times. He crouched down, trembling quietly. 'Uncle?' He was almost crying now.

I was sure he could see me, but his eyes kept darting frantically. I waited a moment longer and stood up and waved. 'I'm right here. Couldn't you see me?'

He wasn't smiling, though, and he did not stand.

'What's wrong, Asa?' I said.

I held out my hand and he seized it. When he stood I saw his shorts were soaked through and his body was shaking. His fingers dug into my palm. I picked him up and felt the moisture seep into my shirt.

'I'm sorry, Asa. I'm really sorry. I was only there.' I pointed, but he wasn't concerned with where I had been. He only wanted to leave. Was this what I was capable of; reducing a child to a shivering wreck? For one dreadful moment it occurred to me I was no better than Uncle Raymond.

'Uncle scared me,' he whimpered to Lucille when we emerged into the open again. He reached for her hand and related the incident to her.

'He's only a boy, Vincent!' she flared, before he had even finished. 'You have to be careful. This isn't me you're dealing with. He's only a child.'

'I'm sorry,' I said. 'We'll get a taxi back, okay?' I was fed up with the whole rotten course of the day, the impromptu decision to fly to London.

They walked ahead of me, hand in hand, in the summer sun. I didn't think the heat would ever end.

# 19

CLAUDIA HAD LEFT two messages by the time I returned. CB and Marie had called. Tunde phoned to say he'd discovered a new club, and we were going on Saturday night. I had missed it, in any case. I phoned Claudia several times, but there was no answer, not even the machine. I guessed she was probably at her mother's apartment.

The next morning Clariss was in full regalia as she swayed along the pavement.

'Hey, Clari!' I called.

'Hey there, sugar.' She waved, but made no effort to quicken her pace, still drunk or high from the previous night. She was staggering down a Kreuzberg street in the daytime, wearing stilettos and chiffon and very little else.

I waited for her to reach the building and she slumped against the wall. 'Honey,' she said. 'This mama is in need of serious sleep.'

'Wild party?'

'Wild ain't the beginning and end of it, sweetpea. I seen some shit a girl ain't suppose to see, you hearin' me?'

Clariss had seen and done things in a single hour most people couldn't accomplish in a lifetime.

'Maybe I'm gettin' old. Seen too much freakery, child.' Gone was the composure along with most of her clothes. I could hear Colonel Theodore Cooper in the background of her drug- or alcohol-induced haze. 'You got your keys, honey? I ain't got nothin'.'

Clariss was anywhere between thirty and fifty, but with the make-up and demeanour it was impossible to tell.

Heads turned and from across the street several rubbish collectors wolf-whistled, but she paid no attention. Frau Lieser began rattling her window for what seemed an unnecessarily long time before she was able to open it.

'You had a visitor,' she called, waving a piece of paper. 'On Sunday. Three thirty-five. I wrote it down.'

Frau Bowker appeared behind her, blinking into the daylight above our heads before she noticed us below. She was wearing her old quilted pink jacket and she held Schnapps against her bosom as if for the warmth. Her face was obscured by the mass of white fur. She glimpsed Clariss for a nanosecond before propelling herself back into the room. Harsh-sounding words were spoken between the two old women, but we couldn't hear.

'People be beatin' down doors to see me,' Clariss complained. 'I need me an office . . . And a secretary.'

'And a job,' I suggested.

'Not you!' Frau Lieser said. 'You.' She pointed to me. 'Pretty girl. Lots of hair.' She made a show of patting invisible curls around her ears. We knew she was concealing a balding pate beneath her floral scarf, but it didn't matter; she seemed like a young girl then.

Clariss stared at Frau Lieser as if she had been slapped.

She slid against the main door and I let her in. 'Only pretty girl in this town is me,' she muttered. 'Me! Don't let nobody tell you no different.'

The door crashed behind her and Frau Lieser sighed, more in anguish than anger. Clariss was her longest-serving tenant. She was the most unreliable payer of rent, but she was also her favourite. She hated to see Clariss drunk and dishevelled, especially when Frau Bowker was visiting.

'Did she leave a message?' I asked.

Frau Lieser shook her head. 'No name, even. Just asked for you. Then "poof", she's gone. Lots of hair. Pretty girl.'

I called Claudia again, but there was no answer.

I took the U-Bahn to *Off the Wall*. Marie and her secretary, Elena, were hunched over Elena's desk, sorting through correspondence. I could see them both, standing side by side, one tall and gangling, the other petite and voluptuous, with calves and a backside that could ruin a man.

'The very man who turned down Kid Creole and the Coconuts,' she said, turning to me.

'I'm too late?'

'Not too late, but it's tonight. I've asked Ernst to do it. You didn't inform me about your return date. I can't very well tell him to drop it now, can I?'

'Is there anything else?'

'Not until the end of next week. How about Thomas?'

'I've only just got back,' I said. 'I'll try him later.'

'You been away?' Elena asked.

'Mystery weekend,' Marie said, tapping the side of her nose.

'Always the best kind,' Elena sighed. 'Champagne, romance, dinners. Did you have a marvellous time?'

'No, not really.'

'Oh, that's rotten,' Elena pouted and continued sorting through the letters.

'Anyway,' Marie steered me towards her office, 'I've made some decisions regarding the Andreas Grob exhibition. We're going for a cover and a few feature snaps.'

'A cover?'

'Yes, why not? It's different. One of the most unusual features we've done. The photograph we've chosen is striking. It's bound to drum up a lot of interest.' She pointed to the prints on the wall opposite her desk. There were several photographs with numbers attached to them, arranged numerically from left to right. The one with Claudia and the child at the piano was number two. The cover was of a boy peering into one of the holes in the wall, not the boy I had carried, but an older, taller child.

'I'm thinking of making some kind of reference to the Wall – "Peering into the Future" – something along those lines,' she explained. 'Elena and I are working on the theme. Jochen is no use. He thinks it's a daft idea, but then he's never any good in that department anyway. If you have any suggestions, don't hold back.'

'Of course. I'll think about it.' I wasn't too sure about her plan myself, but she usually had a good sense about issues. 'What about that one?' I pointed to the second photograph.

'I like that too. Not strong enough for the cover, though, but I like the juxtaposition – the child, the big child, the grand piano. Looks much better in black and white, don't you think? It'll make a perfect counterbalance against the opening feature.'

'The whole page?' I said. It was a mystery how Claudia was leaking into areas of my life.

'The other three we'll sprinkle across the rest of the feature.

If you could write something about what's going on in each, I'll get Elena to phrase the captions.'

I left the magazine perturbed, but pleased I would be paid extra for the cover.

When I returned home I phoned Thomas, who said it must be serendipity because he needed someone to photograph the jazz singer Bessie Corday. She was appearing in concerts over two nights in Berlin before flying to Hamburg. It was only the one commission, but it would be a full-page spread in *Zip*. I told him I would collect the brief, then tried Claudia again, to no avail.

I took the U-Bahn to Krumme Lanke and tried to remember the route Claudia had taken that evening. I must have used the wrong exit because I found myself in a completely different area. There were apartment blocks and shops here and it was slightly less exclusive. I returned to the station and tried another exit. There was the kiosk I had seen that first day and further along the road, a house in the process of being renovated. Two teenaged boys played with a concrete mixer in the driveway until a woman appeared at a first-floor window and shouted at them to leave it alone. Her shrill voice pierced the tranquillity of the neighbourhood.

By the time I arrived at Frau Schlegel's building my shirt was wet with perspiration. I pressed the buzzer and waited and pressed again, but there was no response. I crossed the road and looked up at the balcony. The sliding doors and all the windows were shut. I tried the buzzer a final time. As I was about to leave, a woman answered, 'Who is it?' in a gruff voice.

'It's Vincent. Is Claudia there?'

'Claudia?' she said. 'She's not here.'

'What about Frau Schlegel?'

'No, they're not in,' she replied. 'I'll tell her you came. Vincent, you say?'

'Yes, that's right.'

I walked away and looked up at the apartment one last time. A curtain shifted in one of the rooms, but I couldn't make out a face.

I swam for an hour in the late afternoon. I hadn't kept it up since school and I was only able to swim ten laps. I needed to clear my head. I didn't know why I was pursuing a woman I felt indifferent to, who seemed impossible to reach.

Paint was peeling off the walls and ceiling. The viewing stand was like a mouth, gap-toothed and miscreant, where plastic chairs no longer sat. The pool wasn't crowded, though; I was able to swim several laps without once being interrupted. Later on a section was cordoned off for an aerobics class. As evening approached more people arrived and the pool lost its sense of calm.

Claudia phoned five minutes after I returned, but there was nothing unusual in her tone.

'I came to see you today. At your mum's,' I said. 'Didn't you get the message?'

'You did? Oh, yes. Yes. I almost forgot. I was at the university all day. Mum must have been out.'

'Who was that woman in the apartment?'

'Woman? What woman? Oh, you mean the cleaner?' She sounded unsure and hesitant.

'I was in London at the weekend,' I said. 'I should have told you. You came by the other day?'

'Me? No, not me. I've never been to your place, remember? I don't know where it is.'

'Oh, I thought . . . Never mind.'

We met in a bar off the Ku'damm and moved to a restaurant a few doors along. The food was cheap, targeted at tourists – spaghetti Bolognese and Wiener schnitzel on the same menu – but we were too hungry to care.

Claudia had loosened her hair, combed it out in a would-be Afro, but it was lank and fell across her shoulders and around her face. Eventually she gave up and tamed it in a ponytail. Her mood seemed loose and wild, like her hair, and when I asked where she was staying tonight, she arched her eyebrows.

'You could come back to my place – you haven't seen it yet,' I teased. I was sure she had lied about her visit, but I didn't persevere.

'There's always my apartment,' she said. 'I'd like to see yours, but it's so far away.'

'Far away from what? It's closer than yours is.'

'I mean . . . my place is closer to Mum's. I don't feel comfortable about being miles away from her.'

'What's this with your mum, then?' I asked. 'I don't understand. She can take care of herself.'

'Of course she can,' she laughed. 'It's just that she's alone now. Ever since Dad left and I moved out, I sort of feel responsible for her.'

'It's not as if you can't see her whenever you want. You're in the same city – you can phone or take a taxi anytime.'

'Well, maybe we're closer than that,' she said. 'It's difficult to explain.'

She was wearing the denim miniskirt she had worn at the Atlantic the last time, and a long-sleeved cream blouse through which I could see her bra. She stumbled occasionally in a pair of knee-high red boots, as if she had never worn them before. I liked it when she dressed this way. Trashy. This was the Claudia I had first encountered. The one who was easy and relaxed, who didn't stack up her principles, then reel them off on her fingertips for all the world to hear.

At first I didn't recognize her building, but the interior was vaguely familiar. I remembered fleeing the lobby the morning after our drunken encounter.

'I've run out of coffee,' she said. 'There's tea or cola if you like, or water.' She looked at me, startled, as if I had caught her unawares, as if she had thought we could simply spend the evening exchanging pleasantries, sipping tea. I pulled her hair loose and pushed her against the edge of the counter and kissed her. I could feel her begin to relax in increments until her body went limp. I reached between her legs and slipped my fingers inside her, but after a moment she nudged my arm away.

We kissed some more and I worked my way down her neck, unclasping her bra, feasting, moving on, until I was on my knees and she stood above me in only the boots and the miniskirt. I smiled and she said, 'You're a bad boy, aren't you?' but her expression was uncertain. I nodded anyway and hitched her skirt high above her waist. She leaned back and sighed as I tasted her, gently at first, then lunging deeper with my tongue.

I couldn't wait any longer and stood while she made a feckless attempt to free my shirt from my jeans. But I was already there, hoisting her onto the counter, her elbows raised and banging against the cabinet doors.

'I knew you were bad,' she gasped, and I grunted. She ground her heels into my back, then arched her body, pushing further against me. A roll of fat moved like a Mexican wave from me towards her, back into me again. I blushed, but she only continued to shudder.

When I came, we held each other, tight, then started slowly to slacken. My ankles ached. She lowered her head to my shoulder and sighed. A droplet of sweat fell from my chin onto her thigh.

We undressed in the bedroom and fell horizontally across the bed. Claudia was still wearing her boots. We were both silent.

At length she said, 'Was it all right?'

I nodded. I didn't know why she had to ask that. Her face looked oily and blotched pink and fawn. 'And you?'

She turned and moved her head; all I could see was the mass of hair sweeping back and forth.

I slept for half an hour and woke abruptly. I couldn't force the sleep to return. I eased away and pulled on my jeans and T-shirt. Claudia didn't stir. I traced a finger over the mound of calf where the untied bootlace exposed her skin, but she didn't respond. The window was wide open, the curtains drawn aside. I caught a slight breeze, warm as a woman's breath. I crept out of the room and closed the door as much as possible without shutting it. My feet sank into plush carpeting.

There was milk and Coca Cola and grapefruit juice in the fridge. There were no bottles of beer or wine in any of the cupboards. I longed for a drink. I took a saucepan from the sink and filled it with water and turned the hob to its highest setting. There was a notice board above the kitchen table, with notes and keys and photographs attached to it. A memo read:

**Vincent: 144D Muskauer Str – 615 95 30**

She had my address after all; it was in my own drunken handwriting. I didn't understand why she had lied.

Her father's face stared out of a copy of the photograph I had seen at her mother's apartment: the father, Frau Schlegel and Claudia as a child. There was another one of him looking older, wearing civilian clothes, next to Claudia as a gawky teenager with frizzy hair.

I boiled tea in the saucepan, added milk and boiled it again. I couldn't find the sugar and was forced to drink it unsweetened. Like her mother's place, everything in Claudia's apartment looked pristine and expensive: the furniture, the wide television, even the saucepan I had used. The denim miniskirt, the boots, the garish make-up in the club smacked of a woman who lived in cheaper, shabbier circumstances.

There was a quiet purring from the sitting room. I didn't move until I realized what it was. When I picked up the receiver I remembered it wasn't my apartment.

'Claudi!' A harsh, breathless voice.

'Hello. It's Vincent.' I didn't know what to say to Frau Schlegel, how to explain that her daughter was naked and spent in the next room.

'Come quickly!' she said. She was shouting now. 'Claudi, come!' She dropped the phone, but the connection wasn't lost.

I shook Claudia and she groaned softly and smiled, but did not open her eyes.

'Claudia,' I said. 'Claudia, your mother's just phoned.'

One eye peeled open.

'I think you better go over,' I said. 'She sounded . . . upset. Come on, put on some clothes. Wake up now.' I handed her the skirt, but she raced to the wardrobe and put on clean underwear, a T-shirt, a pair of navy tracksuit bottoms. She had kicked off the boots with ease. She dialled her mother's number and returned the receiver almost immediately.

'The line's dead. What did she say? How did she sound?'
She pushed her feet into white tennis shoes.

'I don't know. Desperate. Maybe someone's broken into
her place . . . You think we should call the police?'

'The police? No, I'm sure it's all right,' she said. 'I'll go
and see what's happened. I'm sure it's nothing.'

We ran down to the lobby and when we emerged into the
evening warmth, Claudia turned and said, 'Okay, Vincent.
I'll call you later. I'm sure everything will be all right.'

'What d'you mean, you'll call me later? Let's go!'

'Please, it's all right, Vincent. There's nothing to worry
about. You can stay here.'

She had tied her hair into a tight bun. With the change
of clothes and the alert stance she seemed a world away
from the clumsy boots and the miniskirt.

'Listen, the longer we argue about this, the more time
we're wasting. I'm coming with you whether you like it
or not. Come on.' I took her hand to lead her towards the
U-Bahn station, but she snatched it away.

'Get in then,' she said. There was a white BMW cabriolet
parked in front of the building, with a navy and green tartan
cloth top.

I didn't say anything.

In less than six minutes we were in front of Frau Schlegel's
building.

'I think it's best if you wait here,' Claudia said. She was
twisting invisible rings on her fingers. She looked up at her
mother's balcony, then back at me.

'Let's go,' I said. 'You didn't hear your mum's voice. I
don't think this is something you should face alone.'

She used her own set of keys to enter the apartment, then
held the door against me, denying me access.

'Claudia, what are you doing?'

She didn't answer. She seemed determined not to let me in.

We grappled with the door for a moment, but she couldn't outmanoeuvre my bulk. For a moment the situation seemed comical. Then I glanced at the sitting room beyond.

There was glass on the floor. Liquid had poured onto the Persian rug. The television had been tipped over and its screen had smashed. The framed photographs I had seen on my previous visit had been thrown to the floor. Shattered crockery and glass stretched from the balcony to the kitchen door. It seemed anything fragile now lay in pieces. It was a miracle the sliding doors were still intact.

'Mum!' Claudia screamed. She picked her way towards her mother's bedroom.

A noise escaped from a corner of the sitting room, by the balcony. Not quite a word; a half groan, half plea. Frau Schlegel lay on the leather sofa. The elegant blue and white kimono had slid from her body, save for a sleeve, which clung stubbornly to her arm. Her legs were twisted up on the back of the sofa and her breasts fell sideways as she leant on one shoulder. She couldn't manage the complication of the tangled kimono, her knotted body and the free arm she was trying to control. She groaned again and raised the arm towards her face. Something slipped from her hand against the sofa and onto the floor. Like everything else it smashed.

The noise seemed to wake Claudia, who tiptoed over the glass towards her mother. I didn't know where to look: at the naked mother, the anguished daughter, the catastrophe of the room?

'Mum,' Claudia said again, but softly. 'What happened?' She worked to free her mother's arm from the kimono, and then covered her with the cloth. She brushed her mother's hair away from her face, then shifted her so that her head rested against a cushion.

'Claudi,' Frau Schlegel moaned. Her head lolled back and forth as if she had lost the use of her neck muscles.

'Where are the things . . . to clean with?' I heard myself ask. I couldn't locate the appropriate words.

'Through there, in the kitchen,' Claudia pointed. 'In the cupboard, behind the door.'

In among the broken glass in the dining area was the photograph of the family – the child, the wife, the lost husband – staring up at me. The glass had shattered and a corner of the gilt-edged frame had come apart.

I used the broom and the dustpan to clear the mess from the sitting room. The photographs and books and items that could be salvaged I placed on the dining table. When a glass-free space had been cleared, Claudia attempted to lift her mother, but the body kept slipping away from her.

'Vincent . . . Vincent, I can't carry her.' Her voice was small, almost inaudible and her face was wet with tears.

I put aside the bucket and broom. 'Now, how do we do this? You hold her legs, I'll take this end.'

We sat her up and Claudia reached down to carry her. I noticed bright spots of colour on the floor.

'Wait – look at her feet,' I said. Her soles were smeared with blood.

'Oh, God!' Claudia cried. 'What am I going to do?'

'You get the bed ready and I'll take her,' I said.

Claudia looked at me wildly as if she didn't understand what I was saying.

'Just open the door. I'll carry her. It's okay, I won't drop her.'

She was light, Frau Schlegel, like a paper plane or a hollow thing that surprised you when you lifted it. I had carried Asa in the park in London, but even he seemed more substantial. A waft of alcohol seemed to seep from her skin.

'Claudi,' she moaned. 'Claudi.' She smiled and her eyes glazed over and then she was somewhere else.

The bedroom was a light, spacious room at the end of the corridor. It overlooked the rear gardens and the houses beyond that. I could make out the street I had mistaken for Frau Schlegel's earlier in the day. I wondered whether she had been drinking even as I had gazed up at the windows.

I lay her down on the bed and the eiderdown seemed to engulf her slight form. Claudia placed a towel beneath her mother's feet and fetched a bowl of water and antiseptic from the en suite bathroom. I held her feet while Claudia wiped away the blood and used tweezers to remove shards of glass.

'She should go to a hospital,' I said. 'They'll know what to do. There might be embedded pieces still in there that you can't see.'

'It's not as bad as it looks,' Claudia said. 'There's not so much glass. It'll be okay.'

I didn't argue. It sounded as if she had done this sort of thing before.

I changed the water when it became too bloody, and replaced the telephone receiver on the bedside table. I held Frau Schlegel's feet again, but she did not flinch in her sleep. Claudia worked with a surgeon's precision and detachment. I wondered what she did at the university. I realized I knew very little about her.

'Who was that woman I spoke to this afternoon?'

Claudia looked up at me and frowned.

'You said she was the cleaner.'

She sighed and began to treat the other sole, her breathing shallow so as not to disturb her work. 'That was Sylvie,' she said.

'Sylvie?' The blonde from the beach. 'What was she doing here?'

Claudia pursed her lips, but didn't respond.

Lining the periphery of the entire room was a neat army of women's shoes of all descriptions, the trail broken by the bed, a chest of drawers, a two-seater sofa and the two doors. I noticed only the left shoe of each pair was on display.

'Were you also here this afternoon?' I asked. 'When I called?'

She nodded. 'We were all here. I couldn't let you in. Mum wasn't in good shape . . . I don't know why Sylvie spoke to you. I told her not to answer the bell.'

She was a woman with secrets, Claudia. I did not know where they began and where they would end. I didn't want to find out. She was as hidden as Lucille was an open book, her pages uncut, unread.

'How are her feet?' I asked.

She put down the tweezers and dabbed the soles with anti-septic, then wrapped bandaging around the worst cuts. 'Good. She'll be all right, I think. She just needs to rest and eat something. Then we'll see. I'll have to stay here tonight. I shouldn't have left her alone today.'

I wondered whether she had left her mother to be with me. I poured the bloody water down the bathroom toilet. I had done a poor job of cleaning the sitting room; pieces of glass lay all around. I opened the sliding doors to the balcony and shook out the rug and draped it over the rails to dry.

I felt compelled to remove every fragment of broken glass

from the apartment. I lifted the cushions and dragged the vacuum cleaner over the sofa and carried the ruined television set down to the lobby. When I returned I placed the glass and mess into old supermarket bags in the kitchen and left them by the television downstairs. When I was satisfied all the broken glass and crockery had been cleared, I returned to the bedroom.

They were asleep, side by side, mother and daughter, on the enormous bed. Frau Schlegel looked peaceful now. Her chest rose and fell evenly, and she did not stir. Claudia was fully clothed. She was still wearing the tennis shoes. I removed the bloody towel from the end of the bed, but red stains had leaked onto the eiderdown. I left the bedside lamp on and turned on the corridor light, switched off all the other lights in the apartment. It was after 2 a.m.

I carried the television to the dustbins outside and threw away the plastic bags. I walked past the cabriolet and looked up again at Frau Schlegel's apartment. I had forgotten the rug on the balcony railing. I hoped it would not be blown away.

# 20

THE TELEPHONE RANG and rang. I was on a ship on the ocean. There were waves rising all around. Gulls were screaming over my head. Someone on deck was raising the alarm, clanging a bell, hollering. I couldn't stop the noise. I had been trying to fuse the telephone trill into my dream, and my waking was gradual and unwelcome. It was barely six o'clock, but the caller would not give up. I dragged myself into the hallway, fearing another emergency.

'Hey, sorry man. Sorry to wake you,' B said. 'We need another hand to help with a job. You have to help me, otherwise it could take all day. I tried to reach you last night, but you weren't in.'

I didn't know what he was talking about. I slumped to the floor. My arms ached, my legs were trembling, my body groaned. I remembered yesterday's swim.

'What kind of job?' I asked.

'Rich people. They're moving to Grunewald. Big house. If we have more people, it won't take so long. It's good money, man.'

I was exhausted, but I needed all the money I could get.

The sky was blue and it was already warm. 'Where do I meet you?'

B was talking to an Asian man when I arrived at the bottom of the Charlottenburg apartment block.

'Tunde was supposed to be here fifteen minutes ago,' B said, as if it were my responsibility.

'He's probably still asleep,' I replied.

Tunde didn't need the money anyway.

'I phoned him yesterday, man.' B was already agitated and the day hadn't even begun. 'This is Suresh,' he said.

I nodded. Suresh nodded back. We stood in silence for a while, waiting to start.

A lorry pulled up and two men wearing blue overalls jumped out. A minute later Tunde strolled up to us. B glanced at his watch and made a show of being cool towards him, but we still had to loiter around for another ten minutes. I wondered what all his anxiety had been about.

Rainer, the man in charge, took us upstairs. The family – a middle-aged couple, their teenage daughter and younger son – didn't seem to be aware a move was imminent. They were eating breakfast in the kitchen, while the boy watched cartoons in the sitting room. Nothing was packed.

Tunde pulled me aside. I thought he might have a plan to get us out of this mess, but he only said, 'Damn, I don't know which one is hotter – the mama or the girly. What do you think?'

The girl was a carbon copy of her mother: straight black hair, parted in the middle, that fell two or three inches short of her waist. Lazy eyes. Nose like a razor blade.

'You can do better in Sri Lanka, any day,' Suresh announced.

'Is that so?' Tunde said. 'So what are you doing here then?'

Suresh shrugged and looked out of the window as if he didn't care one way or the other what Tunde thought. 'Again, it will be hot today,' he said.

I wondered what calamity would occur before evening.

In the end the job was not as daunting as I had feared. An upright piano needed to be winched down from the balcony. There were the usual white goods and the massive items of furniture, but the Metzlers were minimalists; it didn't take long to pack and label their belongings, and load them onto the vehicle. Frau Metzler and her son drove ahead to the new house to ready the rooms for the furniture.

B and Suresh joined Herr Metzler and his daughter in a Mercedes station wagon, while Tunde and I squeezed into the cab of the lorry with the other two removal men.

'That girly, she's fine, fine,' Tunde said. 'Eighteen, nineteen. What do you think?'

'Fifteen, sixteen,' I replied, and he shoved me. 'With her nose in the air like that, I don't think she'll ever notice anyone.'

'That's the beauty of it,' he said. 'She's too, too aware of me. She can't even look at me, otherwise she won't be able to resist for one second. You wait and see.'

I wasn't too sure about Tunde's sexual psychology, but he was so adept at seducing beautiful women, I couldn't discount it altogether.

I was grateful for the breeze of the moving lorry; by the time we arrived in front of the Metzlers' new residence the sweat was beginning to evaporate from my clothes.

'This is Neo-Classical,' Suresh said, looking at the villa. 'It's okay, but in my country there's much better. Even my father's house, it's bigger than this.'

'Is that so?' Tunde said, without looking at him.

'Oh, yes,' Suresh continued, encouraged. 'Small garden, crumbling old house – pah! In Kalutara you can put up your house right on the beach. Old or new, whatever you want. Plenty of land. Even near Columbo.'

B and I glanced at each other and laughed, but Suresh only looked away as if he had spotted some fine art in the distance. I wondered how much the Metzlers' new house had cost, what one would have to do to be able to live here.

I called Claudia from the telephone in the kitchen, but there was no answer. I hadn't made a note of her mother's number. There was a phone book underneath the telephone, but there were too many Schlegels listed and I guessed she might be ex-directory anyway.

The Metzlers agreed to pay us extra to unpack the boxes. They were exhausted by the little they had done and couldn't face the sorting out themselves. I didn't mind; it was early enough in the day.

There were five bedrooms, two sitting rooms, a dining room, a laundry room and a den for the children. I got confused between the daughter's room and a spare bedroom. At one point I walked into her room by mistake and she was chatting with Tunde as he fitted her bed together. They both looked at me with blank faces. I couldn't think what to say.

'I'm roasting,' I blurted. My T-shirt was soaking. I should have worn shorts instead. I could make out the glint of the Havel beyond the window. I hadn't noticed it from the ground floor.

'Ah, ah, – if you were not so extra-large-fries-and-chocolate-milkshake all the time you wouldn't be always complaining now, isn't it?' He laughed. He was trying to amuse the girl, but she didn't understand what he was saying.

I called him a prostitute, who did it for free, who even paid, and he laughed in my face again. I hadn't meant it as a joke.

B, Rainer and the other employee dealt with the precarious jobs, while the rest of us emptied boxes where instructed. When we had finished, Tunde suggested we go out for some beers.

'The devil's nectar,' Suresh said, nodding towards Tunde, as if all his suspicions had been confirmed.

'I can't,' I said. 'Maybe tomorrow.'

'You don't want to know how I handled the girly?' he said, looking from Suresh to me.

'What happened?' I asked.

'She's got my number.' He winked.

'And you think she'll phone?'

He pulled out a Filofax diary page on which was written a telephone number and a name – Leyna.

Suresh said, 'It means "little angel".'

'What does?' I asked.

'Leyna, of course.'

'So, you're going to meet up then?' I said, turning away from Suresh.

'Who knows,' Tunde shrugged. 'She's a young girl, and anyway, the mama is more foxy. She can call me if she wants.' He tucked the number into his breast pocket and patted his chest.

I guessed nothing would happen after that. He had only wanted his ego stroked for the thrill of it. He was so used to women queuing up for him it didn't mean anything any more.

I couldn't face the journey to Frau Schlegel's again, not knowing whether anyone would be in, or what crisis might greet me.

Rainer dropped me off near the centre of town and I made my way to the Ku'damm, to the telephone section in KaDeWe. I glanced through the selection of answering machines and bought the first one that looked appealing.

When I arrived home, I showered and fell on my bed. I hadn't intended to sleep, but I woke up an hour later. Claudia had left a message, but I hadn't heard the phone ring. She said she would call later. I tried her number again, but there was no reply.

I thought I should swim – I didn't want to break the start of a routine – but I was too tired. I hadn't returned to *Zip* to see Thomas about the brief. I had forgotten to provide the information for Elena's captions. I didn't know what I was doing.

I put on clean clothes and hid what remained of my earnings from the removal job underneath the enlarger in the darkroom. As I was leaving, Dieter emerged from the Zimmermans' apartment across the hall.

'Hey, Vinny,' he grinned. 'What's happening? You going out tonight?'

I didn't like it when he was familiar. He was probably high. 'Yeah,' I said. 'For a while.' I didn't ask him what he was doing in the Zimmermans' place. 'And you?'

'After midnight, maybe,' he said. 'It's too early now. First I must get some sleep.'

I went downstairs and he bounded up to his apartment, seeming in need of no sleep at all.

I caught the U-Bahn to Krumme Lanke and walked to Frau Schlegel's building. The cabriolet was in the same position, but the rug on the balcony had disappeared.

'Vincent! What a surprise.' Frau Schlegel greeted me with a kiss. Her hair was pinned back with a butterfly clip. She wore a long tweed skirt and a white cotton blouse cinched in at the waist with a wide leather belt. Her brown boots clicked smartly as she strode across the sitting room. She looked every inch the consummate professional flying into Tegel for a power lunch. 'We're out on the balcony. What can I get you to drink?'

'Um . . . a beer, if you've got one,' I said.

'Of course. I'll bring it out.'

The apartment was immaculate. I hadn't wiped the floor, but now the wood gleamed. There were no signs of breakage, no stains. The books were back on the wall unit and the photographs had been reframed. The dining table was clear of the items I had piled there. The only noticeable change was the gaping hole where the television had been. The Persian rug was back in the centre of the room, the stains evaporated and invisible.

It took me a millisecond to recognize the head of one of the women sitting on the balcony. She had her back to me, but the blonde hair was unmistakably Sylvie's.

Claudia waved and called and I moved uncertainly towards them.

'Hello again,' Claudia said.

Sylvie regarded me coolly from her chair.

'Hi,' I said.

'Hello.' She squinted up at me, which could have been due to the sun or her scepticism. I couldn't tell.

'Sit down,' Claudia said. 'I tried to reach you. You haven't been in all day.'

'No, I was working . . . on a job.' I didn't want to explain. 'Out of town.'

'This weather surely can't last?' Frau Schlegel said as she returned. 'We must take advantage of it before it disappears.'

'True,' Sylvie said. 'What's the point of heading off to the Med when it's glorious right here?' She pulled her mane through one hand, then flicked it up and down a couple of times, like a whip. My heart jumped.

'None whatsoever,' Frau Schlegel said. 'We're spoilt rotten this year. I'm already dreading the winter.'

'We're going to Wannsee tomorrow, to the beach. You should come. You'll like it,' Sylvie said to me. 'Oh, but I forgot – you've already been there.' Her acting skills were as poor as her manners. I wondered when someone was going to mention yesterday's incident.

'What are you hiding there?' Claudia pointed to the carrier bag in my lap.

'It's nothing.' I gave it to her. I felt foolish now. 'It's for you.'

'Me?' Claudia smiled and squinted into the bag. 'An answering machine? For me?' She sounded as if her horse had come in at the races. 'Thank you.' She reached out and touched my arm. There was more of a reaction about the gift than about last night's episode.

Sylvie smirked at Claudia like an older sister. 'Finally, you'll return my calls,' she said, as if it was an old joke.

As the evening progressed, there was still no reference to the broken glass, the missing television, Frau Schlegel's condition the day before. I noticed once when she left for the kitchen, she was almost tiptoeing, but she never alluded to the pain in her feet. After a while I was convinced I had imagined the whole event.

As I was leaving Frau Schlegel asked me to wait while she went to her room. Claudia took the empty glasses and cups to the kitchen. I glanced at Sylvie, but she only looked away towards the pine trees.

'What happened here yesterday?' I asked.

'Maybe you should ask Claudia,' she sighed. 'I'm not the one to say.'

Claudia reappeared, followed by her mother.

'This is for you.' Frau Schlegel proffered a woman's shoe – a canary-yellow brocade with an hourglass heel.

'For me?' I was parroting Claudia now.

'Yes, for you,' she said. 'You can't give us things and not have something in return.'

'Mum designs shoes,' Claudia said. 'In case you hadn't noticed. Lacroix, Gigli – a long time ago she used to work for Vivier . . . Roger Vivier.'

I looked at her blankly; the names meant nothing to me. I turned the shoe in my hand. Light. Expensive. I didn't know what to do with it. 'I can't take this,' I said. 'It's too much, and . . . it's not my size.'

Frau Schlegel laughed and wrapped the shoe in crêpe paper and placed it in a box. She reached up and kissed me once more and when she stepped back the box was in my hands. I noticed her eyes were streaked red. Her touch was as frail as an old woman's. I guessed the evening had been a strain for her after all.

'When will I see you again?' I asked Claudia.

'Soon,' she said. She did not elucidate and I didn't insist. Already I had learned not to depend on her reliability.

I waved to Sylvie who remained on the balcony. She held up a hand; she hadn't moved from her position since I first arrived, and she did not stir now.

# 21

I COLLECTED THE brief from Thomas at *Zip* magazine. It seemed straightforward enough – show up at the Kempinski with one of the staff writers. There was a list of what Bessie Corday did and did not want: I wasn't to photograph her left profile, I could only use soft lighting, I wasn't to mention her first name – she had a temper and her patience was easily tested.

I wrote the descriptions Elena needed and took them into the office on my way to the leisure centre. The pool pitched and crashed with the traffic of the holiday season. I tried to maintain an hour of uninterrupted laps. I was learning to avoid the busiest times, but hadn't quite worked them out. There was a scare at one point; someone discovered a lump of excrement bobbing in the water. People began to flee. The lifeguard fished out the offending article, but it was only a plastic turd from a joke shop. The pool was less crowded after that.

I floated on my back for a couple of lengths, wondering about Lucille and her lawyer in London, Matty and Peju, and the enigma of Frau Schlegel. I didn't know what I was doing with Claudia. I closed my eyes against the peeling paint on the ceiling, the screaming children, the new arrivals. I pushed my body on as if I couldn't work it hard enough, to overcome the ache of the removal job, the fatigue of the past few days.

Claudia was outside my apartment building, pacing on the opposite side of the street. She held a package under her arm.

'You haven't been waiting long, have you?' I asked.

'No, not at all. I've just been to the end of the road and back. I wasn't bored.'

'You should have phoned earlier. I would have come much sooner. I was only swimming down the road.'

She looked in the direction I had pointed as if she half expected to see an open-air pool in the distance. I spotted Frau Lieser and Frau Bowker darting back and forth at the window. They had probably noticed Claudia the minute she arrived, and kept a vigil ever since. As soon as we crossed the road, the net curtain flew back and Frau Lieser called, 'The young lady was waiting – one, two hours! You should have told me – I would have let her in! For tea at least!' Frau Bowker shrilled, 'And strudel!'

'Thank you, Frau Lieser,' I called back. 'It's okay now.'

'Thank you, he says,' Frau Bowker spat. 'If it were winter, she'd be a corpse by now.'

'Pleasant evening,' Frau Lieser interjected. 'Nice to go walking, yes?'

Claudia nodded at her and smiled.

'Always new ladies,' Frau Bowker started up again. 'When will there be peace? Ladies, boys, boys looking like ladies, the idiot girl with no hair.'

Frau Lieser slammed the window shut. They had never seen Claudia before. I wondered who had visited when I had been in London.

'What's she talking about?' Claudia asked.

'I don't know. She lives in her own world.' I smiled up at the two women standing mute behind the closed window, their mouths making shapes.

Dieter was on his way down as we reached my landing. 'What's happened to Caroline?' I asked. 'I haven't seen her for weeks.'

'She's upstairs, sleeping,' he said. 'We're going to *Vengeance* tonight.'

I nodded as if I understood.

Instead of continuing downstairs, Dieter knocked at the Zimmermans' door. I pretended to search for my key until Ingo Zimmerman answered. I turned and waved and said 'Hello'. Ingo was wearing a pinstripe suit and a bowler hat. In one hand he carried a brass-tipped umbrella. He was startled by the audience and shrank back into his apartment.

'See ya later,' Dieter called and sauntered in as if he lived there.

'Your neighbours?' Claudia asked.

'Yes. But Dieter – the one with the mohican – lives upstairs with Caroline.'

I showed Claudia the bathroom and the sitting room, the kitchen area. It took less than five seconds.

'I was going to tidy after my swim,' I said, which was the truth.

'What's to tidy?' she said. 'After the state of Mum's . . .' She checked herself. 'What's in here?'

The bedroom window was closed. The room smelled of stale air and old sweat. 'This is where I work.' I steered her towards the darkroom. 'I have something to show you.' I reached up to the clothesline. 'Remember this?' I held out the photograph of her sitting at the piano with the boy at the Andreas Grob gallery.

'Wow, that's good! Is that really me?' she said.

'It's going in the magazine – *Off the Wall*. In the next issue.'

'Me? You're joking?'

'No, not at all. There are more copies. You can keep that one if you want.'

We returned to the sitting room and I made lemon tea with ice. I thought about what I was going to say while Claudia knelt down and flicked through my record collection. She got up with an Art Blakey album still in her hand and gazed out of the window at where she had earlier been pacing.

'There's a very tall black woman walking down the street,' she said. 'She's hand in hand with a tiny little man. He looks like a professor or something.'

'That's not a woman,' I said. 'Or she didn't used to be. Clariss lives upstairs too.' I went to the window and handed her the tea. 'The man she's with is called Frank. He's a film-maker. Well, he makes porn, anyway. She thinks she's in love with him, thinks he'll rescue her from all this.'

Clariss seemed to be dragging Frank along the pavement. As they crossed the street he had to skip to keep up with her. I could only imagine the expression on Frau Bowker's face.

'Your mother,' I asked. 'Is she all right?'

Claudia drank her tea and continued to stare at the street after the odd couple had disappeared.

'Mum's fine,' she said. 'She just works too hard some-times. It's not good for her health.'

'Yes, but she was drunk that day. More than drunk. She could have really . . . hurt herself.'

Claudia's eyes wandered the room. She picked up the

package and thrust it towards me. 'Here, this is for you. It's yours,' she laughed. 'I nearly forgot.'

It was my old check shirt, washed and ironed. I sighed. I brushed the back of my hand against her cheek. 'You're so mysterious.'

'You smell like a swimming pool,' she said.


Bessie Corday wasn't as difficult a subject as her assistant.

'Mizz Corday requires absolute control,' he warned. 'That's enough from that angle. Isn't that too much light? You speak English, right? What's that accent – Dutch?'

Bessie sat and sipped tea and mineral water and observed everything. She smiled serenely as we flapped around her. The staff writer had interviewed her before the shoot, and now sat to one side and conversed with her as I photographed. They would visit the restaurant terrace afterwards to complete the interview.

'Bessie, could you look down, to one side?' I said. 'A little lower, like this. And, maybe a hint of a smile?'

The assistant hissed in my ear, 'That's enough Bessies from you. It's Mizz Corday. Got that?' his whisper as subtle as a cat's mewl.

Bessie gazed at me through the lens. Her eyes twinkled as if she wanted to explain how used she was to her assistant's ridiculous fussing, and that it didn't mean anything. I found my irritation turning to amusement and let slip another few 'Bessies' solely to hear him screech again.


I spent the night at Claudia's. In the morning it was diffi-cult to get up. My body seemed on the verge of something:

collapse or regeneration. Claudia woke and left the room for a long while. I could hear her muffled voice in the sitting room. I must have fallen asleep again because when I woke there was a note on the bed – *Mum's not feeling so good. Did not want to wake you. Sorry about tonight. Maybe another time? – C.*

I returned home and worked on the photographs of Bessie all morning. In the afternoon I gathered my swimming things and walked to the pool. I didn't think of it so much as exercise, a way to shed pounds: it was a place to stretch out my thoughts and gaze at them, and put them away again, examined. I liked the way the water bore my weight. I could move easily from shallow to deep end and not tire.

I had begun to recognize the regulars: the old woman who took ten minutes to swim a single length; the middle-aged couple who did nothing but gossip as they clung to the side of the pool, not swimming at all; the family whose two boys, round and robust as dumplings, refused to separate. We smiled at each other now and chatted between lengths, called out our *tags*, wondered when the heat would end.

A woman waved from the side of the pool. I stopped swimming and trod water as she approached. She held a small object in the palm of her hand, but I couldn't make out what it was. Rolls of fat undulated beneath her black swimsuit, which seemed several sizes too small. Her thighs shuddered against each other as she drew closer, but she continued to stare.

'You've dropped this,' she said. She squatted and held out a stainless steel Seiko. 'It was at the shallow end. You should be more careful.'

I reached out to the ledge to steady myself. She could see

my own watch on my wrist, but she didn't seem to care. I wiped the water from my eyes.

'It's not mine,' I said. 'See?'

She smiled and continued her gaze.

I looked away, at the old woman just completing a length, then turned back. 'I haven't seen you here before.'

'Never seen you.' Her eyes glinted. 'I'd remember.'

I smiled back. I could feel the spark of arousal. I looked round the pool again. 'Why don't we meet afterwards?' I said. 'For coffee.'

She grinned and looked up at the bathers at the shallow end, then turned towards the windows, to the blue sky, the sunlight. Her neck, stretched out, was wide and graceful. I wanted to reach out and stroke it, pull her into the water.

'Coffee'd be nice,' she said.

'Good. I'll meet you in twenty minutes, okay? At the entrance.' I looked at my watch.

She stood and walked away without responding, her thighs squelching against each other satisfactorily. I pushed against the ledge and swam four laps before leaving the pool.

I couldn't see her in the foyer so I went outside and found her leaning against the entrance wall. She was dressed in tight jeans, narrow at the ankles, which only emphasized her bulk, and a thin baggy white v-neck sweater rolled up at the sleeves. Her hair was thin with moisture, chestnut brown, almost pudding-bowl short around her head. Apart from the unflinching gaze, there was nothing attractive about her. Her eyes seemed so assured and sensual I didn't think about anything else.

'There's the café inside,' she suggested, but she was looking away from the leisure centre.

She didn't give her name and I did not ask. We were strangers. I wanted no more than that. We stood for a moment in silence. She glanced at her wrist, at the watch she had shown me in the pool. It was a quarter past four.

'My place is ten minutes from here,' I said. I let the words hang in the air. 'We could have a drink there. The coffee here's terrible.'

She looked at me and squinted and smiled and we began to move away from the building without speaking. Her jeans chafed as she walked and then, after a moment, I noticed my own shorts doing the same.

'Do you live near here?' I asked, to break the silence.

'Yeah, but that way.' She waved in the opposite direction. 'I'm moving soon. This area's the pits. Me and a couple of girlfriends, we're gonna share a place in Dahlem.'

'Further out?' I said. 'Near the Americans?'

'Yeah, you got it.' She smiled and nodded as if I had understood something.

Fortunately, there was no one on duty at Frau Lieser's window. 'Think I'm out of coffee,' I said. I made a gesture of looking in the kitchen cupboards. I didn't keep coffee; the search was only for show. 'There's tea or beer. I could run down and buy some if you like.'

She shook her head and glanced round the apartment, disinterestedly. 'Nah, not really thirsty,' she said.

She was firm, despite her size, and unrestrained, but we were both removed from the other. It was only sex after all. When it was over we lay apart, staring up at the ceiling. A chair or a stool – something sturdy – fell over in Dieter and Caroline's apartment. After the fury of sex, the ensuing quiet only exacerbated sounds. We listened in silence to the thud of footsteps above. The woman's stomach rose and fell, and then rose higher. She didn't cover herself. She seemed unabashed at her nakedness. I became aroused again.

'Party?' she asked.

'No, I don't think so. They're always like that. I never know how many people are up there.' I reached across to caress her colossal breasts. I was ready for another round.

'I'm meeting someone,' she said and pushed my hand away and sat up. 'I'll be late if I don't go.'

I leaned on my elbow and stared as she squeezed into the jeans and pulled on her sweater. It was simple: no bra, no make-up, no clip for her hair. A woman unencumbered by things. She had kept the watch on throughout.

'Will I see you again?' I asked as she made for the door. 'At the pool perhaps?'

'Maybe,' she said. 'I'm moving, remember.' She didn't smile. She left the room without a word or a touch.

I lay on my back and heard the door slam, listened to the tread of footsteps as she descended the stairs. There were voices again from above. A man shouted – not Dieter – and there was laughter, then quiet again. I was overcome by a feeling of despair. I could feel myself moving from predicament to predicament without the benefit of a lull. I didn't understand this life, the way it ran ahead of you – no beginning and no end – only a shapeless, ragged road with turnings, random as a game of chance.


I lay without moving for several minutes and then pulled on my shorts and T-shirt and went upstairs. Caroline came to the door, her smile skewed and dreamy.

'Hello, Vincent,' she said. She looked behind her as if she were afraid of something.

'Hi, Caroline,' I said. 'Is Dieter in?' I didn't know what I was going to say.

She glanced behind again, her eyes wild and unfocused. But for the candlelight, the apartment would have been pitch black. A woman in a long black skirt and vest crossed the room, and then a man – also in black – followed after her. I couldn't see their faces.

'No, I don't know where he is,' Caroline yawned. 'You could try downstairs: that Zimmerman bitch, or the queer. Dieter thinks I don't know. If you see him, tell him he can screw whoever he likes. I don't care.' She could have been talking about the laundry.

'Are you all right, Caroline?' I asked.

'Me? Yeah, I'm fine.' She blushed unexpectedly and scratched her bald head. 'I have to get back inside now.'

I nodded and she shut the door before I had time to move. I trudged downstairs and looked at the Zimmermans' door for a moment before returning to my apartment. The phone was ringing and I ran for it without thinking.

# 22

C LAUDIA'S MOTHER GOT sick, fast. She had been vomiting blood and had been taken to hospital. I went to the Immanuel where Claudia, Sylvie and a bearded blond man in a suit and spectacles hovered around Frau Schlegel's bed.

'This is my Uncle Julius,' Claudia said. 'He flew in from Frankfurt this morning.'

Julius nodded and looked at me for a moment. A pale, pinched woman tiptoed into the room. She drew him to one side, then left seconds later.

'My wife can't stand hospitals,' Julius snorted, without humour. 'I don't like them myself. Claudi, I'll be just a moment.'

She nodded distractedly and I thought she hadn't heard what he had said.

'I don't know why she bothered to come,' Sylvie grumbled, after Julius had left the room. 'Looks as if she needs more care than anyone in here.'

I didn't say anything. I didn't mind Sylvie's caustic attitude for once. She walked to the window and stood with her back to us. I watched the imperceptible rise and fall of

Frau Schlegel's breathing. She seemed at peace in her sleep, even with the drip attached.

'What happened?' I asked.

Claudia shook her head. 'This isn't the first time, apparently. The blood. I didn't know. She wouldn't have told me if I hadn't seen it for myself.'

As early evening approached, a nurse arrived to check on Frau Schlegel, followed minutes later by a doctor. The doctor looked from Claudia to me and back again. 'Who is this?' she asked.

I wasn't prepared for the bluntness.

'He's . . . he's a friend,' Claudia replied.

The doctor nodded. Julius returned. Sylvie came away from the window. The doctor looked at her notes and then at Frau Schlegel. She spoke with the nurse.

'What we're going to do is this,' she said, folding her hands behind her back. 'We're going to keep her in overnight. Monitor her. There's no real danger at present. There's nothing else we can really do now. If she continues to consume alcohol, though . . .' She hunched her shoulders and pouted. 'There's only so much abuse the body can withstand. After a point it's only a question of time. Some people can continue for decades. Others are not so strong. Or so lucky. But there are a number of options we have here; there are places that have a good success rate, but they usually come at a price.'

'Money is not a problem,' Julius put in quickly.

'Well, that's just a small part of it,' the doctor continued. 'The main stumbling block is often a reluctance to seek help, to even admit there's a problem. If your mother doesn't want to get well, there's no amount of money or goodwill that will change things. You understand?'

Claudia stared at her mother's sleeping face and would not look away.

'We'll talk again in the morning,' the doctor said. 'For now it's best just to let her rest, get her strength back.'

Julius steered Claudia out of the room with a hand under her elbow. 'There's no point staying any longer,' he said. 'We'll come back first thing tomorrow. We should all get some sleep.'

Sylvie and I trailed behind Claudia, her aunt and uncle. She said, 'It's a fine time to act concerned now that she's sick. They stay away most of the time. The family never got to grips with the fact that she married a black man.'

'How long were they married?' I asked.

'I don't know – but he didn't stay long. Went back to America, just like that. They never divorced, but she didn't keep his name. He tried to come back when he heard she was a big shot, but it didn't work out. There was another family in America. Debts. All sorts of things. A real mess. He checked out four or five years ago.' There were no frills with Sylvie. She spoke her mind. She couldn't help herself. What I had mistaken for contempt was an inability not to speak plainly, no matter the circumstances.


When I returned home there was a message from Matty. He said to call back immediately. I retreated to the kitchen. I was famished and had grown weary of bad news.

There was an old tin of beef and dumpling soup at the back of the cupboard. I chopped up some cabbage and parboiled it and added the soup to the pan. I tore off a chunk of bread loaf to use as a mop. Before the soup had begun to simmer the phone trilled. I let it ring until my nerves could stand it no longer.

'Uncle Raymond's getting worse. Aunt Ama wants us to come as quickly as possible,' Matty said. No hello, how are you? 'Why didn't you answer the phone?'

'Worse? What's the matter with him?' I wondered when I would ever get a chance to eat.

'She . . . she didn't say exactly. Old age. She just wants us to come home. Now.'

'Old age?' In my mind he was as irritable and fierce as ever, with a clout that could knock a horse on its side. I didn't want to go back.

I ate the dumplings and the cabbage, but couldn't finish the chunks of beef. My stomach had been filled with other people's illnesses and my appetite had diminished.


Claudia phoned to say her mother had returned home. They would be leaving for a clinic the next morning. I explained about Uncle Raymond.

'I didn't know you had an uncle,' she said.

'I didn't know you had one either. I haven't seen my aunt and uncle in years. I'm nervous about it.' I hadn't realized I was nervous until I had said it. I couldn't pinpoint the source of my anxiety: Uncle Raymond's illness; seeing them after so long; returning home after an absence of over two-thirds of my life?

'How long will you be gone?' Claudia asked.

'Two, three weeks,' I said. 'Maybe a month. It depends. You could come too.' The words seemed to arrive of their own volition. 'Well . . . if you want.'

'I . . . I can't go anywhere at the moment. Not with Mum the way she is.'

'Yeah – you're right. She needs you. I won't be gone for long, anyway.'


I went out for a curry with B, Angelika and Tunde a few days before I was due to leave.

Tunde said, 'Seventeen years!' and whistled as if it was the most ridiculous thing he had ever heard. 'Small pickin wey commot fo ovaseas, come retorn – dey fo sell you, fine, fine!' He laughed and B laughed with him. Angelika looked bemused.

'So exciting to go home,' she said, rubbing her hands together. 'All that sunshine and seeing your relatives again.'

After our freak summer the thought of more intense heat was hardly welcoming, but I said, 'Yes, I'm looking forward to it. I can't imagine how things have changed.'

'Yaoundé too must be very different now,' B said. He had only been away from home two years.

'Yes, dear. Don't forget we're going soon.' Angelika smiled. She turned to me. 'We go in January, to escape the cold.' She looked down and patted her stomach. 'Before I start to show.'

'To show what?' I looked at her blankly.

B's eyes darted about, not settling on anything.

'We will have a baby, of course,' she said.

Tunde coughed into his beer.

'Ah – we've known for two weeks now,' she continued. 'The strain to keep a secret, I cannot tell you.'

I didn't know what to say.

'Congrats!' Tunde announced, raising his glass.

'Yes, congratulations!' I said.

'April baby,' B said, recovering some of his composure.

Angelika put her palms together, as if in prayer, and clapped softly to herself.

It seemed strange to focus on something so far in advance when I hardly considered the next day.

'We must find somewhere to live,' Angelika said. 'My place is too small.'

'And we will marry,' B croaked. He took off his glasses and breathed on them and watched as the fog evaporated.

I put down my beer for fear of dropping it. Tunde gulped at his as if he were dehydrated. B had been married before he arrived in Berlin, in the Cameroon, in his mid-twenties. He hadn't divorced his wife for all I knew, but as far as he was concerned the marriage was never official to begin with.


In the evening I phoned Claudia to find out how her mother was.

'She's not drinking at least,' she said. 'I can only visit on Sundays. I phoned her, but they've got a strict programme. It's never convenient.' She sounded at a loss; she had been too used to caring for her mother.

'Julius was saying – I told him that you were going away – maybe it wouldn't be such a bad idea, to take a vacation. Just for a week or so. He thinks I should go away.'

'Oh, yes?' I said. 'How do *you* feel about it?'

'I think I could go for a few days or a week. Only if you want me to come. I mean, he wants me to stay with them in Frankfurt, but I'd rather go away. Really far away. Some friends are going to Greece. I could go with them. Julius is staying at Mum's for a couple of days.'

'Well, it wouldn't be much of a holiday,' I said.

'That doesn't matter. I just need a change. And only if you want me to come.'

'Yes, of course,' I said. But I wasn't at all sure. I wasn't sure of anything any more.

# 23

THE AIR SHIFTED in thick sheets of moisture the moment the doors of the aircraft fell open. It was still morning. There was no air-conditioned tunnel to help us acclimatize to the heat. We scuttled across the broiling tarmac to reclaim our bags in the little airport building. An official said, 'Welcome to Nigeria,' but the sun was in my eyes, and when I shaded them I saw he was looking at Claudia.

The staff at the baggage reclamation area were suddenly roused from a heat-induced stupor. The sight of the lone aircraft on the shimmering runway, and its pampered passengers, seemed incongruous in the barren atmosphere.

Claudia snatched her suitcase from a pile left on a concrete bank, but an official demanded she open it before we left.

'Why is he doing that?' she asked.

'Security check, I guess.' Already I was irritated.

He peered at her underwear, her magazines, the translation of Baldwin's *If Beale Street Could Talk,* with the air of a man with time on his hands. At one point, he started a conversation with the officer next to him, still holding on to a cassette from Claudia's suitcase – something about blue lights by Roberta Flack, I saw. With his other hand, he began to scratch his belly through a gap in his shirt where a button should have been. Bullets of sweat raced down both sides of his pockmarked face, towards the finishing line of the concrete floor.

When he had ended his discussion he looked back at us and blinked, almost surprised to see us still there. He flashed a perfect set of incisors, as if in apology, and hurriedly closed the suitcase. It wouldn't shut. He pushed hard and Claudia shouted, 'Stop! I do it!' and re-arranged her belongings while the officer looked on. He seemed to be waiting for something, but I only returned his smile, suppressing my anger. In a moment he waved us away.

I changed some money outside, near the airport car park, as Peju had advised. We chose a taxi from an array of competing drivers and drove to the centre of Kano – past the dusty offices and mosques, the emir's palace – until we reached the taxi rank that served the rest of the country. Claudia tried to manoeuvre her suitcase on the untarred road, but, with its wheels manufactured for smooth surfaces, it dragged like a carcass across the ground. I had brought only a rucksack and a sports bag. I hadn't advised her. She stopped and tied her hair back and adjusted her grip on the suitcase. There was a small sweat stain on the back of her dress.

'What are we looking for?' she asked.

'The taxi to Jos,' I said. 'Keep a look out for that name. J. O. S.'

A group of children ran past us, shrieking, spinning a metal wheel ahead of them with sticks.

'But what time does it leave?' Claudia asked.

'Whenever it's ready,' I said. 'I don't think they stick to a timetable.'

There were cars as far as the eye could see. People dashed from place to place, searching for the vehicle that would take them to their destination. Cars trundled by and we were forced to stand to one side.

We found the Jos rank; the obligatory Peugeot station wagon was almost full. Two men leaned against the bonnet. One picked his teeth, the other stared straight ahead.

I asked, 'You go to Jos?' not knowing if either was the driver.

'Eh,' the tooth picker answered. 'Fo two of you?'

'Eh,' I replied. I had no Hausa and my pidgin was poor.

'Fifty naira.' The other man spoke up.

'Fifty? Fo what?' I said. 'Taty naira. No beso?'

The starer turned away. The tooth picker began to converse with him in Hausa. We were two foreigners, Claudia and I, as far as they were concerned, with only a smattering of pidgin, which counted for nothing.

'Forty naira.' The starer still did not look at us as he spoke. He seemed cool and unconcerned.

After the flights, I only wanted to arrive in one piece.

The tooth picker pointed to Claudia, then to me. 'Twenty, twenty,' and he heaved the suitcase and the rucksack onto the roof of the Peugeot without waiting for a reply.

One of the occupants came out so we could sit in the back of the car. Including the tooth picker, who was the driver, there were six of us.

The air was close in the vehicle. I had worn jeans and a yellow chambray shirt rolled up at the sleeves, but even that was too much. Claudia fanned herself with the KLM magazine. The driver returned with a large, elderly Hausa woman, draped from head to foot in damson. A stick-thin girl sat beside her on the passenger seat. A boy of no more than seven or eight glided by, supporting a round tray of heaped oranges on his head. The Hausa woman stretched out an arm, the material falling round her wrists, and motioned to the child to approach. I didn't hear her speak, but the boy lowered the tray and withdrew a paring knife. He began to shave the fruit in a circular motion until, in no time, there were four denuded oranges. Claudia reached out of the window and called, 'Hallo, can we have some of it?' and the boy started the peeling all over again. As soon as she had paid for the fruit, the car began to move. It was as if we had been idling at the taxi rank for no better reason than to pass the time of day.

In the depot the stationary cars did not want to budge and pedestrians refused to quicken their pace. We reversed and proceeded and then circled the rank, dipping in and out of fissures caused by erosion in the road. At one point the Peugeot lurched forward, bumping a woman carrying a basket on her head. Claudia screamed, but the woman only scooped up her goods and rushed onwards as if the car had boosted her energy.

It seemed an eternity before we were on the highway. The relief of the accelerating vehicle was instant; the warm wind buffeted us, quickly evaporating our perspiration. A young woman in front of me dozed against the side of the door, while the man next to her leaned forward and chatted with the driver. Another man gazed out of the window. The girl in the passenger seat squeezed and sucked another orange as if she hadn't touched liquid in days. She gave her last orange to the driver, who drove and sucked and talked at the same time. Claudia offered me one, but I refused it. The others threw their remnants to the side of the road, but she held on to her sticky litter after she had finished.

'It's very bare,' she said. And it was true. There were clumps of trees in the hazy distance, and ragged bushes, but the landscape was sparse. It was the claim of the desert. Sand clouds danced, whipped up by speeding vehicles on the highway.

'It's different down south; much greener,' I said. 'There's a wind here that blows down from the Sahara – the harmattan. Everything gets covered in thick dust. At Christmas time it's cooler, but there's a film of dust every-where – you have to clean all the time.'

'Did you see it?' Claudia asked. 'When you were younger?'

'I can't remember; my brother told me. I think I saw it. I must have.'

There seemed to be a mirage ahead – a crowd in the distance. As we drew nearer a great herd of cattle was traversing the road. Ours was the only car. We slowed and then stopped. Immediately, the wind died and we began to perspire again. I accepted an orange from Claudia and was surprised at its sweetness.

The scrawny cows straggled by. The herdsmen – mere boys – were indifferent to the highway. I wondered about their lives: where they slept, how they eat, their pastimes, what they did when they longed for a woman. I thought of the apartment in Berlin, the Atlantic, the Rio, the crammed super-market shelves; how easy everything was and yet not easy.

One of the men got out of the car and walked to the edge of a bush at the side of the road. He hitched up his caftan and squatted. The other man followed, but ventured further away from the road and remained standing as he sprinkled the ground. The Hausa woman left the car to exercise. The child remained. When everyone had returned, the last of the cattle were still on the road. Claudia wiped her forehead and the skin beneath her eyes with a tissue, and began to sip from her bottle of water. The car crawled around the final cow.

'I'll get used to it in some moments,' she smiled. Her face was puffy and flush from the flights and the heat.

'Don't worry,' I said. 'We're nearly halfway there. It'll be cooler when we get to Jos.'

She nodded and looked out of the window, but the landscape had not changed. 'I wonder what my mother does now,' she said. 'Making baskets or sitting in groups. Talking about things. Problems.' She threw her orange pulp out of the window. It was odd, hearing her speak English. It was like getting used to someone all over again.

'Your uncle, Julius – were they close?' I asked.

'I suppose. Once, when they were kids, but not so much any more. He was, he is four years younger. When he moved to Frankfurt and he was married, he did not communicate so much with us. His wife cannot have children.' She stopped abruptly as if she had said too much.

The sun withdrew, although the heat remained, and then it grew darker still, like an instant nightfall. A sudden, fierce thunderstorm began, and lightning danced upon the land around us. It became stuffy in the car with the windows wound shut. The driver slowed, but only marginally, and I feared we would plough into a hidden pothole. I could feel the anger begin to flush through my veins, something unstoppable rising to the surface. Those lazy, pothole-riddled roads. Within ten minutes, the rain had vanished as if it had been an apparition, and once again the earth was arid.

'This was the road where it happened,' I said.

'What road? What do you mean?'

'This highway, where my parents died. They were driving

the same way. Look! Look at that man!' I pointed. A Medusa-haired wanderer meandered along the centre of the road, naked. He carried no belongings. The filthy matted hair that hung down his back and face seemed his only accessory. The driver braked and swerved to avoid him. As we overtook him we could see his skin, painted with dust. He didn't notice us. His mouth moved rapidly.

No one said anything. Even the driver stopped talking. As we began to accelerate again the car filled with the noise of the wind and the engine. The man in the caftan spoke and the driver roared, but I didn't understand what they were saying.

'Was it bad for you when it happened?' Claudia asked.

'I don't remember. It was too long ago,' I said. 'I can't remember much from that time, only that it was here, this road.'

She nodded and the girl in the passenger seat turned and they smiled at each other. There were more cars now, and tiny satellite villages. One of the byroads led to my grand-mother's village, but she was long-since dead.

I said, 'We went to live with Uncle Raymond and my Aunt Ama. It was okay. We didn't stay for long.' I gazed out of the window.

We sped through Dutsan Wai and then began the slow ascent to Jos. We stopped to eat a late lunch – steaming parcels of *eba* and *egusi* soup washed down with Star beer – at a roadside *buka*. The driver bustled us back into the car to ensure he would arrive before dark.

'I went to visit my father once,' Claudia said when we were on the road again. 'In Atlanta. In Georgia. I was thirteen years. It was not so bad. But my mother, she did not want me to go.'

'Why *did* you go?' I asked.

'He wanted to see me and I wanted to see America,' she laughed. 'New York, California. I wanted to visit him also, of course. I took more classes, to speak English better. My mother tried to stop me – she bought the aeroplane ticket, but she said he would try to keep me there. She said his wife – she was American – would be cruel to me. I think she was only afraid that I would like it there and I would like to stay.'

'I thought your mother didn't divorce him?'

'No, they never divorced, but he married this woman anyway. Two wives. I think, maybe there was another woman after that, but they did not marry. Anyway, I went to this place, Atlanta. They had a small house outside of the city. Three children already. When I telephoned to my mother I did not tell her about these children. One baby girl. Two boys. And my father already not so young.

'I always thought he was a very big man when I was a girl, but when I saw him again I was almost the same height with him. It was all right, but he could see I was already too much like my mother – too far from him to make things easy. The woman – his wife – she was okay. But she was *very* quiet. That's how he liked his wife to be, like a mouse. My mother is not a mouse,' she laughed. 'Sometimes they would fight, this woman and my father. And then the oldest boy – he was five or six – he would take the other boy and the baby into the road to play. No garden. But where they lived there were not many cars. The road did not lead to anywhere.

'Sometimes I waited at the door. It had – what do you call it? Wires? A screen? I listened to their fighting. Wild fights. She threw things at him – pots, bottles, garbage. She wanted to kill him. Always it was because of another woman or not enough money. He would spend money on these other women. It would go round and round, this fighting.' Claudia drew a circle in the air.

'I had only a small taste of it, but it was exhausting. I wanted to remember these fights so that I could tell my mother when I came back to Berlin, so she would not be sad that he had left her. But I never told her. It was too awful, that life. I wanted to forget it.

'I did not go back to visit them. I wrote to my father sometimes, but he never wrote back; he liked only to talk on the telephone and my mother did not allow him to call her house. It was a mess, the whole business, and it was bad for my mother because her family had told her not to marry him. And they were right.' She smiled, but it was not a smile of happiness.

'I always remember those kids playing in the dirt, in the road, and the shouting inside the house, and I was standing there at the screen, listening between them.'

'What happened to the children?' I asked.

She shrugged. 'I don't know. I suppose the mother took them somewhere else after my father died. Maybe they stayed in that house.' She turned to me. 'You think it's awful, that we did not care to communicate?'

'No, not really,' I said. 'You were only thirteen. You were all just children. It's no one's fault.'

'I felt guilty, but I did not want to know them any more,' she said. 'Anyway, it's ten years ago. It's in the past.'

It was strange to see people in Jos wearing coats and sweaters when it still seemed warm to me. It was cooler here, but only fractionally. At the depot we changed taxi and drove to the address Matty had given me. I had never been here before. Uncle Raymond had moved to Jos after retiring. All my links lay in another part of the country now. The houses Matty and I had lived in, the schools we had attended, the neighbourhoods in Lagos – all was left behind. It was like Claudia and the American family; there was no connection. If you left it too long it had no hold on you. Something was broken, and there came a stage when it ceased to mean anything.

A *megadi* at the entrance scowled at us before dragging open the metal gate. He padded to the house in bare feet to report on the arrivals. I hadn't expected a bungalow. Uncle Raymond could have chosen something grander – a two- or three-storey affair modelled on the houses he had lived in during his travels. But this was an old colonial-style bungalow decorated with orange, guava and mango trees and an array of flowering bushes that lent the compound the air of a botanical garden. The light was fading fast, but it was impossible to miss the fact that it was well maintained.

I thought Uncle Raymond's would be the first face I saw, but after the houseboy opened the door, it was Asa who came running towards us.

'It's Uncle, it's Uncle!' he announced to the house, jumping up and down. 'Mummy, it's Uncle and a pretty lady.' He attempted to lift Claudia's suitcase and failed and the houseboy snatched it away from him.

'They've gone out,' Peju said, waddling towards us. 'We weren't sure when to expect you. We drove to the airport yesterday and this afternoon to check. We were going to try again tomorrow. How did you come?'

'You drove to Kano?' I asked.

'No – there's an airport here,' she laughed. 'Ah, ah! – don't tell me you came by road?'

I stared at her.

'Oh dear. Don't you know, every state has an airport now?' Peju continued. 'Soon you'll be able to fly to the villages, I'm telling you. Don't worry – you can catch the domestic flight on the way back.'

The bungalow was larger than it appeared from the outside; the sitting room had been divided into different sections: lounge, dining room, television area. They had been watching a film and the screen had frozen the characters of an animation into a single frame. The top of the television, the side and coffee tables, were covered with lace doilies – Aunt Ama's touch. I noticed a stone fireplace in the centre of the room. For a moment I wondered whether it was used to offset the chill of the air conditioning.

'It gets cold here?' Claudia asked.

'Sometimes – later in the year,' Peju said. 'It used to get really chilly in the old days, years ago. Now it's the same as everywhere else. I don't know why.'

Peju guided us along a corridor parallel to the sitting room, to the bedrooms at the back of the house. The corridor spilled into a hallway almost as long as the sitting room itself, and again there was another passageway after that. There were tributaries that fed into hidden areas.

'I don't know what he wants to do in such a big house,' Peju said, 'when it's only the two of them.'

Asa skated up and down the smooth stone flooring and threw open a door and called, 'Uncle, this is my room! Come and see!'

We peered inside a large room with two metal trunks against one wall, a double bed and toys scattered on the floor, and a view of the driveway. Claudia and I were placed in adjoining rooms. Aunt Ama was everywhere: in the tasselled bedspreads, the lace on the dressing tables, the ornate chest of drawers, the heavy floral curtains. When we were alone in Claudia's room, I sank to the edge of the bed.

'I can't stay here for long,' I said. 'I'll suffocate. I haven't even seen the old goat yet.'

Claudia came and sat beside me, and then lay back.

'You all right?' I asked.

She nodded. 'Only tired. I need a bath.'

I lay on my side, looking at her. I was glad she had come in the end. I closed my eyes and thought of nothing. I heard a car pull up and my heart sank. Claudia was still looking at me. Had I slept or had I only closed my eyes for a moment? I sighed.

'I think it's the old goat,' she said.

# 24

S HE WAS LIKE a bird, a red-throated bee-eater, swathed in snatches of blue and yellow and green. When I held her I was afraid my embrace was too robust. She said, 'You have grown so much! You are taller than your brother. Imagine!'

I had been taller than Matty for over ten years, but I didn't tell her that. Aunt Ama wore a cheap green and yellow head-scarf, like a woman selling peanuts in the marketplace. She had thrown a pink smock over sky-blue cotton trousers, as if she had recently been gardening. When I hugged her I felt how much she had shrunk, or I had grown, or both. I couldn't tell.

She led Claudia and me from the hallway into the sitting room. Asa had commandeered him; they both stood trans-fixed in front of the television screen. I saw him then, an empty shell. The bones so near to the surface. I couldn't breathe.

Asa's eyes left the television for a microsecond and then returned to focus on the film. He said, 'Look Grandy, it's Uncle and the pretty lady,' as if he were talking about the characters on the screen.

When he saw me he arched his eyebrows as if he were mildly surprised. I didn't say anything. I couldn't move. Then darkness arrived. I wondered if I had passed out. Uncle Raymond called, 'NEPA!' in a voice so strong, I was convinced he would be his younger self again when the power resumed.

Matty laughed and Aunt Ama called out, 'Musa!' but the houseboy was already drifting along the hallway with a lighted candle. I could hear generator motors churning into action throughout the neighbourhood, but the bungalow remained shrouded in darkness.

'Your first day and they take the light,' Uncle Raymond bellowed. 'Nigeria, we hail thee!'

'I'd forgotten about this,' I said. It was easier in the dark. We had both escaped the awkwardness of an embrace.

'When does it come back?' Claudia asked.

'Sometimes in a few minutes or a few hours,' Aunt Ama replied. 'Maybe tomorrow.'

'Sometimes for days there won't be any light!' Uncle Raymond boomed as if it were a matter of pride. 'After Easter, they punished us, didn't they? We had to take all our frozens next door. That's when you really need a generator.' He collapsed into the sofa as if the speech had exhausted him.

'I want to watch the movie,' Asa whined, but with a hint of excitement. He would be mildly disappointed when the electricity supply returned.

We ate dinner by candlelight: steak and duchesse potatoes with boiled carrots in butter and parsley. Halfway through the meal, the lights flickered on. Asa screamed, with fear or delight. It was hard to tell.

'Stop that nonsense!' Uncle Raymond snapped and frowned

with disapproval. Gaunt as he was I wanted to slap the stern look from his face. Asa went quiet with the rebuke. I could feel the old resentment seeping back into my bones.

'Where's Kunle these days?' I asked, to break the mood.

'He's in Montreal now. He went three, four years ago,' Uncle Raymond said.

'He studied languages at university,' Aunt Ama added. 'Now he works for a company – what do they do again?'

'Computers,' Uncle Raymond said. 'Computer programming.'

'That's right, computers,' she said. 'I'm not sure whether he's going to do that forever, but he likes the place. Roli is in New York working for a firm of architects, and Bunmi works for Central Bank in Lagos.'

There was a silence.

'And Kayode?' I asked.

'Only Kayode is jobless.' Uncle Raymond spat out the word 'jobless'. 'He's with the sister in New York. I told him he could come and work in petroleum – I can get him a job tomorrow-tomorrow, but he refuses even to consider it.' His children had scattered. That none of them had chosen his own line of work must have been galling for him.

'Kayo's a dreamer,' Matty said. 'He won't work in an office if he can help it. He'll find something eventually, but he'll take his time about it.'

'Yes – maybe you're right, dear,' Aunt Ama said.

Uncle Raymond shrugged and looked at Asa and pouted. The boy giggled and shovelled a heap of potato into his mouth. He had already dismissed the earlier reprimand.

'They tell me you're in Germany now,' Uncle Raymond said, as if he had only just heard. He pronounced it 'Jamany'.

'That's right,' I replied. 'Berlin. West.'

'And London – you didn't take to it? I thought you would

like the place – it's the centre of everything. What is that saying? "To be tired of London is to be tired of life."'

'Yes, that's probably it,' I said. 'But I prefer Berlin. It's smaller. Cleaner. Not so expensive.' I began to nibble the hated carrots I had pushed aside. I could hear Claudia chatting with Peju. I wanted to be involved in their conversation, away from Uncle Raymond's scrutiny.

'Yes, but journalism – it can't pay much?' he said. 'Can it?'

'Photography – I can make a living. It's what I like to do.'

*'Photography?'* He grimaced as if his food were poisoned. He glanced at Matty. 'I thought you said journalism?'

Matty sighed. 'Well, I . . .'

'How can you support yourself?' Uncle Raymond continued. 'Photos of what? Birds, weddings?'

'Well, people mostly. Portraits and concerts . . . and that sort of thing.' I had finished the carrots and there was nothing left to distract myself with.

Uncle Raymond gave Aunt Ama a look as if to say he had been right all along. 'No, no, no, no,' he said. 'When you settle here, I'll put you in touch with Mr Nwabuwe, in the company. I still have some leverage. No more of this nonsense. With your education he can get you something more profitable. I didn't send you to the UK to waste your life.'

'He's doing all right,' Matty jumped in. 'It won't be forever.'

I inhaled, held my breath, exhaled slowly.

'But look at you, Matthew. You are doing *so* well in London, with your career, your fine family.' He looked at Asa and forced a smile. He wouldn't let go. He was like a dog with a bone clenched between its jaws; you couldn't tear it away from him. 'Vincent, look to your brother! Our elders are not there just for the sake of it.'

He had forgotten about his unemployed son in New York, meting out useless advice as he was. I had come to support what I had assumed was a dying man, and here I was bristling as if time hadn't moved on.

'Who said . . .' I started, but Aunt Ama had lost none of her skill for distraction.

'Ray, look at your plate!' she scolded. 'You haven't even touched half of it. Ah! Ah! Eat now and stop talking so that these young people can go and rest. They've been travelling non-stop since early yesterday.'

'Look to your plate!' Asa shouted, mimicking Aunt Ama. He looked from her to his mother, with a wavering grin. Peju couldn't help snorting.

Uncle Raymond glanced across at his wife as if he did not know who she was, then began to fork tiny morsels into his mouth. He had reversed roles with Asa, who had already finished his meal. I wondered again what was wrong with him, but I didn't speak.

I showered next door to Asa's room, while Claudia used the bathroom further along the hall. We had been in the house less than four hours and already I was exhausted, but I could not sleep. I waited until I assumed Claudia had finished changing before knocking at her door. She had laid out her things – a bottle of perfume, lotions, talcum powder, make-up – on the dressing table. A straw hat I had never seen before crowned a chest of drawers. A small framed photograph of her mother, smiling, stood on the bedside table. It was already like a room that had been lived in and cherished.

'You're settled then?' I said.

She was sitting against the headboard, reading the novel she had begun on the plane. She peered at me above the rim of her glasses – I had seen them for the first time during the flight.

'Don't just stand there.' She patted the bed. 'Keep me company. Come.'

She had propped both pillows against the headboard and I had to lean on my elbow for support. She wore a night-dress – beige cotton, decorated with bluebells and daisies. The whole effect – book, glasses, nightie, hair tied back in a bun – was of a prim schoolmistress. She glanced down at me.

'I'm wide awake,' she said. 'It's funny, isn't it? I should be fast asleep by now.'

'I couldn't sleep either,' I said. 'It was a mistake to come. For me, I mean. I can't stand him. I don't know if I can face tomorrow.' I lay back and placed my hands behind my head.

Claudia put the book face down on the blanket. 'You feel so strongly about your uncle. He seems okay to me.'

'That's just part of his cunning. He's charming to other people, but beware if he's singled you out. It's like not being picked for the football team – you're left on the sidelines while everyone else is busy with the game.'

'They didn't pick you for the football team?'

'No – I was just trying to explain. It can be very isolating. It doesn't matter.'

She reached over and lifted my T-shirt and moved the flat of her hand in slow circles across my stomach. Skin barely touched skin, but the effect was both soothing and arousing.

'You haven't been eating?' she asked, and withdrew her hand when my penis stirred.

'I've been swimming.' I could think of no other reason for the weight loss. I remembered the woman at the pool that day. How we lay naked and panting, side by side, like whales on a beach.

'I've been reading this page for about ten minutes,' Claudia laughed suddenly. 'I keep reading the same sentences again and again, but they do not make sense.' She picked up the novel and bent the pages back so that the spine cracked. A minute of silence passed and she said, 'Strange not to hear the cars and the ambulance and people talking in the streets, and the neighbours' television. Just the insects. What are they, crickets, cicadas? I remember this sound from Atlanta.'

'I don't know. Crickets, I suppose.' I was heavy with sleep now. 'When you've got mosquitoes in your ear, you'll happily swap them for traffic, any day.'

She laughed, not realizing I wasn't joking. She spoke, but I could not understand her. Her voice was the song of the mosquito keeping me in this world, when my body ached for unconsciousness.

I half-opened an eye and there was the lamplight and Claudia's silhouette before it. I supposed she was still reading. I closed my eyes and opened them again and the light had changed. It was grey, though I could make out an area of sun beyond the window. Claudia was on her side, facing me, breathing calmly in deep sleep. She had pulled the sheet and blanket over herself until it almost reached her neck. I was surprised at the coolness of the morning. For a moment I wondered where I was in the world; Claudia was beside me, but I could not discern a location. I began to take in the room: the floral curtains, the straw hat on the chest of drawers, the motionless ceiling fan. The memory of the previous evening rose to the surface and I was wide awake with apprehension.

I returned to my room and pulled on a pair of jeans and the faded yellow chambray shirt. The house was sleeping; the slap of my feet against the floor seemed excessive in the silence. Asa's toys and the video containers littered the carpet in the sitting room. It was too early for Musa to have begun his chores.

'Well, this is a surprise,' Aunt Ama said. She was leaning against the kitchen counter, sipping tea. She wore a washed-out blue dressing gown that fell almost to her ankles. The rolled-up sleeves were bunched thick. I assumed the gown belonged to Uncle Raymond or to one of their sons. 'You never used to be an early bird,' she said.

'I couldn't sleep,' I replied. 'I'm not tired, strangely enough. I must have slept soundly.'

'It rained during the night,' Aunt Ama said. 'Sometimes that helps.'

I looked out of the kitchen window at the driveway. Most of the moisture had evaporated, but there were shallow pools where the surface dipped. Aunt Ama said, 'Let me look at you,' and walked up and reached across to hug me. 'Welcome home,' she said. I was embarrassed at the sudden tenderness and didn't speak.

'Come, let us have our breakfast outside.' She took half a bread loaf from the fridge and placed it on a tray with a flask of tea and a tin of evaporated milk with tiny holes punched on either side. She filled two glasses with filtered water.

I carried the tray to the patio near the far end of the sitting room, which looked out at the only expanse of lawn not inter-spersed with trees. Here, there were mainly hedges, garnished with shrubs and flowers: a bloom of magnolias overhanging the concrete slabs; a single avocado tree, pregnant with fruit, at the bottom of the garden. Puddles blotted the patio. We wiped the plastic furniture dry. A breeze stirred the tassels of the folded parasol, but the wind was barely discernible. We sat in the shadow of the bungalow and again I shivered.

'Don't you miss Lagos?' I asked. I was unfamiliar with every aspect of this place. There were no memories attached to it.

'Well . . . yes and no,' Aunt Ama said. 'It's cooler here and quieter, and we don't have to worry so much about armed robbery. But we have left most of our old friends behind. You know how I like to gossip. We are far away from all of that now. It can be dull sometimes. Quiet.'

'You wouldn't want to go back?'

'No, never!' she laughed, but she was resolute. 'Ah, we need peace in our old age. We know enough people here. In time you get used to anything.' She poured the tea as she talked, stirring in generous amounts of milk and sugar for me. She had not forgotten. She said, 'You know, when you leave a place, if you move away in favour of another, you can never completely forget the first.' She held a fist against her chest. 'It is like a stone tied around your heart. It keeps you from floating away from yourself, from losing something essential that once belonged to you.'

I wondered whether she was remembering Lagos or her own country, Ghana, which she had left as a child. I tore off a piece of bread to dip into the tea. When she had refilled her own cup, she pulled the lapels of the dressing gown closer together and sat back in the chair, looking out at the trees beyond the lawn. There were no clouds in the sky.

She began quietly. 'Claudia's a nice girl. Have you been together very long?'

'No, not really. But it doesn't matter.'

She looked across at me sharply. I couldn't afford to be flippant. 'I mean, we still don't know that much about each other.' I thought of other words to say, but they would have sounded strange here, away from what I had grown used to. I grew desperate. 'I don't know how long it will last. We're not married, if that's what you're asking.'

'Of course I know that. Matthew told us. You don't tell us anything.' She spoke looking out at the bougainvillea as if she was furious with it. 'You could have been dead or alive all these years. But for your brother, we wouldn't know. Just like those Ajegunle boys who take off – not even a word to the mother, even on the deathbed. As if you don't care, eh?'

I put down a clump of bread. I hadn't expected this, at least not from Aunt Ama. She made no attempt to disguise her rage. I made no reply. I let her simmer for a while, hoping the storm would pass. I noticed breadcrumbs swimming in my milky tea and felt queasy.

'I don't understand, Vincent. Not even telephone calls, or letters. Not *one* Christmas card? What were we supposed to think? Even your cousins, not a word to them – ah, ah! What is that?' She picked up her cup and stared at it and put it down again as if she could not understand how it had got there. She gathered the lapels again and pulled harshly. That she was ordinarily placid made her anger all the more alarming. 'Only now that he is sick do you come back. How does that happen, Vincent?'

'What's wrong with him?' I snapped. I could match her anger with ample reserves of my own.

'Ah, ah!' Aunt Ama looked at me. 'You hate him *so* much? You don't care if he lives or dies?'

I could not think in this chaotic, broiling state. If I spoke I would regret my words. Aunt Ama was the last person I would want to hurt. I could feel my anger turning in on itself, flowing back through my veins, like a venom, searching for a place to rest.

'Is it that you don't care, Vincent? That you stayed away for so long? Eh? Answer me!'

I stared ahead at the unbroken skyline. Such a piercing blue. A blue to love and hate all at the same time. I suddenly remembered that Claudia was asleep, that there was a house full of people behind us. My jaw was trembling.

'What do you say?' Aunt Ama persisted.

Lawn, trees, sky, sun. There was no escape.

'I thought . . . you didn't want me,' I said. My voice was thin with strain.

A barefoot man appeared on the lawn wearing corduroy trousers cut off at the knee, and a T-shirt promoting a Prince concert. The T-shirt would have belonged to Roli or Kayode at one time. I noticed a limp as he walked. One leg was thinner than the other, markedly so, and slightly bowed. He carried a trowel in one hand, an aluminium watering can in the other. He called out a greeting to my aunt and she answered him. He looked not far from his fiftieth birthday. A houseboy, a gardener, a *megadi*, a cook. Four to watch over two. I wondered if there was a chauffeur.

Aunt Ama sank back into her chair and sighed. We watched as the gardener attended to the plants and the soil. He was talking, but only to himself.

'He has had two strokes already this year,' Aunt Ama said. 'Who knows when the next one will arrive.' A tone of resignation had replaced the umbrage.

I thought for a moment she was referring to the gardener.

'Between that and the cancer, I don't know.' It was her turn to stare ahead.

The chattering gardener put down the trowel and began to gather individual flowers from the periphery of the garden. He stood in front of the foliage, turning his head this way and that, before deciding whether a flower would compliment the bunch in his hand.

'Cancer?' I stared at her. 'I didn't know.'

Aunt Ama nodded slowly, as if there was something to comprehend. 'Well, now you are here. That's all that matters.'

'Do you mean he could go any day now?' Panic was rushing in, sweeping aside the anger. 'Why didn't you tell me before?' I regretted the words even before they had left my mouth, but I was powerless to stop them.

Aunt Ama gave me a look and smiled. 'With the cancer he is managing, but this other illness . . . well, we can never tell. Kunle, Bunmi, your brother – they come and go. Kayode and Roli were here only last month. We never hear from you. He just wanted to see you, you understand? For you and for him. He is angry too, and he cannot afford to be angry when he is like this. He needs peace, in himself. You understand?'

I nodded, but all I felt was confused. This, the man I had hated for most of my life, reduced to a husk, the membrane of a husk. What point was there in hating now? I had hated for years in vain. 'How long is he expected to live?'

'Months, a year. No one can say,' she sighed. 'It is possible that he could live for years. It all depends. It could be tomorrow. But then,' she smiled, '*I* could go tomorrow.'

I wondered how it would be for her when Uncle Raymond died, alone in this vast house. I couldn't imagine either one of them without the crutch of the other. I pushed the thought away. The gardener approached with the flowers arranged in the watering can. Before he stood on the patio, he stepped into a pair of pink plastic slippers that lay to one side. He swung the withered leg further and higher than the healthy one as he propelled himself forward. The watering can swayed from side to side. The whole effect seemed guaranteed to end in disaster.

'Good morin', Ma,' he panted. 'Morin', sah,' he nodded to me. At close range he seemed nearer to sixty.

'Good morning, Clement.' Aunt Ama sat forward to inspect the flowers. There were alligator peppers and orchids and the yellow lilies I thought, as a child, were sprinkled with the blood of their victims. 'Very nice indeed!' She selected three alligator peppers for herself before Clement proceeded to the kitchen to arrange the displays.

'There was some money left after everything was settled,' Aunt Ama said, nodding to herself. She was searching for something on the tray, but could not find it. In the end she simply snapped each stem a few inches from the head of the flower. She drank her water until the glass was almost empty. 'Your mother and father did not leave a will, but it was what they wanted – Matthew won the scholarship. He was going away; it was his wish to go. And we did not want to separate you.' She placed the stunted flowers in the glass of water, then wiped her palms on the dressing gown. 'I thought you understood. Maybe you were too young. I thought we had explained it properly. If it had been my choice, and your uncle's, you would have stayed with us. You were always wanted. You shouldn't say such things.'

I had been too young at the time; now I was too old to remember. It seemed a waste of a life, of an experience. What could I say? There was no longer justification for the anger. I had not expected to hear her words.

'I . . . I didn't understand,' I said. 'Or maybe I did, but it didn't make any difference. I can't remember.' It was like an empty train pulling out of a station, this feeling. It had forgotten its passengers on the platform; there was nothing inside, but still it was heavy.

Clement returned. He was singing this time. He released the watering can and picked up the trowel and swung it from side to side as he moved. An ersatz conductor in the lush garden.

'Claudia must be awake now,' I said. I sat on the edge of the chair. 'I think I'll go in. She'll be wondering where I am.'

Aunt Ama nodded again, but she did not speak. I shrugged and stood up and went back inside without another word.

# 25

THE DAYS PASSED. The hours limped by without incident. We drove to town, the museum, to the crumbling zoo. In the evenings we climbed the hill to the hotel where they served cold beer and dried bush meat. There were poor imitations of western fare: hamburgers and pizza served with French fries thick as thumbs. The children of the privileged swam in the pool overlooking the town, or played tennis and games on the tiered lawn in front of the adults. Asa was always excited to arrive, racing to the edge of the revelry. He nervously circled the other children, but didn't join in and they did not encourage him. When he grew tired of this, sleep would usually overcome him. We never stayed long – the arrival of darkness heralded the reign of mosquitoes; it was more pleasant to return indoors.

It seemed as if we had been here for months, not days. The variety was endless: rain, sun, heat, the chill of evening and early morning, the sudden black clouds, the brilliant blue sky.

I slept late, and often when I rose, Claudia would already be dressed or reading. One morning I discovered her drinking tea on the patio with Aunt Ama and Peju. I stood behind the glass of the sliding doors, unseen, and wondered about their conversation. I thought of the balcony at Frau Schlegel's apartment, how the women sat and talked there. My uncle and aunt had taken to Claudia in a way I hadn't expected. The women laughed, and at one stage Claudia stood and wandered bare foot into the garden to pick flowers. As she returned a hand touched my shoulder.

'Most of the time it's only the two of us,' Uncle Raymond said. 'It's good that you are all here. Now the house is full of life.'

Each time I saw him my breath fell away. I couldn't believe how the years had reduced him, like a piece of stick whittled from a tree trunk. His eyes held mine.

'You have your mother's face,' he said.

I smiled.

'But still jumbo like your papa, eh?' he laughed. Always giving and taking away in the same breath.

My anger rose, but I held it now, and felt it withdraw. He couldn't change; there was no point in countering him. The old resentments would flare up repeatedly, but they were like candle flickers now rather than forest fires. Uncle Raymond had been older than my mother, by five years at least; now I wondered how she would have aged. I searched his face for a trace of recollection, a clue to how time might have moulded her.

'How are you feeling?' I asked.

'Better. Much better,' he replied. 'Some days the pain is more severe. The drugs they give me, eh, I don't know whether they do more harm than good. I never took medicine until I was fifty. Even for a cold or a headache. Now they are pumping me full of drugs, enough to last several lifetimes.' His laugh could not disguise his bitterness.

The women turned and called to us, their voices muted by the sliding doors. We waved, but didn't venture outside, and they resumed their conversation.

'What will you do when you finish in Germany?' he asked. 'Will you come home or return to London?'

'I'm not sure,' I said. 'What do you mean by "finish"? It's where I live. I've made no plans to live anywhere else.'

He nodded slowly. 'And the girl – you're going to marry her?' He was looking at Claudia through the glass.

'No, we're not serious. I haven't known her very long. I don't know how things will turn out.' I was thinking of Lucille. Had I made a poor choice in Claudia, or Claudia in me? I remembered our meeting in the Atlantic, her mother steeped in alcohol, the secrecy. 'It never turns out the way you expect.'

'And how did you expect things to be?' he asked.

'I don't know. Not like this. Different . . . I didn't think. I just let it happen. Isn't that the way it works?'

'Perhaps. But you have to know what you want, otherwise you could be scattered to the wind. Look at Kayode now, he doesn't know his left from his right. He's a burden to his sister in New York. Law, accounts, graphic design – every time we speak to him it's a different pursuit. I could get him a good job in the company even tomorrow morning, but he just turns his nose up.'

Uncle Raymond had made no reference to the fact that my cousin was struggling. He had raised his children to succeed without the grace of making necessary errors. It was no surprise they had all dispersed. I would write a letter to Bunmi and Kayode when I returned. I wasn't sure whether I would send it.

\* \* \*

We arrived downtown shortly after eleven, but already the marketplace was bustling. Matty manoeuvred Uncle Raymond's Peugeot past vehicles parked on streets and paths hours ago. People traipsed along the side of the road and ran in front of the car, risking their lives in order to reach the centre stalls. Asa jumped up and down on the back seat while Claudia tried to calm him, but he only became more boisterous.

'Daddy, look at that boy! Look at his teddy!' he squealed. And in the same breath, 'Daddy, where's the video man? When will we stop? I'm thirsty!'

'Asa, sit down and keep quiet,' Matty warned. 'If you don't behave I'm not buying any videos, you hear?'

Asa was silent for a moment. Then his head started to sway from side to side and he was up on his feet again. 'Daddy, look at that boy! Look at his funny teddy!' He had dismissed the threat or it was already forgotten.

A boy sauntering beside the car was swinging a dead cat by the tail. It looked hard; rigor mortis had already set in, but that did not diminish his pleasure. He swung it as happily as a child might play with a favourite toy.

There was no available area of shade left in which to park so we left the car in the full glare of the sun. Asa wanted to see the dead animal again. He looked as if he might shoot across the road, but then seemed uncertain about separating from us.

'Asa, I'm telling you now, you better behave,' Matty said. 'You don't want to get lost in this place. Come and hold my hand.'

He ran back and held his father's hand, then detached himself and clung to Claudia.

'It's hot today, Asa,' she said. 'Do you think it will rain?'

He looked up at her, then at the ground, giggling, then raced back to his father. He gazed at her from a distance, suspiciously. I laughed and Claudia reached for my hand instead.

She bought a cup of boiled peanuts as we wandered among stalls selling bags and shoes and batteries. Table fans vied for space with Chinese flip-flops and pineapple pyramids. In the alleyways and under cover of the main building the temperature was marginally cooler. We bought a gallon of groundnut oil for Aunt Ama, and bunches of green and yellow plantains. The stallholders assumed Claudia was from abroad and called out to her, but she did not respond until we came to the materials section.

'I must buy some of this cloth for my mother,' she said. 'She's good at designing clothes. When I was a girl, she made many of my dresses.'

The stallholder sat back and appraised us. He spoke in Hausa, then Yoruba, and when we didn't respond, said, 'Yes? Which one do you like? Best material. Choose any one.'

Matty and I had no grasp of the language. If Peju had not been feeling unwell or Aunt Ama had joined us, we would have been treated differently. Instead the stallholder considered us tourists.

'I give you fine price,' he said, curling his fingers theatrically.

'This one.' Claudia pointed. 'And this one. How much is it?'

'Twenty naira, taty naira,' he said. He pulled down the two bales of cloth and stretched them out. Claudia touched the material and her eyes danced. He could see that. He had made a sale without the effort of enticement.

'Nonsense,' Matty snorted. 'I no 'gree tourist price. Oya, oya. Ten, ten naira. Make we commot.'

But already it was futile. The stallholder sat back on his stool and sighed. He hitched up the sleeves of his *agbada* and scratched his biceps, and left his muscles on display.

'Pickin!' He spoke directly to Asa. 'Come and eat sweet!' He reached back and fetched a saucer of bonbons from the top of a bale of cloth.

Asa stepped forward, his eyes devouring the fluorescent colours.

'You like?' The stallholder pointed to the material again and laughed.

Claudia nodded. Behind us two women wearing wrappers and head ties stopped to glance at the stall. The stallholder folded the bales of cloth into two striped plastic bags and held them out. 'Oya now, forty-five naira only. Special price. I get plenty-plenty customa.'

Asa had gobbled a couple of sweets and was working up the courage to request another.

'Which one you like?' the stallholder asked the two women.

They ignored him and continued to search for themselves.

Claudia handed the notes to the man, despite Matty's protests, and Asa received a third bonbon. We left the concrete shelter of the main market and wandered among the outdoor stalls in search of videos.

'He might not be here today,' Matty said. He stopped and stared back in the direction we had come from.

Asa looked to where his father's gaze fell and then screamed, 'Noooo!' as if he had witnessed some atrocity. 'It's there!' He pointed towards the outdoor market, his arm wavering a hundred and eighty degrees.

The sun was almost at its zenith. The shopping grew heavier with each step.

'We could go to the shop in town,' I suggested. 'Or try tomorrow.'

'Noooo!' came Asa's cry again.

People stopped to stare at the wailing child.

'Asa!' Matty gave him a look. 'That's enough, you hear?'

The boy frowned and grew quieter and his body shuddered with unspent tears.

'But we came for the video, yes?' Claudia said. 'We can try one more time, it's okay.'

'It's okay,' Asa mimicked and reached for her hand.

We trudged along the lanes and in a few minutes came across two separate video stalls.

'Can I have two?' Asa was shifting from anguish to high anxiety in his search, seduced by the images and colours on the boxes. 'I like this one, and this one.' He was skipping a little in his decision making.

'Asa, just choose one,' Matty said. 'Don't be greedy.'

'This one, too?' he asked, not hearing or choosing not to hear. He looked to Claudia for support, and then his eyes darted across the counter, wanting to scoop up the entire stock. His little fingers flapped back and forth, not making fists, but opening and closing as if his palms were on fire.

'You want filim?' the video seller goaded. The sight of Asa dancing and waving, intent on all the merchandise, amused him. 'Come and take it. Choose any one.'

'Really?' Asa screeched. He didn't wait for his father. He grabbed a cassette close to hand and began fingering others on display.

'This one?' the stallholder laughed. 'You like Bombay filim?'

'Noooo!' Asa screamed. '*Lassie!*' His breath was coming fast now and he was beginning to pant.

'Pickin like filim,' the stallholder chuckled, but his eyes had narrowed and he was looking closely at the boy.

'*Bugs Bunny*, too!' Asa pointed aimlessly at the whole display.

'Okay, Asa. Time to go now,' Matty said. The warning note in his voice had disappeared and he was now trying to guide him through the frenzy. 'Which two do you want? Choose quickly and let's go.'

But Asa's fists clenched and unclenched as the hysteria grew. It had gone beyond the issue of videotapes. For a moment, when he opened his mouth there was only silence. Then a wail arrived with such force I flinched. Matty's head seemed to sag and his shoulders slumped. He was so good, so attentive to Asa, it was a shock to see him fold in this manner. He picked up his son and carried him, the little legs jabbing downwards, his arms flailing. It wouldn't be long before his energy unravelled. I paid for two videos and walked with Claudia towards the car.

'It's not so healthy for them to be in the sun too long, without their own agenda, just waiting,' Claudia said in German. 'It builds up tension when they're hyperactive. They need release.'

I looked at her. 'How do you know about it?'

'It's part of my training,' she said. 'Child psychology. But I'm not an expert, by any means. I still have a long way to go.'

'I didn't know what you did,' I said. 'Your work, I mean. Your studies.'

'You didn't ask. Anyway, I haven't qualified yet.'

'What else don't I know about you?' I asked.

She looked at me and smiled and was quiet for a moment. 'Well, when I was maybe four or five, there was another child. A brother. Mum had a baby boy. But he was sick, right from the beginning. In the end he died. He wasn't even a year old.'

We waited for a lorry to trundle past before crossing the road.

'I didn't mean for you to tell me that,' I said. 'Or anything. I'm sorry.'

'I don't mind telling you. It's in the past now. Besides, I don't remember it well.' She waved away the memory as if it didn't mean a thing.

The car doors had been flung wide open. There was still no breeze and the sun had magnified the heat inside. Asa lay dazed on the back seat, his shirt unbuttoned and his sandals removed, sucking at a bottle of water. Matty leaned against the bonnet, a lit cigarette in his hand.

'I thought you'd given up?' I asked, leaning beside him.

He glanced at the cigarette as if it did not belong to him, then tossed it into the ditch. 'I have,' he said. 'We should go now. They'll be waiting for us.' But he didn't move.

# 26

I WOKE EARLY the next morning and watched Claudia as she
slept. There were times when she was still for so long I
was afraid she wouldn't breathe again. It seemed at one
moment she was in deep sleep and the next she was watching
me. We gazed at each other and then my hand began to
rove.

'I have no protection,' I said. 'We've used it all. I should
have thought of it yesterday.'

'It's okay,' she replied. 'But you'll be careful?'

We lay side by side with the temperature of our bodies
raised by the friction of our slow movements. I watched her
watching me. We kissed and held each other, then relaxed,
hardly moving at all. It seemed to go on in a kind of dream,
making us drowsy and careless. The moment was unexpected
and too intense and it was over before I withdrew.

'I'm sorry,' I said. 'I wasn't thinking. I'm really sorry.'

Claudia didn't speak and because I thought she was upset,
I said again, 'I'm sorry. You shouldn't have trusted me. Why
did you trust me when you know how I am?'

'How you are?' she said. 'It was an accident. It's okay.

I'm not blaming you. Look, I'm here as well. You're a funny one.'

I rested on my elbow and looked at her and wondered whether there was ever a time when she was mean and selfish.

'We should go back,' I said. 'There's no point in me staying here any longer than you. My uncle's not going to die tomorrow, and I'll be bored.'

'Bored if he doesn't die?'

'No!' I said, but we were both laughing.


We piled into the station wagon with Aunt Ama behind the wheel. It felt like the excursions we had made in childhood, but now the only child was Asa. We were travelling out of Jos in search of a site not marked on any map. Uncle Raymond and Aunt Ama had discovered it by accident years ago and had not been able to locate it since. Asa slept between Claudia and me, while Peju and Matty sat in the rear. I passed Uncle Raymond my complimentary Bessie Corday cassette.

'The landscape . . . it is very unusual,' Claudia said. Out of town the land was largely devoid of trees, encrusted with bare rocks and gorges.

'We used to be one of the main producers of tin,' Uncle Raymond said, turning to talk to us, 'in all of Africa. In the world, for that matter. Until the Seventies people from overseas used to mine the land. After they left no one bothered to clear up the mess.' He looked out of Aunt Ama's window and pointed. 'You see those hills there? Those are man-made. The craters around them – they're the result of years of careless tin mining. They took what they wanted, and left, but they did not clean up; neither the overseas companies nor our government. The abandoned mines should have been filled and closed down. Now they're polluting the rivers and streams everywhere.'

'Ray is on a committee of retired executives,' Aunt Ama explained. 'They're trying to force the government to take action in order to reverse the environmental damage – the government and the companies concerned.'

'But no one wants to listen.' Uncle Raymond massaged his neck and turned to face the road ahead.

The car swerved onto the Miango road and we began to feel every flaw on the surface, every pothole Aunt Ama failed to avoid.

'Shagari's government refused and now Buhari won't listen. They're telling us to join the War Against Indiscipline while all the time they're lining their own pockets.' The grind of the tyres against the road seemed to reflect Uncle Raymond's emotions.

'But why do the people put up with the corruption?' Claudia asked.

'Well, it's not a government of choice,' Uncle Raymond said. 'It's a military regime, even though everyone was glad to see the last lot go. There was no democracy in it.'

'But people are growing restless again,' Aunt Ama said. 'Every day there are rumours of another coup.'

'Coup, coup, coup!' Peju complained from the back of the car. 'Only God can save us from all this nonsense!'

'Look at the aeroplane!' Asa called from his half-slumber.

In the scrub a third of a mile beyond the road, a small propeller plane had come to rest. It seemed improbable, this symbol of technology in the midst of this wilderness. As we drew closer we could make out figures: two or three white men and a clutch of herdsmen swathed in cloth. Cattle grazed in the scrub for hundreds of metres in all directions. A few lean cows had wandered onto the road.

'What are they doing out there?' Matty asked.

'Evangelizing,' Peju said. 'Bringing Christianity to the people of the bush. You see them from time to time, but they don't come to town so much any more.'

'But it's the Eighties,' I said. 'I didn't know that still happened.'

'No, it goes on quietly,' Aunt Ama said. 'And it will continue.'

As we drove past, the missionaries glanced towards us, then looked back to their flock. Bessie sang *The Oyster and the Deep Blue Sea*. I remembered how tiny she was, a woman who hardly spoke, and now her rich voice filled the car.

Single flame trees burst into view by the side of the road, their brilliant red flowers rivalling the intensity of the sun. As we climbed higher we could sketch out the pattern of the hills and the expanse of land in the distance.

We passed through a village – a dozen mud-spattered buildings on either side of the road. There was no market visible, only a small wooden hut with soft-drink bottles and tubes of sweets displayed on its front ledge. I could see no vendor. Villagers appeared intermittently along the roadside. A woman carried a baby on her back held in place with a wrapper, a tray of produce balanced on her head. Her movements were steady and she did not seem burdened by her load. I remembered a moment when I was a child, playing with our neighbours in the garden of my parents' house: a woman walking along the road, beside the garden, carrying a tray on her head, calling out 'Fine bread, fine bread!' in a shrill, tinny voice. After listening to her chant, the words began to lose their meaning for us. We started to taunt her as she passed. 'Fine bread, fine bread!' we called after her, mimicking her sharp nasal whine. My mother emerged from the house at the sound of our voices. She looked at the retreating figure carrying the bread loaves, then turned to us. 'Be kind to her,' she said, but without anger. I felt ashamed, more so than if she had been annoyed, had scolded us and told us to stop. She was wearing a pale yellow shift dress, bleached by the sun and repeated launderings. Her hair was wrapped in long straight plaits that rose from her head like a crown of black quills. She was smiling then. I could see her now as clearly as I had seen her then and it startled me. I had thought of the past as something that could be wiped, sluiced away by the wash of the present.

In a moment – less than ten seconds – we had entered and left the village, a whole world in which people existed. They were born, they grew and then they departed. I thought of my own world, in Kreuzberg, of Frau Lieser and B, Tunde, Marie, Arî, Clariss, the others. How far apart life could be. The streets of Berlin were more familiar to me now than anything here, and it discomfited me.

Aunt Ama slowed down beside an old couple walking towards the village we had passed. They did not pay attention to us as we stopped, but when Uncle Raymond called to them, they hurried to the car. He spoke to them in English, then in Hausa and Yoruba, but they didn't understand. The old man's eyes were clouded with cataracts; the old woman held on to his elbow. Aunt Ama leaned across and mentioned a name. The old woman shook her head, but the man began to mutter and argue with her. His companion motioned for us to continue in the same direction, flinging her arm at the road ahead. She spoke, but her words were lost to all of us.

'When we were young engineering graduates,' Uncle

Raymond said. 'We used to travel all over the country, working on different projects. These people here, they were completely cut off from the rest of the land. All over Nigeria there were people, communities like this. They had no idea they were part of something larger. Their world was only where they lived.'

I looked behind at the old couple as the car sped away. The woman was still holding on to the man, but it wasn't clear who was supporting whom.

'There was no road as such,' Uncle Raymond continued. 'They used to live below the ground; in dug-out caves. Naked. And it was cold then. Not like it is now, with global warming or whatever. You would see them walking by, completely naked, with ashy skin. The children too. We didn't know what language they spoke.'

'Who's naked?' Asa asked, rousing now. He had been leaning against me, and now my shirt creases were outlined on his face.

'No one's naked,' Matty said. 'We were only talking.'

'Where are we going?' Asa asked.

'Over there.' Aunt Ama pointed. A boulder the size of an apartment block lay a few hundred metres off the right-hand side of the road. She turned and drove along a dusty track, bordered by wispy bushes, until we came to a clearing. There were no signs of life: no cars, no sounds, no litter.

'Time to walk,' Uncle Raymond announced.

'Walk? Where to?' Matty frowned. 'Up there?'

'It's not far,' Uncle Raymond replied. 'I will be seventy-one this year. If I can climb, then anyone can.'

Matty looked across at Peju, who only patted her stomach and said, 'Oya now, let's go.'

We shared out the bags of food and drink between us and

began the gradual ascent. The sun disappeared for a moment and returned. Then minutes later, it was replaced by vengeful clouds. Asa raced forward, then ran back to meet us. He asked, 'Is it night-time now?' looking up at the sky, and ran on before awaiting a reply.

'We should take shelter,' Aunt Ama said. 'It will rain soon, I'm sure of it.'

We waited beneath an overhang of rock for several minutes. Peju had found the climb straightforward, but Uncle Raymond leaned against the stone, breathless, and closed his eyes.

'We should go back,' Matty said.

'Go back? For what?' Uncle Raymond's eyelids flicked open. 'We're going to the top, isn't it, Asa?'

'Yes, Grandy.' He reached out for the old man's hand. The uncle, the nephew, the nephew's child. My brother had clung to Uncle Raymond as if our father had never been. It had appalled and moved me in the same breath, this need.

The crash and sparkle of the storm drew near and when we thought it must surely rain, no rain fell. The first stones bounced playfully on the outskirts of our shelter. Asa reached out to retrieve them before they melted, and cried when they disappeared. Then, as if a pillow of sky had split, the hail came down without the deliberation of rain. It simply poured as if it had been tipped out. Claudia shouted at me, but I could only see the movements of her mouth. Asa fled to his father, looking away from the tumult. We all shrank back. The noise was in everything and everywhere. In less than five minutes it was over and the storm had moved on.

We edged out, away from the protection of the rock. All around us – the granite boulders, the cinnamon earth, the sparse vegetation – the land had blanched, blanketed in a thick layer of hailstones. For a moment we could only stand and survey the white landscape before the hailstones began to melt. As the clouds retreated, the intensity of the sun and the warmth of the earth removed all trace of the storm. By the time we reached the summit of the hill, the granite surface was almost dry.

'We made it!' Aunt Ama cried. 'I thought we would never find this place again.'

'We discovered it by accident years ago,' Uncle Raymond explained. He inhaled deeply and let out the air in degrees. 'We've tried to return here before, but we always get lost.' He looked round, his hands resting on his stomach. The incline had not been far or steep, but the short walk had exhausted him, even with the interlude of hail.

'It's further than I remember,' Aunt Ama said.

'I can't recall driving so far last time,' Uncle Raymond concurred. 'Maybe we took a wrong turning, eh? Anyway, let us sit and rest.'

What seemed like a precipice from a distance was merely a change of direction; the rock continued at a downward gradient, rolling gently to a meagre lake at the bottom.

We sat looking down at the water, at the hills on one side, the undulating land stretching out on the other. A few clouds skittered by, but we were soothed by the warmth of the sun. Asa skipped down the boulder towards the lake, then seemed to lose confidence and pattered back. Peju and Claudia dished out fried rice and peppered chicken, while Matty and Aunt Ama leaned back against the rock.

Uncle Raymond kept an eye on Asa as he fled down the slope again, then called out when he thought he had gone too far. Uncle Raymond had softened with age or perhaps the change was in me? I had tried to get away, but where was I going? Was there sense in any of it? Aunt Ama and Uncle Raymond were older now, more fragile with age. I had hardened my heart for too long.

'How did you find this place?' Claudia asked. 'It's so far – in the middle of nowhere.'

'Well, you know, I can't remember,' Aunt Ama replied. 'I don't know what it was we were doing in this area then. We discovered it by accident, isn't it Ray?'

'Actually . . . no – it wasn't completely by accident. It was your father's discovery,' Uncle Raymond said. He was looking at me. 'He brought your mother here before you or Matthew were born. I can't even remember whether they were already married that first time, but they came several times in their lives. Oh, yes. It wasn't so accessible in those days – we didn't have proper roads – but there was a way from Jos. It was a long, long journey in those days.'

I drew closer then because, after all, I was greedy for more.

'That's right!' Aunt Ama said. 'We came one time. Later. A group – about eight of us. Kunle was three or so, Matthew – you were just a baby. I always thought that was some-where else.' She was remembering something that was half forgotten, with the surprise fresh news brings.

'There was very little water – like today – when we came that time,' Uncle Raymond said. 'In the rainy season, the lake stretches all around, even to where we parked the car. We were afraid to enter the water, except for Kunle – and your father, of course. Only the two of them swam. We were sitting further down there. We watched them, but we didn't even get our feet wet, remember?'

'I don't remember any swimming,' Aunt Ama laughed. 'Who would swim in that dirty water?'

'Exactly what we said then,' her husband continued. 'But

my sister said that they might not see this place again, that they would regret it if they didn't swim. So they went ahead and swam. And she was right.'

No one spoke for a while. I could see him then, Raymond as a boy, his little sister, hand in hand, fiercely protective. I saw how much he still missed my mother. I wondered whether the landscape had altered at all since my parents were here, whether it recorded the passage of time. It was strange and comforting to know I was seeing what they had seen, sitting on the same rock, viewing everything that lay between here and the horizon.

'Are we going swimming?' Asa asked. He looked from his father to Peju to Uncle Raymond.

'No, not today,' Matty replied. I was sure he was about to say 'the water's dirty', but he did not say anything else.

Asa stood up and looked shyly at Claudia, avoiding his parents' eyes. He began to edge away from them.

'You want me to come with you?' Claudia asked.

He nodded, but didn't speak. I pointed towards the lake with my chin, and Claudia and I walked down the boulder while Asa darted ahead. He stopped halfway and waited for us to catch up before resuming his sprint. The distance between us grew shorter as we reached the water's edge. By the time we arrived at the lake, he was standing behind us.

'You won't swim?' Claudia asked. 'I thought you wanted to go in the water?'

Asa shook his head. He picked up a pebble and threw it as far as he was able. It fell, at most, two metres away from him, making a dull splash.

'Asa's afraid of water,' I explained. 'Wild horses couldn't drag him in there.'

'It does not look so clean,' Claudia said. 'Perhaps it's not safe.'

We walked along the perimeter of the lake, skimming stones across the water.

'Is it hurting them?' Asa asked.

'Hurting who?' I said.

'The dead boys, in the water?'

'The dead boys?' Claudia frowned.

I had to think for a moment before I remembered the afternoon at the Serpentine. 'No, Asa,' I said. 'There aren't any dead children in the water. I was just joking. Do you understand?'

'But where did they go?' he asked. 'Did someone take them away?'

'No, Asa. I was only joking. I was telling lies. Like the boy in the film – *Pinocchio*. Remember? It isn't true.' I had a fear the lie would haunt him for the rest of his childhood.

'No children are in the water, Asa,' Claudia said. 'There is nothing here. You must not be afraid. Look!' She kicked off her slippers and waded into the lake ankle deep. She scooped up a handful of pebbles and skimmed them, one by one, across the water. 'Now you try.'

Asa drew back his arm and threw. The stone soared higher this time and fell heavily into the water near the edge of the shore.

'You see,' Claudia shrugged. 'No one is here. No one gets hurt.'

'No one gets hurt,' Asa echoed.

We ambled along the shoreline and when we could walk no further, turned back to the hill. Asa grew tired halfway up the slope, so I carried him piggyback to the summit. As we approached I examined their shapes: my aunt, my uncle, my brother, Peju lying back against the rock. I thought, as my mother had once thought, that I might never return here. But I would remember it.

# 27

I HAD EXPECTED things to change, but life remained much the same as always. Frau Bowker scowled at me, forgetting who I was, until Frau Lieser, in a rust-coloured cardigan, called out a muted, 'Hallo!' from behind her closed windows. It was cooler now. Summer was fading fast.

'Can't stop to talk.' Clariss strode past wearing white flannel trousers, a cream silk blouse and an ivory headscarf. Her plimsolls slapped clumsily against the pavement.

'Jogging's no good,' she said. 'My legs are too long. They're too beautiful to be ruined. Next week, I'm taking up karate.'

'You could come swimming with me,' I suggested.

'I couldn't do that,' she grimaced. 'Naked bodies, kids, old folks, freaks – all in the same tub. Uh, uh. Hell, no. Not me, sweetpea.'

'Why all this exercise all of a sudden?'

'This isn't exercise, sugar. This is self-preservation. A girl has to protect herself. Look what happened to Henkelmann.'

'What happened?'

She gave me a look. 'You're kidding, right?' She was all lips and legs and flailing arms. Her bright pink lipstick seemed manufactured for a child.

'No, *really,* Clariss. I've been away.'

'Well, hon,' she began. She took on the self-important air of a person with news. 'Someone came forward – the killer's wife or the girlfriend, some lady. Anyway, she wanted the reward. And who can blame a girl – a whole bag of cash or a psycho boyfriend? Not a difficult choice. Turns out he'd been visiting the lanes in Lübars. Car cruising, apparently. Supposed to be big out there. News to me, and I know everything.'

'Clariss, what happened to Henkelmann?'

'Well, hold on honey. I'm getting to that. As I said, Henk's in his car. He meets someone. They go into a field to do the nasty, and bingo – the guy's some psycho killer. Splits Henkelmann's head wide open with some sort of machine.'

'A machine? I thought it was a wheel lock?'

'Yeah, that's it. How d'you know?'

'It was in the papers . . . just after he died.'

'It was? But if they knew . . .'

'They didn't know *who* did it. Only *how.*'

'Oh,' she said.

'But . . . why?' I asked. 'People don't go round killing for no reason whatsoever.'

'Whatever,' Clariss sighed. 'Me, I'm sick of hearing it day in, day out, like there's nothing going on in the rest of the world. He was out cruising, he picks up a maniac, and now he's dead. Shit happens. "Wicked 'ole world", my grandma used to say.'

She glanced at her fingernails and winced as if they were no longer there, then looked up and waved to Frau Bowker who was still standing guard at the window.

\* \* \*

I arrived early at *Zip* for a meeting with Thomas. The Bessie Corday issue had worked out better than expected; they had used my portrait of her on the cover and sales were higher than average, although there was probably no connection between the two. Thomas was eager to involve me in a more structured schedule.

'At least until Christmas,' he said. 'You can commit to that?'

'Of course,' I said, even though I was still working for Marie.

There was a diary of confirmed assignments for the Christmas season and a loose line-up of concerts and festivals in the run up to the holiday, some of which would be dropped, others shared among staff and freelancers. There was the opportunity to travel to the Dominican Republic in the new year, but that was still a long way off. Whether I was in the city or halfway across the world, I was to remain in constant communication. Telephone and facsimile numbers of where I could be reached were a priority. People had been fired for proving elusive, Thomas said. 'I run a tight ship and people think I'm a cunt, but we win awards. I'm not in the award-winning business, mind, but I don't tolerate bad behaviour. You understand?'

I envisaged running battles ahead.

On Sunday I caught the S-Bahn to Wannsee, then took a taxi to the sanatorium. I asked a staff member where I might find Vanessa Schlegel, and a woman walking past overheard.

'Schlegel? She went for a walk.' She pointed through an open window. 'Out the back, over there.'

I left the building and walked around its perimeter. There was a neat herb garden at the front, and acres of fields and forest behind. I could see moving figures in the distance, but

I didn't know where to begin. At the back, on a wide terrace, people sat in quiet groups or on their own.

I waited on the steps at the edge of the terrace and closed my eyes against the sun. The only audible sounds were the cries of children playing on the grass. I wondered about them, the homes they came from, their individual stories: a drug-addled mother, an alcoholic father, a child who had lost the desire to eat. Did their laughter and games camouflage carefully concealed horrors? A girl called out, 'Claus, stop that!' and I remembered the Rio, which I hadn't visited since leaving for Jos three weeks ago. I thought how strange it was being back already, the anticipated trauma of the visit receded now, in another kind of existence, a fresh catalogue of anxieties.

'Look at him – not a care in the world!' a voice called.

I opened my eyes and watched Frau Schlegel and Claudia walking towards me; it was like a shaft of sunlight filtering through rain clouds, the feeling I had. I must have loved her then.

'I couldn't find you, so I waited here,' I replied.

'We've been walking all over,' Frau Schlegel said. 'I must know every square centimetre of this place. Why don't we sit and have coffee?'

Claudia chose a nearby table, but Frau Schlegel pointed to the side of the building. 'Over there,' she said, 'is better.' There were chairs at the edge of the terrace, further away from other people.

We drank tea and coffee and fruit juice, and I thought how much a beer would suit the late afternoon. I wondered at the strength of my desire in a place where alcohol was forbidden, how much more ferocious that need would be for the patients here.

'They never leave you alone,' Frau Schlegel said. 'All day

long they shove you in groups. You do exercises, lectures, counselling, all sorts of programmes. You go back to your room at the end of the day, forgetting there's someone else there, sharing your space. In my case, Frieda Meisner. Drug addict, or used to be. There's simply no privacy. None at all.' She retrieved a packet of cigarettes from her bag, tapped it on the table top before opening it. 'Still . . . every day is a new day. You have to remember that. Sometimes it feels like a victory just waking up; the previous day has been and gone, and you're all right. You're getting stronger. Apart from this.' She waved her cigarette in the direction of the occupied tables.

'Couldn't you ask for your own room?' I said. 'After all, you've paid enough to be here. You should at least be allowed a few comforts.'

'That's what I said, but no.' Frau Schlegel waved away the smoke in front of her face. 'It's all part of the treatment, they claim. Everyone has to share: rooms, responsibilities, stories. If they see you wandering off on your own, they'll come and grab you. It's hardly the real world.'

'Mum, remember there are only two more weeks of this, then it's over,' Claudia said. 'Two weeks isn't that long, is it?'

'Claudi, every day is like two weeks in here. A lifetime. You can't *go* anywhere. There's nothing to read apart from tattered newspapers and old books. There are fights over what to watch on TV. You look at the clock; you realize only one minute has passed. It's excruciating. And the things people say here, in front of other people. It's truly shocking. I could never be like that. People saying terrible things about what happened to them when they were young, what happens to them now, what they do. That Frieda, she sold her body for drugs, you know. Can you imagine! I'm living with a prostitute.' She turned to check no one had heard, then whispered, 'She's had children who have gone into care because of her. I don't know if she even thinks about them. And I'm sure I haven't heard the end of it.' She sank back in her chair and took a long drag on her cigarette. 'Listen to me going on. I'm so sorry to hear about your uncle, Vincent. It must be hard being here, knowing he's not well.'

'No, it's all right. He's not critical at the moment,' I said. 'But I think about him – about both of them – all the time. I always have, I suppose. We never used to get on, you see, and I could never understand why he didn't like me. He always loved my brother.'

'Families,' Frau Schlegel laughed. 'Like me and Julius. I was always the favourite. Father adored me. Until I met *your* father, that is.' She turned to Claudia. 'Then I understood what it was like to be on the outside. Only Mother came to the wedding, and you should have seen her – stiff as an ironing board. Julius got her good and drunk on the day, though, and she softened up a bit. But my father . . . we didn't speak again, not properly. Not as before. Always, there was this awkwardness. And he rarely phoned. But he loved Claudi. He always played with you when we visited. You were his joy. Maybe if he had lived, things might have improved. Now it's too late. He'd die if he could see me in here, though!' She clucked at the thought.

A middle-aged man with yellow shoulder-length hair and red spectacles approached our table. His scalp shone pink along his centre parting and his hair swung back and forth each time he bobbed his head. 'We'll see you at ten tomorrow, I trust, Vanessa?' He shoved his hands deep into his blazer pockets, then withdrew them almost instantly.

'I expect so.' Frau Schlegel squinted up at him.

There was a moment of silence as he stood there, his hands scampering from his hair to the pockets and back again.

282

Frau Schlegel continued to stare at him. 'This is Claudia and Vincent,' she said. 'Ulrich.'

'Oh, so great to meet you,' Ulrich said, his head bobbing enthusiastically. He reached out and shook our hands in turn and beamed.

'Yes, well I'm sure you're very busy, Ulrich . . . and as you can see, we *are* in the middle of something, you understand.'

'Oh, of course. I'm sorry. How silly of me,' Ulrich said, backing quickly away. 'Another time then, Vanessa. So good to meet you both.' He waved, then hurried down the steps.

'Ulrich!' she laughed. 'You see what I have to put up with? He's completely mad!'

'But he seemed sweet to me,' Claudia said.

'Oh, he's not so bad. He just pesters me relentlessly. I came here for rest and relaxation, not romance. You know what someone said to me the other day? We had a group exercise – out there on the grass. These two women were looking at me, whispering. Then one of them was paired off with me – it was a game of trust, but I wouldn't have trusted her to throw away my rubbish. She says, "You're Vanessa Schlegel, aren't you?" What could I say? I couldn't deny it in a place like this. Where would I run to? She says, "Hannelore Kohl wears your designs, *and* Lady Di. I could never afford a pair, but I love your shoes. I've got clippings from all the magazines." Afterwards she runs back to her little friend and off they go, tittering like school-girls. How can you trust anyone in a place like this? The Chancellor's wife – of all the people she could think of.'

'You should have ignored her,' I said, 'or denied it.'

'What's the point?' She shook her head. 'The whole thing's exhausting and besides, I'm tired of running.'

Claudia chewed her lower lip and tried to smile. 'So, what else has been happening since I've been away?'

'Well, Edward is in charge, at work. Edward's my right-hand man, Vincent. At my company. I just hope the responsibility doesn't go to his head or there'll be trouble when I get back. Ah, and I did save you some papers – some stuff about the Henkelmann affair. Messy business. I'll just be a minute.' She went inside to fetch the articles.

Claudia put her elbows on the table, rubbed her fingers against her temples and sighed.

'She's doing all right,' I said. 'Don't worry.'

'I know. She's trying.' She looked directly at me. 'Don't say anything, but this isn't the first time it's happened. She's done this before and it didn't work.' She couldn't stop the words now that she had begun. '"The people are strange, they're going to tell the papers, the treatment's all wrong." Always the same excuses. It's as if she doesn't really want to get well, or she does but it involves too much effort. If you don't really want to change, well, no one can force you, can they?'

Frau Schlegel returned and dumped a bundle of newspapers on the table. 'They're from all over,' she said. 'I've marked them all. You can tell how bored I've been.'

Police investigating the mysterious circumstances surrounding the death of SPD politician Heinrich Henkelmann last night ended months of speculation by formally charging a Schöneberg dental technician with the murder.

'Dental technician!' Frau Schlegel said. 'It's almost comical.'

The man, named yesterday as Karl Kessler, 43, was placed under police custody for the brutal slaying of Henkelmann, after his wife, Annika Kessler, came forward with fresh information about the case that has baffled the authorities and stunned the city.

'What about this?' Claudia separated another newspaper from the pile.

The full extent of the tragedy has yet to be uncovered as criminal investigators piece together details. These are the known facts: at 8.05 a.m., 6 July 1985, farmer's wife Agnes Bischof called emergency services in a state of distress after discovering the deceased's body while walking the family Alsatian in the picturesque fields of Lübars in an area frequented by sexual adventurers.

'It's not something I ever expected to witness,' Bischof later told reporters. 'I didn't go too near, though, but I knew something was very wrong. You couldn't tell it was a body even from a short distance away – it was so badly beaten – I couldn't make out what it was. Effie was barking . . . out of control. That's not like her. I couldn't quieten her . . . I'd never seen a dead body before – I didn't go too near . . . The police, they arrived in no time, though. Very prompt. I was very impressed. It's not so easy to find us out here. It's horrible that anything like this can happen.'

Sources close to Henkelmann's wife, Eva, suggest their 16-year-marriage was in a process of reconciliation – there had been reports that the couple had been experiencing marital difficulties for a number of years. Police have exhibited an instrument – a car anti-theft device – believed to be identical to the weapon used in the July attack. Forensic tests have confirmed that blood traces taken from the interior of Kessler's Volkswagen Passat match Henkelmann's.

'The whole thing's a bit gruesome,' Claudia said. 'It's enough to kill someone, but to hack away until the head is just . . . just pulp. That's really sick.'

'And since when has Lübars become a hotbed for sex?' I asked. 'I thought it was all farmland and the odd village.'

'A man can go there and take a lover, day or night, they say. If you know where to look,' Frau Schlegel explained. 'Like in the supermarket – you browse, you like, you select. But there's no charge. At least I'm receiving an education; ask Frieda – she tells me all about it.'

'I still don't understand why he was killed,' I said.

'They're not sure, either,' Frau Schlegel shrugged. 'All sorts of possibilities are flying about: political assassination, homophobia, blackmail. I read somewhere that Kessler's been detained before, for assault. Frieda thinks the man's a mental case.'

'For someone you don't like, you and Frieda seem to have a lot to talk about,' Claudia said.

'But there's nothing else to do! At least she's good for some gossip. When I get out of this place I'll never see her again. She thinks we'll continue to meet outside, but she's mistaken. Look, there she is!' She waved to a couple walking towards the side entrance of the building. Frieda's wavy auburn hair fell to her shoulder blades. She wore a grey polo-neck sweater and a long chocolate-brown skirt. She looked more like a chic Wilmersdorf housewife than the slattern Frau Schlegel had described.

# 28

D IETER WAS STANDING at the bar in the Rio that evening. Claus said, 'Vincent, you've been away, don't think I haven't noticed. I had my suspicions for a while, but they've caught the Lübars murderer, so I'm giving you the benefit of the doubt.'

'Shut up and pour,' I said. 'You're well, I trust?'

'Who me? Nothing changes; how could I be otherwise? This is Martine, by the way.' He nodded towards a woman standing next to Dieter: blue beret, pink sweater, brown leather trousers. 'She's a dancer, but she won't tell us where she performs, will you?'

She smiled as Claus made the introductions.

Dieter and I carried the drinks back to the table where Tunde, Clariss, B and Angelika were sitting.

'Who's the chick at the bar?' Tunde asked, peering at Martine.

Dieter proceeded with the details.


I didn't stay long. I needed to make a telephone call. Ever since Frau Schlegel had returned home, Claudia and I had spent less and less time together. The decision to leave the sanatorium prematurely had been Frau Schlegel's. Everyone concerned had tried to persuade her to finish the treatment, but she had been adamant. Now Claudia felt unable to leave her mother alone for too long in case she relapsed. An illness like that was vampiric; it drained you. It had cost Claudia her health and her freedom and there was a part of Frau Schlegel I could not help but despise.

I sat with the phone in my lap and dialled slowly. When I heard her voice my heart leapt.

'Vincent!' she cried. There was no bitterness in her tone.

'Hello, Luce,' I said. 'What's happening?'

'Oh, this and that. I've only just got in. This is a surprise. I'm *so* glad you've phoned.'

'I thought I'd call. I just wanted to hear your voice again; it's so good to hear your voice, Luce.' The words were running out of me, unrestrained.

'It's a good thing you did call,' Lucille said. 'If you'd left it another few weeks, I wouldn't have been here.'

'Why – you moving?'

'To Westbourne Park. I'm finally buying a place.'

'That's great – you always wanted to buy, didn't you?'

'A bit more than I'd planned to spend, though. It needs *a lot* of work, but it's a fair size and there's a garden. Bags of potential. And you? How are you?'

'Good, good. Still in the same place. Work's picking up, though. I went to visit my aunt and uncle.'

'Yes. I saw Peju – we bumped into each other in Tesco the other day. I'm glad that you've seen them again. Peju said you all had a good time out there.'

I wondered whether she had heard about Claudia.

There was a moment when I thought everything might

work out: Frau Schlegel would stay sober; Lucille would come back to me; Claudia would find someone else to love, someone kinder, less muddled. But I knew I simply wanted things to revert to the way they had been, for certain events never to have taken place. And I realized that was something I had always done; flee from an unmanageable present to an imagined perfect past.

She said, 'I'm going to live with Colin, Vincent. We're buying together. I wasn't going to tell you, but you phoned . . . I think you should know.'

'Oh, Colin . . . that's sensible. The lawyer, right?' I said. The rubber ball of my heart came to a standstill. 'Anyway, the weather's changing now . . . we had a good summer.' I looked out of the window into the still night air. A woman was reading to a child tucked up in bed in the building opposite my kitchen. I didn't know what I was saying.

'Yes, we had a good one too,' Lucille said. 'Vincent, are you still there?'

I said I was.

'Vincent, there was no need to tell you about any of this, but you phoned. It's not like me to hide things, you know that.'

'I know, I know. Listen, Luce, I have to go.' I couldn't get enough air into my lungs.

'Don't be like that, Vincent. Talk to me. Just say what's on your mind.'

'What's there to talk about? There's nothing I can say that's going to change things, so what's the point?'

'Why did you phone, then?'

I hung up and lay on the linoleum with my eyes wide open. My head throbbed. The glare from the bulb was like car headlights on a country road, but the effort to move was too great.

289

When the phone rang I leapt for it. I was certain I would hear Lucille's voice, but instead it was Tunde.

'We're going to Jacaranda!' he shouted. There was a clamour of voices and music in the background. 'Dieter says some dancer was asking for you – Martine – she's coming too. You want to meet us here or head straight for the club? We're leaving in thirty minutes.'

'Okay, I'll see you at the Rio.'

I washed my face and changed into my Hawaiian shirt and baggy chinos. A night of revelry seemed like a godsend. When the phone rang again I did not think.

'You're in, thank goodness,' Claudia said. 'I tried before, but it was busy. I can't find Mum. I've looked everywhere.'

I wandered into the hallway searching for my left shoe. 'What do you mean, you can't find her?'

'I fell asleep and when I woke up, she was gone.' She had begun to cry.

'Hey – wait, wait, wait . . . how long has she been missing?'

'Nearly two hours now. I wasn't worried at first. I thought she'd come back soon. I don't know what to do.'

'But . . . she's an adult. She can go out if she wants to. Maybe she's gone to a friend's house or for a walk.' I didn't sound convinced myself. 'You've checked the building?'

'I've looked everywhere. The car's still here, but her coat's gone.'

I yanked the telephone cable into the bedroom as I searched for my shoe, and knelt on the floor and squinted under the bed. 'She didn't leave a message?' I was thinking only of my own desire for drunkenness, for oblivion. I shifted my dirty clothes and my suitcase, still half-unpacked and saw only balls of dust and dirt rolling away from me. I sat up, still kneeling.

There was the canary-yellow shoe Frau Schlegel had given me sitting on the window ledge.

'No message. Nothing. She could have gone anywhere.' She didn't mention what she was most afraid of.

I crouched down, my forehead against the bed and closed my eyes. The dancer with the blue beret, the possibilities at the Jacaranda, a night of abandon ahead. In the end, what did it mean?

A weekday night. Zehlendorf was deserted. There was no litter, no anarchists loitering on the streets. Kreuzberg was like a circus on speed compared to this. Zehlendorf felt safe, but desolate. I couldn't imagine Frau Schlegel wandering about on her own.

As I approached the building a battered Citroën pulled up.

'Vincent – what are you doing here at this hour?' Frau Schlegel called.

I peered at the vehicle, at a bearded man behind the wheel.

'Claudia said you'd disappeared. She was upset. She didn't know what to do.'

'You didn't tell her?' the man asked.

'My God! Claudi. I completely forgot. I didn't think – she was fast asleep.' She held a cigarette away from her face and looked up at the balcony. Claudia was leaning against the railing, looking down at us. She didn't move. For a moment no one spoke.

'I should go now, Gaspar,' Frau Schlegel said. 'Thank you for all your help.'

'No thanks needed,' he replied. 'Only remember what we talked about. Patience.'

She nodded and emerged slowly from the car. 'We were driving,' Frau Schlegel said as we approached the building. 'It was easier than sitting still. I couldn't sit any longer. I needed ... movement. Sometimes I get so agitated. What must she think of me?'

'She was worried, that's all,' I said. I couldn't elaborate, could not say what had been at the forefront of our minds: that she had gone to the nearest bar and ordered a double vodka and then another, and had lost herself in drink.

Frau Schlegel headed straight for the balcony to speak to Claudia. How did it feel to be mothered by a daughter who needed mothering herself?

I went into the kitchen to make coffee – a kitchen for a large family, with table and chairs and a vast cooking range capable of conjuring a feast.

'I'm sorry you had to come all this way,' Frau Schlegel said as they returned from outside. 'I felt ... not so strong. That's how it was. I had to go for help – Gaspar heads our meetings. He helped me to ... to calm down a little. I've been trying to keep busy, but it creeps back again ... work, worries, everything. It's all my fault. I've been neglectful.'

'It was no trouble,' I said. 'Besides, I like coming here.' And I realized, as I said it, that I did after all.

'Don't worry, Mum,' Claudia said. 'There's no point in worrying now.' But her face was drawn and pale.

Her mother nodded slowly. 'One day at a time, they say. We have to remember that.'

'You look like you've been to a party.' Claudia turned to me.

'Sorry?'

'Your clothes,' she said.

'No,' I laughed. 'Not really a party. Just . . . it doesn't matter now.'

I remembered the dancer, Martine, the prospect of a night of pleasure. A drifting into the unknown. It seemed so easy to swerve off the ledge, down the cliff face, without apparent thought. Life seemed a process of maintaining equilibrium, from tipping too far in either direction, from inertia to absolute chaos. Often it was easier to allow things to develop at their own pace, with their own agenda, so that nothing and everything was culpable. It was a way to manage without making sense of anything, a habit as addictive as any drug, as necessary as sleep.

# 29

F RAU LIESER FELL the second week in September. A warm
spell floated in – a scattering of days – before being
chased away by an autumnal breeze. No one trusted the
Indian summer – we kept our sweaters and umbrellas close
to hand – and it was gone before it could be fully appreci-
ated. Frau Lieser had been mopping the stairs, eight steps
from the landing. She tripped on her own foot, the right
playing hide and seek with the left, spraining her wrist,
twisting an ankle, her soft, ageing body bruising easily as
overripe fruit.

Ezmîr Özdemi fell the very next day. Eight floors this time.
His body split like a dropped watermelon. He had not fallen,
of course; he had gone of his own volition. There was a
piece in *Der Tagesspiegel – Asylum Seeker Leaps to Death*
– but it was tucked in the centre, in a column so small it
was easily missed. He jumped at the conclusion to an interview with immigration officers that had not gone in his
favour. It was one of the warm, floating days; he ran through
a wide-open window. I thought as I read the piece I could
see his soul drifting one way, heavenward, the shell of him

racing the other. A cheerful man. I recognized his photograph; I had taken it, after all. Arî's one-eyed compatriot. I remembered the hostel of only a few weeks ago, the men on the bunk beds, the Somali family, subjects in my portfolio. There was a burial shortly after the event. Arî left his apartment for several days and when he came back he did not speak to any of us, only to Frau Lieser, whom he visited in hospital. He told no one where he had been. He went out and returned, but he seemed angry and afraid.

Frau Bowker visited our building every day now. She flung open Frau Lieser's front windows when the weather turned mild. Usually she stared wretchedly behind the panes, clinging to Schnapps. Once, when returning from a meeting at *Zip*, I spotted her sentinel form gazing into the street. She had already dashed into the hall by the time I reached for my key.

'It's you . . . I thought perhaps it was Marianne,' she lied. She glanced over my shoulder theatrically, as if Frau Lieser was hiding behind me, and said, 'There's tea and milk. The milk mustn't be wasted. I have much too much to think about. Sit anywhere; just don't sit in Marianne's chair. She'll be back any minute, and what would she think, me entertaining all and sundry, morning, noon and night? Silence Schnapps!'

I had no choice but to enter the fussy minefield and make small talk, while Schnapps pattered between kitchen and sitting room, utterly bewildered. She attempted a couple of feeble yaps, then a low growl, which fizzled into a whine, but her mistress only ignored her. In a moment she lay on the rug and focused on nothing, confused and defeated.

'A few more days and she'll be back,' I said. Clariss and I had visited Frau Lieser in hospital the day of the accident.

Now it took all of Frau Bowker's reserves to prevent herself scaling three flights of stairs in order to engage Clariss who seemed to have become her confidante. She was lonely; she missed her old friend, we could see that clearly. Perhaps her panic-stricken features bore witness to a terror of permanently losing Frau Lieser.

Clariss tried to stay away from the building until she was sure Frau Bowker had left for the day, but often she was caught out when the old woman visited at odd hours. Frau Bowker spoke to anyone now – Arî, Dieter, even Caroline whose cold look rivalled her own hateful glares. We were all unnerved by her need; we trusted her more when she had been cruel and cunning.


One night I was woken by a telephone call. 'We have a new government!' Uncle Raymond's voice was thin and distant. 'Again!'

'When did this happen?' I shouted back. It occurred to me that I too might sound stretched and far away.

'This morning, or yesterday! I'm not sure. We are under curfew. Did you see it on TV?'

'No! I don't have a television. I didn't hear it on the news, though. No one's said anything!'

'Oh.' He sounded disappointed. 'Anyway, it's normal. It's what we are used to. Don't worry! I wanted to let you know that we are all right. I spoke to Roli and Kayode in New York just now. Only Bunmi I can't reach. Imagine, I can call you, but I can't even reach Lagos. Your aunty wants to . . .' We were cut off. I listened for a while in case the connection returned. I hung up and waited ten minutes, but he didn't ring back. I phoned Tunde.

'Yeah, I heard,' he said. 'This afternoon. Non-stop palava, eh? Listen, Linda wants to party. You want to come out tonight?'

I hung up and phoned Matty, then dialled Uncle Raymond's number, without success. I tried eleven times before I slept. He had said not to worry, but I could not help thinking of the two elderly people alone in the large bungalow.

When it began again it was silent or noisy, or both. I don't remember. Perhaps we only noticed the absence of things – words and phrases and gestures we had begun to rely on. Maybe it accrued gradually; no one was fully aware. Frau Schlegel fell – it seemed a time for falling – but Claudia didn't discover until the next day when her mother limped home from work. She said it was 'nothing' – she had slipped on a polystyrene food container 'some fool' had discarded in the street. It didn't matter. It provided the impetus for her to draft a new kind of sole – a combination of sports and formal footwear. Something to focus on, she said. Ideas were gathering and ideas kept her occupied.

And when I called Claudia one evening and Frau Schlegel answered to say her daughter was at a friend's house, her words and sentences dragged. I asked if everything was all right.

'I'm just tired, Vincent. We're launching a new product tomorrow. I've been working day and night to make sure everything's perfect for the presentation. I was just dozing when you phoned.'

I apologized. 'Just make sure you get a good night's sleep,' I said.

'I'll try and do that, my dear,' she said. 'Sleep well yourself. Remember, every day is a moment to treasure.'

But I did not hear that phrase again, nor any of her favourite words and maxims. She began to drop her crutches like an invalid who wants only to run when she can barely crawl. No more 'patience and humility' and 'time is a healer'. 'One day at a time' seemed an age away.

It had begun long ago, only we had been unaware. We had been charmed into relaxing because of her initial zeal. We felt like fools, like the boy in the blindfold who tried to strike the *piñata*: we were in the wrong room, the wrong town, the wrong country. There were signs, like telegraph poles, for all to see. We did not see them.

Claudia had made dinner for Sylvie and me: braised beef with garlic mushrooms and roast potatoes. The telephone rang and Claudia went to answer it.

'I thought she was with you,' Claudia said. Then silence. 'But she was going to the meeting tonight. That's why she's not here.' Her voice was small and disbelieving.

Sylvie and I looked at each other.

Claudia didn't speak when she returned to the table.

'What's wrong?' I asked.

'Gaspar wants to know where Mum is.'

'She's not with him?' Sylvie asked.

Claudia shook her head.

'Maybe she had somewhere else to go,' I said. 'She can't attend meetings all the time.'

'He says this is the second week she hasn't shown up.' A cloud crossed her face, a puzzled, angry nimbus. 'What's she been doing all this time?'

When Frau Schlegel returned, Claudia was falsely breezy. 'How did it go?' she called.

'Fine. Same as always,' her mother replied.

'Any newcomers tonight?' Claudia reached for the table mats and shook them hard.

'No, just the usual crowd. Gaspar says two new people are coming on Monday.'

'You want some coffee, Mum?' Claudia half-shouted.

Frau Schlegel missed the tone in her daughter's voice. 'No thanks. I think I'll just have a soak. Turn in. It's been a long day.'

'Mum, where were you tonight?' Claudia asked. 'You weren't at the meeting, I know.'

'What . . . you're checking on me now?' Frau Schlegel glared.

'No, Mum. I just . . .'

'I won't have you spying! I won't have it! You under-stand?' She was shouting now and her hands were shaking. 'If it's so important to you, I went to visit Kirsten and the boys. Phone her if you don't believe me.' She marched to her room and slammed the door.

Claudia shrugged and cleared the table. No one spoke.


I still could not get a connection to Jos. I phoned Matty, who couldn't get through either. Probably everything was fine, he said. I wasn't to worry. B and Angelika continued to prepare for their wedding and for the trip to Cameroon. Tunde stopped seeing Linda soon after bumping into Martine again at the Jacaranda.

The Zimmermans moved out a week after Frau Lieser returned. Dieter had given up the pretence of seeing them separately. He grew bold. He began to visit their apartment when they were both in. Sometimes he would dart back upstairs wearing only a dressing gown and army boots, and hurry down again while Caroline screamed at his retreating figure. What had started as an adventure had developed into an obsession.

One evening Dieter knocked on their door and there was no reply. I no longer heard the jangle of keys or the clunk of their door in the early morning or late at night. Dieter tried again the following day. Frau Lieser lent him her spare key on the third evening after he frightened her with tales of accidental deaths, gas cookers left on, tenants swinging from pendants. They had left most of their furniture behind, but everything else had vanished. There was an envelope addressed to Frau Lieser containing one month's rent, but no note. Dieter shrugged and said, 'That's fucked up. I wonder if Clari's down at the Rio?' He never mentioned the Zimmermans again.


Frau Lieser hobbled about on aluminium crutches and declared she couldn't do a thing for herself. She hovered by her window and ensnared whichever unlucky tenant she happened to spy. She seized anyone she recognized – Claudia or B or one of the punks, even the mailman – who was able to carry a tray from her kitchen to the sitting room, to turn her mattress, to sit for five minutes of conversation. Concern about her friend seemed to have drained Frau Bowker. Perched and alert one minute, her chin would slowly sag and her mouth would slacken.

'She's getting on now,' Frau Lieser said to me. 'Elsa's so much older than me, you know.' She shook her head sadly and the bows of her headscarf flapped like the ears of a cocker spaniel. 'I didn't notice it before.'

'I'm two years older than you, Marianne,' Frau Bowker growled, but she did not raise her head. 'I hear every word you're saying.'

Frau Lieser jumped and reddened. A moment later, Frau Bowker was snoring fitfully again. Frau Lieser squinted, but couldn't decide whether her friend was genuinely asleep.


When next I visited Frau Schlegel's apartment, Claudia put a finger to her lips and indicated the leather sofa. Her mother lay sprawled along its length, a blanket covering her legs.

'She's tired,' Claudia said, matter of fact. 'Thought she could manage a glass of wine at work yesterday. She didn't finish her lunch or her work, but the empty bottles are there for you to see. I found her on the bathroom floor when I came back.' She pouted as if it was all beyond her now. She had tried and she had failed. What more could she do?

Frau Schlegel woke an hour later, eyes bloodshot, face crumpled. Haggard.

'Claudi . . . you're back. Vincent? I must have dropped off. What time is it?' Her eyes scanned the room as if she had lost something.

'D'you want me to run you a bath, Mum?'

She shook her head and yawned. 'No. No, I should really get to bed. There's a marketing meeting first thing tomorrow.'

Claudia glanced at me, waited a moment before she spoke. 'It's Saturday tomorrow, Mum. Edward phoned. It's all right, about the meeting. Don't worry. Let me run you that bath.'

Frau Schlegel winced and stared at her watch. She sighed and shook her head. Perhaps it had seemed like a dream, the previous day, the inebriate plunge, the vanished hours? Could it kill a part of you to know you were ill and unable to help yourself? She was quiet for a long time. I retreated to the kitchen to make coffee, to give them some privacy. When I returned Frau Schlegel was kneeling on the rug, rocking back and forth, Claudia beside her, an arm round her torso. 'I can't do this any more,' Frau Schlegel cried. She was like a girl who had been forbidden to attend a dance, disconsolate and maddened.

I backed into the kitchen and waited. I wanted to be away from the raw emotions, the tears. When I emerged Frau Schlegel was on the sofa, dabbing at her eyes with the hem of her sleeve.

'Come, let's go and have that bath,' Claudia whispered.

But Frau Schlegel did not move from the edge of the sofa even after Claudia had entered her mother's room. We could hear the gush of the filling bath.

'I don't know why she puts up with me,' her mother said. 'Why does she do it when she could be enjoying herself – going to parties, travelling, focusing on her studies, anything – instead of looking after an invalid?'

I shrugged. 'Maybe she *would* rather be doing that if things were different. But they're not, so she does what she does. Maybe she has no choice. She loves you.'

'She does? Yes . . . I suppose she does.' She began to cry again.

# 30

S HE DRANK BECAUSE it was what she had learned to do. It was the unlearning that came at an infant's crawl, moving forwards, backwards, backwards again. As Frau Schlegel succumbed to the alcohol once more, I noticed how much calmer she seemed. She didn't jump at the slightest noise, and though her words were often slurred, she was more relaxed, gentler. Sometimes her eyes betrayed an inner panic. They scuttled back and forth, unable to settle. She was full of the guilt and tension of the hidden drinker now. We never saw her touch the alcohol, but she was always under its influence.

When she returned from work she made straight for the bedroom. There were places where she hid the drinks, which were dumbfounding. Sylvie found bottles of whiskey in the hanging baskets on the balcony. After we discovered how devious the mind could be, there was no place we didn't look: the back of the new television set hid bottles of warm wine; the deep cracks of the sofa could swallow more than dust and pfennigs; the tops of cupboards; beneath the mattresses in the spare rooms; the cisterns in all the bathrooms; little bottles of spirits stuffed into the shoes that lined her room. Frau Schlegel never asked about her disappearing bottles. She didn't appear upset by their loss, but she grew more cunning in her efforts to hide them.

I took Claudia out to dinner several nights a week, to the cinema and the Rio – now Club Carnival, Claus's latest venture. She had lost her appetite – she hadn't been eating properly for weeks – and I worried about her self-neglect. I wanted her to surface from the constant anxiety of her mother's illness. Frau Schlegel was no longer permitted to attend the AA meetings, where sobriety was insisted on, but Gaspar visited regularly to try to convince her to return to the sanatorium.

'And part of me wants to stop,' she confided in me one evening. 'Part of me prefers it this way.' She looked down at Claudia who was lying on the Persian rug. I wasn't sure if she was awake, if she was listening. 'It's a bit like sleep,' she said.

'What do you mean?' I asked.

'Well . . . it's not really like . . . like being awake. You're hardly conscious. Days pass – you don't know what's happening some of the time, but you can function. Nothing seems so very important, and I like that. When I was in the sanatorium and soon after I left, every moment felt so real, so harsh, for such a long time. It felt brutal. I don't know how to explain it well. I hated feeling that way; as if my whole body was electrified and I couldn't switch off the current.'

Claudia sighed and turned, but did not wake.

'Have you made a decision about the reassessment?' I asked. The sanatorium had agreed to readmit her on the basis of another interview.

'I have no choice. I have to try again, for Claudi. And for

myself,' she said. 'No one says it will be easy. They may not agree to take me this time, but I suppose it's better to try and fail, and then try again. Better than to give up, no?'


She had been so near to beginning a period of recovery, but I never saw Frau Schlegel again. It was in the news and on the radio. Clariss announced to all her friends that Vanessa Schlegel's apartment block had been razed to the ground, along with her warehouse of shoes in Spandau. Frau Bowker claimed an explosion had destroyed all but the ground floor of the Zehlendorf building. The truth was less horrible, but just as devastating.

She died on a Saturday afternoon. Claudia was in town, shopping for a raincoat. Frau Schlegel retired to her room to lie down. She fell asleep with a cigarette between her fingers. She hadn't reacted quickly enough to save herself from the flames that raged all around her. A bottle of malt whisky was found beneath her pillow. We hadn't once thought of looking there.

People I had known or had once had contact with were appearing regularly on the news – Heinrich Henkelmann, Frau Schlegel, Ezmîr Özdemi – in the space of a single summer, the span of several weeks. All in the effort of getting along in the world: the casual sex, the alcohol, a place to call home. The endeavour to make life more bearable. Sometimes the sheer exertion of living drove a person beyond their limits.

A batch of people I had seen in the press or had heard of attended the funeral: the actor Otto Ostermeyer and his wife; the playwright Clara Kohlhaase; the actress Sonja Mieke, who had once been married to Otto; half a dozen fashion designers. The Chancellor's office sent a representative, but in truth Vanessa Schlegel's star had been waning for at least half a decade. Few could afford her shoes and the styles had changed anyway. She had been reluctant to adapt to the times.

It was strange to see the Schlegel clan: Julius and his sickly wife, Frau Schlegel's still-sturdy mother, the aunts and uncles and some of their children. It was odd to see Claudia among all those white faces. With her mother gone she seemed alone in their midst. But Sylvie and her friends were there, as were B and Angelika, Frieda and the yellow-haired man from the sanatorium. Ulrich. Marie came out of journalistic curiosity, even though she had not been invited.

At first Claudia could only cry, but later she seemed better able to cope than either Julius or her grandmother. In a way she had been preparing herself against calamity for much of her life. She had expected the worst and the worst had happened and still the world did not end.

Julius and his wife remained in Berlin until the end of the week before returning to Frankfurt with Claudia's grandmother. Frau Schlegel's apartment was salvageable but, once it was restored, Claudia wanted only to sell it.

It began to rain and the cold closed in. I remembered the hot summer, how we sat on the beach and our blood boiled.

'We could go somewhere,' I said, 'before B gets married. Get away from here.'

'You have somewhere in mind?' Claudia asked. She hadn't slept in her own apartment since the funeral. She did not want to be alone.

'I don't know. Greece, Spain? Somewhere warm. I miss the sun already. I'm not ready for another winter.'

'It's possible,' Claudia whispered. 'It's possible.' She stood, staring out of my sitting room window as tears spilled down her cheeks.

'Listen – anything you want, just name it. We'll do it together.' I went and held her. 'Don't worry about money.'

She frowned and said, 'But you haven't any money,' and then she laughed and cried and then somehow managed to laugh again through her tears.

'I've got enough,' I said, closing my eyes, and as I held her I felt a searing pain. It seemed I had never truly loved before. If this was love, what a terrible, brutal thing it could be. Not an experience to run to, but to flee from. I wanted to embrace it, yet cast it aside at the same time.

'She should be here!' Claudia cried. 'There's no need for her not to be. Sometimes it hits me so hard, that she's not coming back. Not ever.'

'Let's go outside, let's walk,' I said. 'It'll take your mind off it.'

She didn't move. She hadn't heard me. She inhaled as if she had just walked up the stairs, and wiped her face with the back of her hand. 'You didn't tell me,' she said, still staring out of the window, 'what exactly happened to your parents. You didn't say.'

'You don't want to know about that,' I said.

'No, I do. Really. Tell me. Tell me something, anything.'

I walked away and sat on the edge of the table. There didn't seem any point in keeping it from her then. I told the whole story: of a grandmother left behind, and the rain and the car as it bounced like tumbleweed along the road. The last words spoken. How Matty's ribs were smashed, his left leg broken at the tibia. How the scar across his torso remained to this day. How my father seemed unscathed apart from

309

the awful whistling in his throat. How my mother lay half outside the car, her body twisted impossibly. How I screamed and screamed and screamed and no one heard. How I was untouched.

I had never told Lucille what had happened. I had never told anyone the details as I was telling Claudia now.

At the end she only nodded. She looked out at the stone-grey sky, which had shone so blue only weeks ago. 'We could go far away.' She turned at last. 'Maybe Barbados or Hawaii.'

My heart fell. I didn't speak.

'Money's no object, remember,' she smiled. 'Only if you want to, Vincent. We can use some of Mum's money. We don't have to go if you don't want to.'

'Why did you say Barbados?'

'Barbados? I don't know. It was the first place I thought of. Why?'

I shook my head. 'It doesn't matter . . . Say we go some-where. We come back. I return to work, you continue your studies. What then?'

Claudia sighed. 'I don't know, Vincent. I don't know anything right now. The future . . . I can't even concentrate on today.'

'So . . . what is this?' I said. 'This back and forth? It's tiring. I want to stay with you.'

'You do?'

'Well . . . yes.' I had strayed from the shore and now the ice was thin. 'I thought, maybe we . . . we could try at some-thing – life, you and me.'

She bit her lip and nodded vigorously as if she hadn't quite taken something in, but was agreeing nonetheless. She came away from the window and placed her palm against my temple. 'I never know what's going on in here,' she said.

I shrugged. 'Nothing much. It's not such a mystery.'

'I thought you hated me, in the beginning,' she said. 'I didn't know how you felt.'

'I didn't hate you. Maybe I hated myself, but I could never hate you.' I could feel the strength in her body despite her frailty.

'We should go for that walk,' she said, 'before it gets dark.'

I glanced outside. 'It's dark already.'


Frau Lieser and Frau Bowker were shuffling into the hall as we descended the stairs.

'You're walking, Frau Lieser,' I said.

'Oh, no – it's only the physiotherapy. It won't last. If I collapse before I reach my door, don't be surprised. Now, I'll need a young man's shoulder to assist me.'

I helped her into her apartment while Frau Bowker and Schnapps clattered behind. 'The sun disappears as soon as it arrives,' I heard Frau Bowker complaining to Claudia. 'The summer never lasts . . . and a good thing too.' Already the heatwave was forgotten.

'Now, a cup of tea would be perfect,' Frau Lieser exhaled as she sank into the overstuffed chair. 'Don't you agree, Elsa?'

Frau Bowker scowled, then looked up at us desperately, but we were already backing out of the door.

'I hope they don't come to hate each other, stuck in the apartment like that,' Claudia said.

'It'll be all right. Frau Lieser will be well enough soon. She'll be making tea for the other one in no time. Things will return to the way they were. She's just enjoying the attention.'

I looked back at the building, to the window where Frau

Lieser and Frau Bowker had stood watching passers-by all summer. I looked up to my window out of which Claudia had been staring only minutes ago. Everything seemed settled and quiet, yet I knew that behind the walls life pitched and twisted, and sometimes it was calm for a while, but often it was not.

'What are you looking at?' Claudia asked.

I turned from the building. 'Nothing, just nothing. Which way should we go?'

Claudia shrugged. We glanced both ways as we waited on the pavement and then stepped into the road.